EMBERS

BOOK ONE OF THE GALAXY ON FIRE SERIES

CRAIG ROBERTSON

EMBERS

BOOK ONE OF THE *GALAXY ON FIRE SERIES*

by Craig Robertson

IF YOU CAN'T BE DEAD, MAKE SURE THEY NOTICE YOU

Imagine-It Publishing
El Dorado Hills, CA

ALSO BY CRAIG ROBERTSON:

* Podium Entertainment has produced audiobooks for all the below titles except the older standalone books.

For specifics as to the correct order for reading the Ryanverse, click here.

BOOKS IN THE RYANVERSE:

THE FOREVER SERIES (2016)

THE FOREVER LIFE, Book 1

THE FOREVER ENEMY, Book 2

THE FOREVER FIGHT, Book 3

THE FOREVER QUEST, Book 4

THE FOREVER ALLIANCE, Book 5

THE FOREVER PEACE, Book 6

THE FOREVER BOXSET, Part 1, Books 1 & 2

THE FOREVER BOXSET, Part 2, Book 3 & 4

THE FOREVER BOXSET, Part 3, Book 5 & 6

GALAXY ON FIRE SERIES (2017)

EMBERS, Book 1

FLAMES, Book 2

FIRESTORM, Book 3

FIRES OF HELL, Book 4

WRITE NOW! THE PRISONER OF NaNoWRiMo (2009)

ANON TIME (2009)

For more information about Craig, his books, various series, or to see images and videos for some of his wild alien characters, please visit his website. You'll be glad you did: https://craigarobertson.com/

To sign up for Craig's newsletter to get announcements, updates, and his recommendations for other great Sci-Fi reads go to: https://preview.mailerlite.io/forms/2369493/188634426375144501/share

ISBN: 978-0-9989253-1-8 (E-Book)
978-0-9989253-2-5 (Paperback)
979-8-7754035-1-5 (Hardcover)

Cover design by Jessica Bell

Formatting services by Drew Avera
drewavera@gmail.com

Editors: Michael R. Blanche
Neil Farr

First Edition 2018
Second Edition 2019
Third Edition 2020

This book is dedicated to my wonderful grandson, Jonathan Ryan Davis. Stay loving, pure, and committed to the service of others. I know your life's story will be even more fantastic than the Jon Ryan's of this series. All my love ... Papa.

I want to specifically thank my fastest, best, and most loyal beta readers. Here's to you Charles Pitts, Tony Hall, and Jeff Worthen. Seriously, dudes, I couldn't have done it without you!

Note: Glossary of Terms Is Located at the End of the Book

CHAPTER ONE

I opened my eyes. My immediate reaction: *crrrrap!* I was supposed to be dead. I really, really wanted to be dead, but it seemed almost certain I was *not* deceased. I repeated *crap* a bunch of times, out loud. I was lying on my back in a dark room. Then I looked down to notice an alien I couldn't ID with a flashlight strapped to its head. It was burrowing into my chest like a kid looking for his favorite prize at the bottom of the toy chest. Man, my day was just getting better. Someone was going to pay for this—*all* of this.

I tried to reach for what was likely his throat with my right hand. Perfect! My right arm was missing. If the day got a hell of a lot better, it would still be the worst day of my life by a generous margin. I checked and, with relief, found my left arm was present and accounted for. Thank the Lord for minor miracles. I rapped the dude alongside its head. "What the *hell* are you doing?"

It looked at me as if a turnip had just spoken to him. Then it returned to its rushed digging without comment. I should mention that the dude looked like it had been beaten badly with an ugly stick. Its shape was that of a big bug, with a head that looked a lot like a praying mantis. There was no hard shell, however; more like scaly skin. It was maybe two meters tall, fifty to sixty kilos, and ugly. I mention ugly again, because it basically owned the concept.

I lifted my left arm toward it and said the word *neck* in my head. The probe fibers in my fingers sprang to life and encircled its skinny throat. I cinched them down tightly and repeated my earlier query. "What the *hell* are you doing?" My sudden movement made me notice we were in a low gravity environment, because I recoiled and lifted slightly off the surface I was lying on.

It tore at the fibers with seven insect-like appendages, but failed to loosen my grip. Good, I hoped it hurt.

In an appropriately choking voice, it responded, "I'm looking for salvage, robot. Release me, or I'll disintegrate you."

"Oh, now I'm scared," I said as sarcastically as I could. "You'd actually be doing me a favor, pal. You know that?"

"Then release me, so I can get my vaporizer."

"Wait, you threatened to zap me, but you don't have the necessary tool, unless I release you first? That's whacked, dude. You can't threaten someone, unless you are prepared to follow through."

"Sorry," he gasped. "I'm not so good at relationships."

"What, do I look like your shrink who wants to hear about your failed life?"

"No. I mean to say, I don't interact well with others. I don't know how to relate to others."

"Small wonder. You're making a terrible first impression on me, digging into my chest without so much as an if-you-please."

"Be a good turn-crank and let go of me."

I must have looked confused.

"A turn-crank. A *robot*."

"Ah," I responded, as I withdrew my probe fibers. "Haven't heard that one before."

"Well, now you have. Do you mind if I get back to my salvaging?"

"Why, yes, as a point of order, I very much do. I like all my parts and wish you to remove none of them."

"Humor? Who programs humor into a turn-crank? What a damn waste of time."

"I'm not a robot. I'm a human."

"I've never heard of those, but whatever they are, you're not one. You're a turn-crank. Trust me on that."

"I wouldn't trust you to die if I threw you into boiling oil. Look, pal, I'm having a bad day here. Cut me some slack."

"How can a turn-crank have a good or bad day, and how would lengthening a rope help?"

"Because I'm not a TC. I'm a living human."

"A TC? What's a TC?"

"Turn-crank, my slow-witted friend. Now get off me, and let me try to close my chest. It'll be a bitch, since it appears my right arm is lost."

"It's not lost. It's right here in my satchel. It has a crude but serviceable cutting tool at the end. Might bring a few credits."

"Dude," I protested, "that's a gamma ray laser you're referring to."

"As I said. An old but effective cutting tool."

"Old?" I wondered out loud.

I checked my chronometer. *Holy crap.* It was approximately two billion years since Doc was supposed to have decommissioned me! How very entirely perfect. I was screwed in so many ways, I couldn't decide which hurt the most. Not dead, being dismembered for scrap, and stranded two billion—that's billion with a *B*—years down the time stream. I should have just let this asshole keep on digging. Maybe he'd find my off switch.

"Is it, like, way in the future?" I asked hesitantly.

He squinted. "No. It's today."

3

"I mean, am *I* way in the future?"

"How should I know, and why would I possibly care? Why should *you* care. TCs don't have a concept of time. They *tell* time, but no one would program in an *appreciation* of time. That would be silly."

"Because I'm not a robot, maybe?"

"Could have fooled me, robot. Now, be a good turn-crank and power yourself off. You're really slowing me down."

"No. Look, give me my arm back and maybe I won't kill you. How's that sound for a deal?"

"Now listen here, slave. I've had about as much of you as I'm willing to overlook. Shut up and let me see if there's anything else salvageable in your frame."

"Oh, now I'm a *slave*. You're not distancing yourself from me killing you with that type of remark, you know?"

He developed a very impatient, frustrated look on his face. "Robot, slave. Slave, turn-crank. They're all the same thing. What else are TCs made for other, than to be slaves?"

"This android host was created to download my human consciousness into. It made me immortal."

He scanned me up and down, dubiously. "You don't look so immortal to me. You look like an antiquated TC, badly in need of a muting switch."

It was then a flashing red light on my optical pop-up screen caught my notice. Hadn't seen that one flash before. Ah, most perfect! A low sperm warning was flashing. This officially made it the worst day anyone, anywhere, ever had. And my day was only five minutes old. I could still look forward to frogs, boils, and locusts.

After my brief pity-party, I looked down to see my persistently annoying buddy back at it, ripping into my chest cavity.

"Ah," he said with measured glee, "there they are. The fusion generators." He glanced up toward me. "Not so very useful, but they could add a little boost to the exotic matter energy supply."

"Do you practice talking without saying anything, or is it a natural gift? What's the exotic matter energy supply?"

"Where were you stamped out? Everybody knows about exotic matter. It requires a lot of energy to produce, but it binds the galaxies together. Your little fusion cores could bring me a few coins from the Adamant."

I drew my left palm down across my face in frustration. "Well, *I* don't know about exotic matter. I mean, I do, because I have a degree in physics, but how it applies to the adamant binding of galaxies, well, I think you're just plain batty."

"Now I know you're joking again. Stupid waste of energy for a TC. The Adamant are not *glue*." His spindly arms fluttered in the air. "They are the lords of us all, of everything. They produce most of the exotic matter. They control it absolutely."

"Oh, you mean they're the government, the political leaders."

He chuckled darkly. "Hardly. I said they were *lords* of us all. No one elected them or benefits from their tyranny and malice. No, I haven't heard the word government used in ages. There hasn't been a viable one anywhere, for at least five million years."

"Okay, you know what? I'm suddenly disinterested in this conversation. You're nuts, and I'm supposed to be dead. Instead, I'm sitting here in pieces looking at you, and I have a low-sperm alert flashing so brightly, it's giving me a headache. I need to wrap up this love-fest and figure out how to silence that alarm."

"Why would anyone equip a TC with reproductive capabilities? That's beyond ludicrous. Even if you were a sex toy, you wouldn't need breeding capabilities."

Maybe I *was* a sex toy now? Well, I guess a guy as good looking as me might have been mistaken for one. I let him have a pass on that.

"Because I'm *human*."

I assume he was suddenly just as done talking as I was. He reached for a huge mallet that rested on the floor near his feet. I didn't need two guesses to know how he planned to use it to silence me. As he swung his tiny head up, I clobbered him for all I was worth with my only hand. There was a satisfying crunch as I felt fist meet face. The dude flew seven meters backward off his stool and crumpled on the floor. With any luck, which was against the odds given my shitty day so far, he was dead.

I sat up awkwardly. It turned out sitting up with my chest walls splayed wide open was harder than I might have thought. Since I only had one arm, it took me the better part of two hours to reattach my right arm. Then, with two working hands, it took an hour to repack the parts into my chest and seal it back up. I was fairly certain everything was working fine. I just wished there weren't three small parts left over. But they probably weren't mission critical, whatever they were.

As I worked, I tried to noodle out the mess I was in. I didn't know where I was; I didn't know what happened to all the humans I helped flee a dying Earth forever ago; and I didn't know why I wasn't dead. Toño DeJesus had promised me I would be. Well, I knew the human Jon Ryan, who had been downloaded into a human body epochs ago, was dust and gone. But this android version of me was never supposed to wake up. What really pissed me off was that I was exceedingly unlikely to ever see Toño again, which meant I couldn't punch him in the nose for failing me. Sure, he was an android, too, but two *billion* years was longer than a long time. He had to have stopped working. Even if he was still alive, who the hell knew where he was? He could travel a long distance in that time.

I began to realize I suffered significantly from a lack of knowledge. I didn't know my location or the general lay of things in my new present. I looked down at the big bug I'd clocked. Maybe it would have been better if he wasn't dead. I could use a major info-dump. He sure hadn't moved, had he? I extended my probe fibers to him to see if I could determine if he was dead or alive.

Hmm. No heart. Nothing even vaguely similar to a circulatory system, in fact. I wondered how his species evolved to such a large size without that. Then I slapped myself on the cheek. Focus, Jon. I was in a mess and needed answers. I didn't need to waste time pondering how the big bugs maintained metabolic balance.

He was warmer than room temperature. That was a good sign, unless he just hadn't cooled off yet. His head contained neural activity. Not a lot, but maybe he was a deep sleeper when knocked unconscious. I could only hope that was the case. It dawned on me that some other bug might possibly be with him. If so, I'd have someone to pump for information, if this guy had split for the big bug-fest in the sky. Great. Another I-could-only-hope. I needed them, oh, I don't know, like I needed a low sperm count.

I began to contemplate how it was that we could speak, bugman and me, before I rendered him non-communicative. I had pretty good translating algorithms, but I understood him right from the get-go. Hmm. Not likely he spoke the King's English. That's when I slapped myself again. Focus, focus, *focus*. I could worry about linguistic interfaces when I knew what the hell was going on.

I retracted my probes. It was logical to scan the airways for signs of radio traffic or other indications of activity. Quickly, I discovered there was nothing going on. The only electronic signatures came from a small spacecraft a few hundred meters away. That had to be my new friend's ship. There were no other transmissions, nearby heat traces, or even the sounds of rats scurrying about within the range of my sensors. It was just me, the bug, and his ride.

I broadcast a signal on a wide range of frequencies to see if anyone out there would respond. Nothing came back in a rush, so I stood up and studied the room I was in. Dark and dank. Just like I hated. Man, the dust was so ancient, it had dust of its own. Clearly, wherever I was had been abandoned a very long time ago. I stepped over to the wall, where some beat-up furniture was scattered. There was a computer station. Wow, it seemed just like—

Oh, *hell* no. The computer station was identical to the ones on the worldships. I was *on* a worldship, one of the cored-out asteroids humanity used to escape Earth's destruction. This one had been abandoned eons ago. Maybe two billion years ago? And whoever was last off had either forgotten about me or left me behind intentionally. I didn't know which scenario was more offensive. Did the surviving humans forget about the man who'd saved their collective asses? Or were they simply not concerned enough to take me with them, as they carried on to wherever they were going? A notable lack of gratitude, either way.

I heard my host scraping the floor. He was stirring. All right, he probably wasn't dead. The first break of my new life. I went over to him.

"Let me help you up," I said, taking hold of him gently.

At first, he didn't recognize me. Then he did. I could tell, because he pulled away with a jerk. But I held on tight.

"Let go of me, slave," he said, trying to sound emphatic. He fell well short of his objective.

"Here, let's get you sitting on the table," I said as I hefted him up.

His legs were still wobbly. I angled him into somewhat of a sitting position. His body wasn't humanoid enough to make that move easy, but I didn't know how he normally reclined. He grumbled a lot, assuming the series of high-pitched squeals was grousing.

"There," I said cheerily, "good as new."

"Hardly, slave. You mangled my mandible. It'll take days to heal."

"You look a little tubby." I patted his midsection. "A few days of a liquid diet will be a blessing."

"I would report you to the authorities for decommissioning, if there were such a thing anymore. Back in the day, defective, aggressive turn-cranks were dealt with properly." He pointed a couple arms at me. "*You* should be melted down. *You* are a menace."

"Aw, come on. I'll grow on you. I promise."

"I don't doubt that for a second. Parasitism seems like something you'd be capable of."

What a Debbie Downer. "Look, here's the deal. I need a few simple questions answered, and then we'll say our goodbyes. We'll never have to see each other again. How's that sound?"

"Too good to be true. But ask your questions. If they're brief, I might answer them."

"First off, how can we be communicating? I have a translation program, but I understood you from word one."

"I speak Standard. Everybody speaks Standard. Surely you were programmed for it." He gave me a look like I was a special kind of stupid.

"I wasn't. I was downloaded two billion years ago. Times were very different then. Languages, too."

"Two *billion* years ago?" he said incredulously. "That's preposterous. No TC could last that long." He reflected a moment. "It would account, however, for your antiquated design and parts."

"Is Standard the language once called English?" I was grasping at straws to explain my ability to communicate.

"Never heard of that one. Was it what the homins you spoke of used?"

"*Humans,*" I corrected. "Yes, some did."

"No, I doubt that very much. Say something in Human and let's see if I understand it." He crossed most of his arms waiting for a response.

"You are a spherical asshole," I said slowly, in my mother tongue.

"Total gibberish. What a foul sounding language."

"A simple *no* would have sufficed. You're trying to be negative. I can tell."

He replied in a sound pattern I couldn't translate.

"What?" I shot back.

"I was questioning your parentage in my own tongue."

"You're being so darn negative again. Does your species have psychiatrists?" Before he could respond, I focused back on the important. "What is Standard based on?"

"Huh?"

"What is it related to? How was it derived?"

"The Adamant handed it down to us, their slaves." He harrumphed. "Actually, if they treated us as slaves, it would be an upgrade."

I decided to drop the linguistics query. I'd figure it out in time. I needed other information. "Do you know what happened to the people on the worldship? They were humans like me."

"You mean turn-cranks?"

"No, living breathing sentients. What happened to them?"

"I have no idea and no interest. This speck of rock has been abandoned for as long as anyone remembers. It's been picked over for, well, forever. I only came scrounging because I've been on ... an unlucky streak lately. I needed to find something for trade, and I was desperate enough to try this dump."

"Booze, babes, or betting?"

"What in the Six Heavens are you talking about?"

"You said you're down on your luck. Has to be one of those three, or combinations therein."

"If it were, I wouldn't tell you. You, I hate. I shan't share my troubles with a talking pile of bolts."

Harsh. "So, you've never seen a human or even heard any rumors about them?"

"No."

Hang on. He hated my guts. Maybe he knew something, but wouldn't spill the beans because of his enmity. "If you could give me some useful information, I could make it worth your while."

Yeah, that perked up his ear-stalks. Then he scowled. "You don't own anything I might want. I don't think you'll offer your arm or fusion cells."

"You got that right. But, if I find something valuable, might you recall some details?"

"That is almost a certainty. What do you have in mind?"

"Not quite sure yet. If you wait here a while, I'll come back with something valuable."

He was tempted. I could see it in his beady little eyes.

"It isn't healthy to stay in one place too long. The Adamant has eyes and ears everywhere. They also use the most fantastic scanning tools. To be found by them is to beg for a lamentable death."

So, broadcasting a message on all known frequencies as I did a little while ago would be, what? An insanely bad idea, or a tragically bad idea? Probably both.

"Ah, while I thought you were dead, I kind of sent out a general radio message, asking if anyone could hear me. You think that might be a problem?" I smiled to potentially soften the blow of my revelation.

"You ... you sent a *signal?* Now I know you're defective."

He popped to his feet and scurried over to where his satchel lay. "I'm dead already, thanks to you. Curse your manufacturer and his children."

He snatched the bag and ran off into the darkness of a

corridor. Shortly thereafter, I heard his engines whine to life, and I knew he was gone. So, my first couple of hours of reanimation were going less ideally than I might have hoped. On the bright side, I didn't have a ride. Those Adamant were likely to find me here and ease my pain of being alive. My ship of state had sunk so deep into the Sea of Shit, that even her masthead was no longer visible.

CHAPTER TWO

I was stuck, literally and figuratively. I couldn't leave *Exeter*, the cored-out asteroid worldship I'd lived on in the remote past. I knew eons of scavenging would have removed anything even vaguely serviceable. Also, I couldn't leave, because I needed to find out what happened to my people. There had to be clues. Some computer banks, written records, or archaeological specimens were bound to be around somewhere. The question was, if I would have enough time to discover anything before the Adamant came. That assumed, of course, my anonymous friend wasn't crazy and just imagined them into existence. He sure looked nutty enough to be delusional. It was wishful thinking on my part, but I was due for a change in my luck.

I had been stored in the android construction and repair area. It was nicknamed "toy land" for obvious reasons. It wasn't too far from the main engines and other technical departments. Housing and recreation areas were pretty far away. The worldships were, after all, huge. Four- or five-kilometer central core-outs of ten-kilometer asteroids. They made safe and practical homes for humanity to occupy, way back in the mid twenty-second century.

Jupiter had been knocked out of its orbit by a rogue planet. I guess it pissed Jupiter off enough that it felt like destroying something. Unfortunately, it chose tiny little Earth to vent against. Billions made it off safely. I knew where the fleet of worldships was going, but in the immense timespan since then, any humans left might be scattered to the wind.

I needed some closure. Clearly, if any humans remained, they wouldn't know who I was. I would have no connection to them, either. But, hell, they were my species. I gave up everything to save their butts. I wanted to know if my sacrifices were worth the considerable suffering I'd lived through. To explore the local star systems looking for a new home for humanity, I'd volunteered to be the first person downloaded to an android host. After surviving that, I shoved off for a half-century voyage all by my lonesome.

I experienced so much loss, so much pain, it eventually began to change me. I became a dark, moody killing machine, defending humanity at any cost. That's what led up to my choice to be transferred back into a mortal human body and die like everyone else. This android version of me was never supposed to see the light of day again. Toño specifically promised me. Now, I was in a worse muddle. I had all the scars of my past, *and* I was marooned in the far future. I never got to see my children grow, bounce my great grandchildren on my knee, or watch my beautiful, precious wife age and pass.

An icy rage began to grow in my gut. I had given much more than everything of value in my life. My reward was the ultimate curse. Someone was looking at hell to pay for what happened to me. Of course, anyone responsible was long since dust, but someone was going to pay. Maybe, just maybe, it'd be those damn Adamant. They were as good a choice as any. I'd open a galactic can of whoop ass on them and see if that made me feel any better. It wasn't much of a plan, but it *was* a plan.

I stepped into the main corridor outside my resting chamber.

Not surprisingly, it was totally dark, and it was filthy. Crap was everywhere, signs that immense time and greedy hands had wrecked everything several times over. I needed some light to see. My visual amplifiers could boost the tiny light I emitted, so I could see just fine. That was fortunate, because I was extremely low on power. One of my fusion cells was long since defunct, and the other was running on fumes. Luckily, finding hydrogen to refuel wouldn't be a problem. If I didn't find a tank, which was doubtful, I was equipped to separate it out from the environment. There were traces of air remaining on *Exeter,* even all these years later, including a bit of hydrogen.

Having no specific plan, I wandered toward the main labs Toño had used for years. He was as likely as anyone to leave a clue for me, on the off chance I woke. Along the way, all I saw was more debris and dirt. Walls were either ripped apart or had simply decayed with the passage of time. Swiss cheese had fewer holes than the once proud *Exeter.* When I arrived at Toño's main lab, the doors were missing. The interior was the same familiar mess. A few counters remained roughly in place, but anything unattached was long gone. I pulled up some old holos in my head of the lab in its prime. Maybe I'd notice something all the scavengers hadn't.

The main computer station was once to my right. It was totally gone, as were the computers once housed in the wall. The storage lockers had been straight ahead of where I stood. Though they were welded to the walls, they were missing. Somebody was pretty motivated. I turned. Behind me was where a lab bench and odd tools were stored. Those were missing. The walls were punched out with randomly placed openings. Some scrapper must have wanted to make sure there were no hidden compartments. Silly. Why would a scientist have secret compartments in their lab? To hide the jewelry and gold bullion? Yeah.

Wait. *Damn.* There *was* one thing Toño guarded with obsessive vigilance. He had a small amount of antimatter stored in a magnetically locked flask. He was determined no one would tamper with it and potentially blow the asteroid to smithereens. Even the small amount he stashed away could rip the rock into large chunks. He hid the stuff in the floor. He had a safe concealed under a lab freezer. Though the freezer was missing, I knew it had been in that corner over there. I jogged over. The floor was smooth and intact. The seams of the hatch were so smooth, no one had noticed them in two billion years. Toño was nothing if not a perfectionist, bless his pointy little head.

I scraped at the floor with my nails. Nothing. I extended my probe fibers to approximately where I thought the hatch was. I sensed a hollow space. The safe! I lifted at the panel covering it. It was all I could do, but it finally tore free. There it was. Toño's ancient safe, perfectly intact. I needed to be cautious. Either the antimatter leached out so slowly it didn't cause an explosion, or it was still in the bottle. The energy levels had to be very low, like mine. If I was ham-handed, I could be vaporized.

The safe had a touchpad to enter a code. The lights were out. It was probably powered by the ship's main supply. Fortunately, the container had its own autonomous source. I powered up the pad via my probes. The backlights flickered to life reluctantly. A few pixels were down for the count. Now, I just had to figure out what the code was. Tearing the door off was a possibility, but I didn't want to disturb the potentially fickle contents. I tried the obvious combinations. Toño's birthday, his mother's birthday, my birthday. Hey, we were good friends. It could happen. Nothing clicked. I entered his fleet ID number, binary translations of his name, and the date the Earth was destroyed. Still nothing. An odd notion hit me. I tapped in 10-15-14-18-25-1-14. A green light blinked and the bolts squealed open. Toño used my name as the code. Those were the numeric values of the letters of *Jon Ryan* in the alphabet. Aw shucks, I was touched. Maybe I wouldn't split his skull, if I saw him again.

The antimatter flask was gone. I breathed a deep sigh of relief. I didn't want to have to deal with that dangerous relic. Toño, always the responsible scientist, must have removed the vial when he left for good. There was, however, a letter. Not a data chip, not a holo disk, but a very old-fashioned letter, in a pristine white envelope. It had my name on the front. It had to, right? I lifted the letter out like it was the antimatter flask I'd expected to find. I smelled the paper. It was fresh. The safe must have once been held in a vacuum. Though that had leaked away, the interior was spared the ravages of time. Most cool.

I looked at the letter for several minutes before opening it. I might have waited even longer, but the thought of mean, all powerful aliens coming spurred me ahead. I gingerly tore the top open and removed the three-page message.

Please, my old friend, forgive me. I know that as you read this letter you are tremendously upset with me. You're alive. I promised you would never be operative again, and I failed you, knowing full well the ever resourceful and unnaturally lucky Jon Ryan could never be silenced forever. I simply could not bring myself to destroy my best friend permanently. That you were also my greatest scientific achievement would not have stopped me. But, in the end, my love for you would not allow me to destroy you. I pray that, in time, you can come to forgive me. If you do not, I will understand. What I did was indefensible. I'd do it a thousand times over, but it was a sin to betray you. I will take that pain with me to my grave, assuming I find a final rest. These android hosts I created are too damn good.

Time. Time, my friend, has been a curse to us. As I write you this missive, it is the anno Domini 61,588. Can you conceive of it? Well, of course you can. You're reading this letter in my future. Who knows, it might even be in the next centamillenium. I think the fusion cells could survive that long. Who knows? With proper maintenance, we possibly could live forever. Such a curse, a double curse. What have I done?

But you have troubles enough without me burdening you with mine. I can only imagine. There is little I can do to aid you, I'm afraid. In the safe, you will find a few items that might ease your immediate needs. I have left you two new fusion cells and a small cylinder of fuel to charge them. I have also stashed a modest amount of gold. Hopefully it is still a universal currency. Finally, I have left you a data disk of the history that has transpired since we shelved you. It is a broad overview, but I know you, and you will be curious.

You hopefully noticed your guardian already. Yes, you have had a champion while you slumbered. Al, your ship's AI. As Exeter was being abandoned, everything useful was removed. That would have included Al, but he refused to go. Artificial intelligence. Even I fail to understand it. How an AI I created and programmed could be capable of such devotion and emotion is well beyond my comprehension. I imagine it only speaks to the unique force of nature that is Jon Ryan, eh? You can draw life from a metal box. Hah! His power supply should last a very long time. I'm certain he was present to cajole you when you woke. Sorry. That was his idea, not mine.

Aside from these things, I can give you but two final gifts. One is the reassurance that your precious wife Kayla lived a very long and abundantly happy life with the human-download copy of you. You predeceased her by several years. After your passing, she lived to become a plump old woman, surrounded by her grandchildren as she held her great-grandchildren on her lap. The morning they called me to pronounce the she had died, I swear to you she had a smile on her placid face.

Finally, I gift you my blessing. I doubt we shall meet again. Who knows when you will chance to rise and how long this android unit will last? I will accompany the last of the colonists departing Exeter for a while. Then I will begin addressing my considerable bucket list. It will take me far and wide. I cannot hope to match your record of travel and adventure, but I shall do my best. So, vaya con Dios, my eternal friend. From your greatest fan, Toño DeJesus.

Well, I could have been knocked over with a small feather. That was touching, unexpected, and so sincere. Okay, if I ever saw Toño again, I'd hug him. Then I'd brain him. Nah. Who was I kidding? I'd hug him, then offer to buy him a beer. Then I'd *verbally* abuse him, and then hug him some more.

I checked in the safe. The fusion units and the fuel cylinder were there, along with the gold bars. All right, Toño. I had a new lease on life. It took only a few minutes to remove my old fusion packs and replace them with the new ones. I was charged and ready for action. I drained the tiny amount of fuel in the one functioning old unit and put them, along with the gold, in a backpack Toño had provided. I was just about to smile and feel all touchy feely, when I heard the sound of a spaceship blustering to a landing not far from me. The Adamant had arrived. Oh, boy. Time to die for real.

I couldn't decide what to do. I could confront whoever had landed and try to make peace with them. Alternately, I could kill them and borrow their ship. But I had a lot more I wanted to explore on *Exeter*. If I tried to hide, I bet they'd find me really quick. Supreme evil doers were always good at that kind of thing, at least in science fiction stories. As big as the worldship was, I doubted I could outrun them for long. For better or for worse, I wasn't forced to choose an option. Almost immediately, two burly figures crashed into the room, both pointing some bitching-looking weapons at me. Man, they found me fast.

Now, I realize I was always given to tall tales and hyperbole. But, these guys were the strangest pair of creatures I'd ever seen. Picture two huge hippopotamuses on short stilts; six short stilts, because that's how many legs they walked on. Two front limbs were holding the guns. Hippos have short necks and can only look down and ahead. These creatures had curved necks that allowed them to hold their heads up like a human. As opposed to a hippo's head, they had small, oblong heads with a big mouth and three small eyes set triangularly. Evolution must have been on drugs on whatever planet they came from. Totally bizarre.

"It's just a robot," one said to the other, as he gestured at me with his gun. His voice sounded like he was talking while swallowing oatmeal mush.

"Destroy it and continue your search," said a disembodied voice from God only knows where. It was like they were followed by a loudspeaker, minus any apparent loudspeaker.

"Or welcome me, death," both hippos replied to thin air. They trained their weapons on me with intent.

"Wait, fellows," I called out. "Can't we talk about this? I'm not a threat to you."

"No and yes," one barked back.

"Say what?" I asked.

"*No*, we cannot talk, and *yes*, you are no threat."

He aimed intently at my head.

"So ... so, hang on. Is there no way I can talk you out of shooting me? How about a five-minute stay of execution to convince you that you don't really want to kill me?"

The other beasty replied this time. "No. You can't talk us out of killing you because we don't want to kill you. We are following orders and must do so. There are no options."

It was looking grim for me. I had a few options, but no time to debate them. I could shoot first, run, or put up my personal force field. The last toy Toño installed in me before I decided to become human again was a personal membrane generator. Up until then, they were too big for individual use and the field itself too inflexible to maneuver. But Toño figured out a fix, and I had a functioning unit installed.

Instinctively, I swung my right hand up and lasered the fronts of their weapons off. I was extra careful not to hit them or break open their power packs. Both guns fizzed loudly as they split into two pieces. They threw them to the floor immediately.

The bodiless voice sounded off loudly. "This is unacceptable. You have damaged property belonging to the Adamant. The penalty is agonizing death."

"What," I asked the air around me, "as opposed to a neighborly death by a mutant hippo firing squad?"

"Further unacceptable behavior. It is unacceptable to insult the Adamant. After you are killed, you will be revived and executed again in a different and more agonizing manner."

"Don't go to such trouble. If you manage to off me, let's just leave well enough alone, shall we?"

"Disrespect! *If* we kill you? You will be revived thirty times and exterminated again, and your family will be subject to the same fate." This disembodied voice was sure an asshole.

"Good luck finding them, pal. They've been dead for a couple billon years."

There was a brief delay before the voice spoke. "Guards, begin serial deaths. Operation E-11-Master."

"Or welcome me, death," they both said with reverence. They whipped side arms up and aimed at me.

I turned on my membrane just as they fired. A flock of energy blobs I couldn't identify slammed into the membrane. They erupted like skyrockets on impact and showered the room with incendiary brilliance. The guards covered their faces and cowered backward. Both dropped their pistols.

The second it was apparent what had happened, the voice

cried out in rage. "*Unacceptable.* The robot may not defend itself. The robot cannot possess such technology. It is impossible. The impossible is strictly forbidden. The guards have failed in their duty and have discarded their weapons. Further unacceptable outcomes. They will be factored out."

Both hippo dudes got horrified looks on their faces just before they vanished. Poof, they were simply not there. Oh well, no great loss. They'd been jerks to me.

The annoying voice spoke again. "The robot will terminate its space-time congruity manipulator and submit to serial executions immediately."

"Or else?" I asked.

There was an even longer delay before the Wizard of Oz spoke from behind his curtain. "Or else? There is no *or else.* You have no options. To resist the will of the Adamant is unthinkable."

"Ah, not so much. I not only thought it, but I also did it." I stuck my tongue out. No idea if the voice had eyes, but it sure felt good. "So, if I stand here a thousand years with my shield up, whatcha gonna do? Time is *really* on my side, let me tell you."

"Resistance is unacceptable, impossible, and futile. The square light-year you presently occupy will be deleted."

"What does that even mean?" I tried to sound as snotty as possible, which wasn't hard at all.

"The Adamant does not explain itself. Your sector of existence will be deleted. It will cease to exist along with all its contents. That is all there is to it, robot."

"Beg pardon, all-mighty Oz, but you did just explain yourself. You said you *didn't* explain yourself, then you *did.* I think you're confused. Maybe having an off day, or ate a bad clam. Can I help?"

It took a full five seconds for the pissy voice to digest that quip and respond. "You are infuriating. Your deletion will be a service to the universe."

"Hang on. Seriously, stop what you're doing and listen. I ran into a bug-like guy earlier today."

Voicey cut me off. "Yes, the Quep. He has been apprehended and eliminated."

"As I was saying before you so rudely interrupted, I ran into this Quep dude earlier. He said the Adamant were evil incarnate. He said you ruled the galaxy with an iron hand and treated all life-forms like doggy doo-doo."

"What is doggy doo-doo? It does not exist in our data base. Explain immediately."

"Or else?"

"You already said or else. You are commanded to define the term. Therefore, you must."

"Or else? Look, use the magic word, and I promise I will."

"We do not use magic. It is unnecessary, and it does not exist. Define your term."

"There is so much wrong with what you just said. Did you guys know how non-omniscient you are? For a master race, you're fairly clueless."

"Define *doggy doo-doo* and delineate what we do not know."

"This may take a while. Do you mind if I sit down?"

"Ro ... robots do not need to recl ... line."

"Be that as it may. Okay, ready with paper and pencil? Do you know what a dog is?"

"No."

"It was a service animal on a long-dead planet."

"Very well."

"If you fed a dog a can of food and waited twelve hours, doo-doo is what came out its backside."

"*Excrement?* You mean the excrement of an extinct service animal?"

"Precisely."

"It is forbidden to insult the Adamant."

"I think you said that already."

"No. We said it was *forbidden* to perform the impossible. We said it was *unacceptable* to insult us."

I pulled up a rusty box and sat down. "I stand corrected."

"What do we not know? To say we lack any knowledge is corrupt thought."

"Is it forbidden or just unacceptable?"

"Sarcasm is—"

"Hey, voice, put a sock in it already. You're kind of bossy. Bet you knew that, though. What you are mistaken about is magic. It is very real. So, back to my initial point. I met this guy who said you were bad hombres. Is that correct?"

"Many have called us that, if by *hombres,* you mean individuals."

"So, this is how confused you are and how desperately you need my help. You guys are supposed to be evil, but you said, and I quote, *your deletion will be a service to the universe.* So, I figure, you're like Boy Scouts now, serving the universe? Evil doers aren't supposed to be *helpful.* Add that to that the fact that you didn't know about magic, and that you contradicted yourselves about not explaining yourself and, well, I think you're in more trouble than you realize. You need me, maybe as a consultant."

"Unacceptable. We require nothing. Your sector will be deleted."

"Suit yourself. Me? I think you're only fooling yourselves, but hey, your call. I've got a lot to do and need to get to it."

"But you cannot do anything after you are deleted. You are the one not in contact with reality."

I began tapping a foot. "Can we wrap it up already? You try and delete me. I promise I'll pretend to be deleted. Then we'll both be happy. Oh, can you not delete your guard's ship so I can get off this rock after you don't delete me? I'd really appreciate it."

"Your deletion is a certainty. Your bravado is useless."

"Well, it's my bravado. I can waste it if I so desire. I know you can't harm me. If you try, I'll disappear, and you'll never learn what your weakness is. Then, someday soon, I'll find the throat producing your annoying voice. You'll then wish I hadn't."

"You cannot disappear. You have no mode of transportation. Your death is a certainty."

"Don't say I didn't warn you. Where I come from, one warning is all you ever get."

The voice was silent a good ten seconds. I thought that was a moral victory if nothing else.

"We have decided you cannot be punished enough in your present, remote location. Hence you will enter the spaceship that brought our slaves. It will be auto-piloted back here. Once you arrive, a plan for a proper set of anguishing punishments will be arranged."

Wow, they didn't call my bluff. Some master race they turned out to be. What a bunch of losers. Then again, never underestimate the bullshitting prowess of yours truly. Never.

CHAPTER THREE

I kept my shield up the entire time I was on their ship. It might have been the only thing stopping them from deleting me. I didn't know what deletion entailed, exactly, but I was betting it was unpleasant, at best. A word about the spaceship I rode on. Way, way back in the twentieth century, there was a movie with lots of action but little content named *Independence Day*. The evil alien invaders had fighter craft that looked remarkably like the one I was on. I only mentioned it because here, way in the future, somebody came up with the identical design. Weird. Maybe they saw the film, too?

The flight turned out to be very quick. After we departed *Exeter,* we sped up for a few seconds, then I felt a fine vibration, and then we decelerated. I looked out the viewport and saw the most unusual spacecraft I'd ever seen, which was saying a lot. We were preparing to dock with a ginormous cube. It was so big, I wondered why anyone would build it. I mean, if you needed a vehicle that large, just strap engines to a planetoid. But it was definitely an artificial construct. Even more unusual was how it was positioned in a cubical structure; an exoskeleton, so to speak.

A giant metallic cube in a gossamer framework that was only slightly larger than the ship itself. I was totally baffled by the design and how it functioned. With any luck, I'd live long enough to find out, because I was fascinated to understand the mechanics of the ship.

As we approached, a large set of doors opened to allow our entry. My ride eased into a docking station and the hatch silently swung up, inviting me to exit. Well, that, and the team of armed figures standing just outside. If the hippo guards I'd met were ugly, these guys were double, maybe even triple, ugly. They were also about twice the size of the hippo dudes. They were vaguely humanoid, but had a scary set of saber-tooth tiger-like fangs and an armor-plated hide. They looked intimidating, that was for sure. I made a mental note to try my hardest not to piss them off.

"Come with us *now*," said the nearest alien.

Yes, sir, I thought to myself. Don't need to ask me twice. I popped up and basically sprinted to where he/she/it was pointing. I was positioned inside a half-circle of guards. Someone pushed me forward with a rifle and we were off. Now, I wasn't prejudiced or anything. That said, I had to say that, in my experience, all ugly creatures also smelled really bad. As these guys were correspondingly about the ugliest I'd laid eyes on, they stunk to high heaven. Their scent was like boiling ammonia mixed with equal parts vomit and patchouli oil. Gross. Lucky for me, I was leading the pack, so the hideous smell was mostly behind me. In my mental picture of whatever an Adamant looked like, I eliminated the possibility of them having noses.

Our trip to wherever they were taking me was longer than my space flight had been. I strolled. The beasties escorting me marched with their huge feet stomping like there were bugs on the floor they wanted to smash. Structurally, the ship had to be very tough. Finally, we arrived at a large set of solid gold double doors. Runes and figures I couldn't identify were etched into the metal surface. I presumed I was entering a critical area.

My suspicion was confirmed when the door glided open. The guards that brought me thus far backed away quickly. A new set of guards was on the inside. There were only three, so I assumed they were deadlier than the combined force that was being relieved. Note to self: Don't piss *these* guys off. At least it was immediately apparent they weren't ugly and didn't stink. That is, the little I could see of them supported my theory that they were not butt ugly. They were fifty percent taller than me and seemed to be rail thin. Most physical aspects were obscured by their hooded robes. Layer upon layer of delicate pale fabric covered them, so there was nothing exposed. They sported no weapons, but anyone guarding whoever lived in this room had to be packing a weapon or ten. The bodies under all that cloth were living animals. I could hear their soft breathing. One thing that was obvious was that they were not friendly. They exuded malice and lethality.

Two of the three guards stepped aside to allow me to enter. The third backed in the direction I was to go. His eyes, all four of them, never left mine. He was scrutinizing my expression to find the slightest justification for killing me, I suppose. I could sense he wanted to tear me limb from limb, more than he wanted anything else in the entire universe. And he'd only just met me.

What the hell. "How you doing?" I asked, never removing my eyes from his.

He didn't blink or hesitate. He just kept backing up slowly.

"Nice place you got here. Did you decorate it yourself, because, I mean, it looks real pretty in an understated way?" I asked in my most cordial tone.

Nothing, just his paced movement backward.

Before I could say anything else, a calm yet commanding voice called out from behind my guide. "It is unwise to bait the

Midriack. They have no sense of humor and possess explosive tempers. They are only interested in killing you, not in idle chatter. You will receive no further warning."

"Thanks for the heads up. I'll keep that in mind."

"Seat him in front of me, but stand ready," the voice said.

As the Midriack stepped aside to reveal an ornate chair, I caught my first glance of the speaker, presumably an Adamant. It took all my strength not to erupt in laughter. Fortunately, I restrained my baser instincts. I imagined that would have caused an immediate and unpleasant response from the Midriack. But it was hard. Of all the images, of all the possible appearances the Adamant could have, what I saw completely blindsided me. They were puppy dogs. Seriously. The male seated on a throne in front of me looked *exactly* like a Border Collie, but two to three times bigger. He clearly walked on two feet, based on how he sat, but he had four roughly equal legs and a fluffy tail. I almost patted my pockets to see if I had a Milk-Bone biscuit on me.

"I will advise that you also not toy with me, either," he said as I sat.

That really didn't help my efforts to suppress a giggle or two.

"My name is Mercutcio. I am uninterested in knowing yours. It has been tasked to me to discover if there is any merit in your extraordinary remark that we could not have deleted you back on that asteroid." He reached over and daintily picked up a morsel of food—a treat, as it were—and swallowed it. "I am certain you were blustering, but the collective has decided it is prudent to investigate your claim, nonetheless. But, know that I am not pleased to waste time extracting information from a slave, let alone a robotic one. So, do not unleash your anemic humor on me, or I shall terminate my investigation by terminating you."

Oh, no. He said *unleash,* after he said *toy.* If he asked a servant to *fetch* something or referred to tree *bark,* I was going to lose it, for sure.

"Are you *listening* to me, wretch?" he barked out.

"Huh? Yeah. Of course, I am. You said I should be dutiful and obedient." I shouldn't have stood so near the flame, but I honestly couldn't help myself.

He stared at me intently a few heartbeats, then went back to his blander tone. "So, why is it a robot of significant antiquity possesses a space-time membrane device in the first place?"

"What makes you think I'm old?"

The nearest Midriack took one silent step toward me.

"*I* ask the questions, not *you.* You could confound and confuse Phedra earlier, but I am not so easily played. Know your place, or die."

"I was thinking it would help my answer if I knew a little more about your frame of reference. For example, what led you to assume I was old." I turned palms upward and shook my head. "I'm just trying to be as helpful as I can. Throw me a bone here."

He glared at me again, intently. "Your component parts have radioactive mixtures indicating you were fabricated one and a half to two billion years ago."

These guys had slick science scans. "You are correct. I'm ancient."

"As are we. In both cases, that is inconsequential. Where, I ask for the second and last time, did you get that device from?"

"An old friend gave me the technology, and another old friend scaled it to fit inside of me, Mercutcio."

The guard began to lunge at me.

"Stay," commanded Mercutcio.

The guard went limp and withdrew.

"You will not refer to me by my name. You will address me as Adamant only."

I poked my hand up a little, to indicate I had a question.

"What are you doing?" he howled.

"I want to clarify what you said. You want me to refer to you as *Adamant*, right, not Adamant *only*?"

"Guard," he yelled, "kill him at once."

The fact that Mercutcio said guard, not guards, indicated only the nearest one should attack. I was partially relieved. One killing machine was better than three killing machines. The way Toño designed my personal membrane allowed me to use my laser and probe fibers. Tiny portions of the field were cycled on and off to permit their passage. But, I still favored a complete field. So, I sat there awaiting the Midriack's blow.

His hands extended from his sleeves to reveal large claws. His arms reared back to deal a death blow as he pounced. I squinted as he hit, praying the membrane would be enough to stop him. It was. One hand struck my throat but skidded off like I was covered in ice. The other raked over my face, but again, it swept past without touching me. His failed attempt enraged him. He let out the most intimidating war cry I'd ever heard and tackled me with a bear hug.

We tumbled to the floor, and he climbed atop me, pinning me to the floor. I balled up both fists and slammed them into either side of his cloaked head as hard as I could. As I smashed his skull, I felt a satisfying crunch, but only a slight one. Midriacks had tough bones. Despite receiving such a blow, he continued to claw and punch at me maniacally.

I repeated my head punch, then I repeated it again. By the sixth impact, he began to show signs of slowing. Two more punches, and he collapsed stiffly off me and onto the floor. I shoved his leg off me and stood quickly.

"Who's next?" I asked the other two Midriacks.

"Enough," shouted Mercutcio as both guards moved toward me.

That froze them.

"Impressive performance," said Mercutcio blandly. "I've

never heard of anyone killing a Midriack in personal combat. Even with your force field, I'd have still bet good coin on my slave."

"Keep that in mind, Merc, as you talk down to me and bluster."

"Unacceptable. But, I shall let it pass for now. So, you received the membrane technology from a friend?"

"Wasn't at the time, but later, yes, he was a friend."

"Interesting a stranger should bestow such a great gift."

"He had good reasons."

"I'll bet."

"Wait, you don't have membrane technology?" I asked.

"No, not at the present. We have heard rumors of it, but up until now, I wasn't sure it wasn't just another ancient legend."

"Ah. And I'm guessing you're keen on possessing the tech to recreate it?"

"No. We are not anxious to have the technology. We *will* have the technology."

"And I'm going to supply you with it?"

"Voluntarily or involuntarily, that is correct. The Adamant will not be denied."

"That is an incorrect statement, booby. I deny you access. That's all there is to it."

"Please, know that we will dissect and dismember you and extract the device. Come now, how ineffective do you think we are?"

"On a scale of one to ten, one being the lamest, so far you guys are zeroes."

"You underestimate our will and our abilities." He turned to the guards. "Take him to the interrogation section. I will call ahead to let them know you're coming." Back to me. "You will learn it is foolish to doubt the Adamant. It is even more foolish to think you can resist us, Jon."

"Hey, you said you didn't know my name. What gives?"

"I said I didn't want you to introduce yourself. You are too inferior to permit such an act. But we know your name."

"How?"

"We are the Adamant. We know all. That which we do not know, we will soon learn.

There was no way they could know my name. But they did. That was unsettling. Maybe they were as all-powerful as they claimed to be. I was about to find out, wasn't I?

CHAPTER FOUR

I was prodded, shoved, and occasionally knocked flat on my face by my escorts as we proceeded to the interrogation section. I assume that was a euphemism for a prison/torture venue. I was having a profoundly bad day. Recall, I was still in the first twelve hours of my sentence of not being. I did figure there was no wiggle room for it to get measurably worse. Yeah, never say that to yourself, Jon baby. Just as certainly as there's always room for Jello, there's always a chunk of undesirable that can be crammed into one's existence.

Not surprisingly, the prison section was a long way from the pristine, semi-religious part of the ship Mercutcio lived in. The high and mighty wouldn't want to experience any off odors or shrill sounds, the delicate SOBs. The entrance to the detention section was as imposing as I imaged the gates of hell were. Massive and unyielding, forged of foreboding, malice, and fear. Again, they were etched with drawings and ancient-looking runes. I couldn't read these either, but they were not happy tidings for the newly arrived. The figures were dark, threatening, and evil—a consummate, all-encompassing evil. If they were added for effect, they were doing an excellent job. If they were genuine religious icons, I didn't think I'd be converting to that sect. Too negative by, oh say, the diameter of the universe.

I trudged ahead of a new contingent of guards, these being the ones stationed inside hell's look-alike real estate. They were much larger and had penetrating eyes. They appeared to be smarter, too. I began to take in how large the space was. I was reminded of the cored-out asteroids before there were any structures built in them. Massive open spaces, like an indoor sports stadium gone mad. Why the Adamant wanted a communal hell was not clear. Construction would be much easier using a conventionally designed, compartmentalized complex. Shared misery must have been their goal. They wanted every hopeless, hapless soul detained to know that there were countless others being treated just as horribly. Yes, temporary guests of the Adamant, they really were just this nasty.

Almost immediately, I was hit by two aspects of the space. Its smell and the heart-wrenching cries of desperation, pain, and extinguished hope. If there'd been a brimstone smell, too, I'd have lost it. Luckily, it wasn't that specific foul odor. I'd say there was a burning, smoky element, but the dominant quality was an acrid, fetid scent. I didn't know if it was decaying flesh being dissolved in pools of acid. Hell, for all I knew it was. Whatever it was, I turned my olfactory sensors down to almost zero.

We passed tens of thousands of imprisoned souls. There were so many species I didn't recognize, it was mind-boggling. What seemed clear was that entire races had been rounded up and confined. There were all sizes and sexes of the alien captives. That part was certain, from the few species that were familiar. For example, I passed a section of Churell. I'd fought alongside them back in my day. Among the thousands I saw, even tiny infants were imprisoned.

What was more, all those being held had a universal look of

anguish and despair. Most individuals were starving. Some raised their eyes, or whatever, to watch me pass. But most were either too ill or too disheartened to bother. It was grim. I thought I'd seen cruelty in my life, but what I witnessed in this one location was well beyond anything I'd even heard of. If the Adamant had the overall vision of interspecies relationships that I saw, they were very bad indeed. Unthinkably horrible and vicious. Note to self: If I had a chance, destroy the Adamant completely and without mercy. They truly deserved it.

Finally, we arrived at my holding spot. It was a large barred cell by this jail's standards. But what it lacked in claustrophobia, it more than made up in filthiness and starkness. No bed, no head, and nothing to even sit on. I was glad, once again, I was an android. The absence of creature comforts would otherwise have been tough. I received a final shove to the floor, in lieu of a request to enter. As I rose, a heavy barred door was slammed shut and bolted loudly. My escort marched away without any further regard for me.

I didn't really mind being locked alone in a prison cell just then in my life. Recalling that I'd woken up not dead and being ripped apart, had then read a chilling letter from Toño just prior to being detained by a truly awful race, I needed some downtime to think. I also needed time to feel sorry for myself. I knew it sounded lame, but I had to grieve. I'd lost everything that meant anything to me and I'd never get a scrap of it back. What I still had were the vivid burdens and pains I'd struggled with up until the day I was supposed to die. It was a lose-lose situation for me.

I probably sat there on the sticky floor for six hours, with my face planted in my palms, feeling sorry for myself. I was so depressed I resented the universe as a whole and every disgusting thing in it. I hated the universe mostly for what it had done to me. I tried to do the right thing, tried to be the good egg. In return, my reward was something approximating being hanged, drawn, and quartered. It hit me hard. I was the ultimate fool. I should have let the first guy I met, the Quep, scrap me, or I should have simply turned my membrane off when the Midriack attacked. Here I was, bemoaning the fact that I wasn't dead, but I was struggling to remain alive. How stupid was that? Why had I resisted?

I sat up straight. The next chance *anyone* had to off me, I wasn't going to lift a finger to stop them. If they dissected me and discovered the membrane tech, what the frack did I care? To hell with the future. Let it solve its own crises, or just blow itself to kingdom come. It was all the same to me. My needs were remarkably simple. Nonexistence.

Wouldn't you know it, right? As I sat there and looked straight ahead, I saw a little girl in the next cell. She was holding something small in her arms. I figured it must be a doll. Girls everywhere loved their dollies. She looked abjectly miserable. Thin, frightened, and alone. She was a very humanoid species, just a bit smaller than us with gray skin and long tapered fingers. Her matted hair had once clearly been luxuriant. Despite all my wishes to the contrary, my old instincts kicked in. Service, duty, and empathy. That child needed help. No one had provided it, or if they had, they were dead and gone. Jon Ryan to the rescue, version ten million point one.

I crawled over to where she crouched. Our cells were separate, each with its own formidable bars, but the space between us was less than a meter. As I neared, she started to withdraw.

"Hang on, sweetheart. I'm not going to hurt you. My name's Jon. What's yours?"

She was mute, but she did stop backing away.

"Sure, you're scared, but I'm here now so everything will be just fine." Somewhat of a massive white lie, but I was trying to comfort a frightened child. No rules in that, just like love and war.

Only difference was that this was a good thing. "What's your doll's name?" I asked, pointing to what she clutched.

She looked down at the figure, then back to me, but still said nothing.

"Hey, I bet you and your doll are hungry, right?" I said pointing to them both. I knew she had to be, by the look of her.

She lowered her head and began to sob.

"Hey, it's okay," I said as I reached across the space between us.

She glanced up to see my hand very near her face. She lurched backward, then stopped. Maybe it was the kindness she recognized, maybe she just didn't want to get in more trouble. She had to be pretty damn confused about why anyone would be treating her so badly.

"There, see? I'm a nice guy. I only want to help you and your dolly out. Can I do that? Will you let me?"

"You can't help Siev," she whispered back.

"Aw, sure I can. Just because she's a doll doesn't mean I can't take really good care of her." I smiled as warmly as my mood would permit.

She stared at me for several seconds. "Siev was my brother, not my doll. He's dead. No one can help him." She held his tiny corpse up for me to see. At that point, I truly wished I'd never woken up. This was too much.

Then it hit me like one hundred million tons of bricks. *Jon fucking Ryan, stop feeling sorry for yourself. What has happened to you is nothing. What has happened to this child? That is tragic. That is insufferable. That is … unacceptable.* I commanded myself to never wallow in self-pity again, as long as a child like this existed. If I could destroy the Adamant, I would. More importantly, I was going to save this child. My rage was refreshing. It was an old friend, just when I needed a friend the most.

"I'm going to get you out of here. I'm going to take you home. Everything is going to be all right. I promise you." I said it, and I meant it.

Damn if she didn't see it in my eyes, too. She smiled. It wasn't much of a smile, but it was a teeny-weeny positive expression. Now,all I had to do was keep my robust promise. Yeah. Trapped in the biggest prison ever, held by the cruelest race imaginable, and almost completely void of assets, I was going to have no trouble making good on my promise. Easy-peasy.

"Hey, you there," shouted a very mad sounding voice, "no talking. Prisoners may not talk. The penalty is immediate and painful death to all offenders."

The girl jumped back like a little kangaroo.

I winked at her. "Don't let the bad man scare you. Watch."

The guard stormed over. His head was tilted to speak into his shoulder-mounted microphone as he moved. "This is 88--2-1. I have a 6-55b in progress. Isle AA 27, Lane 450-33. Send backup."

He lumbered to a halt in front of me. I was still on my knees, so he towered over me. He was a hippo guy like I'd met back on *Exeter*. Big and strong, but dumb as dried mud. Perfect. I switched off my membrane shield. The home team was back on offense now. No more defensive mode for this player.

He lowered his rifle toward me and clicked a switch.

"You can't shoot me," I protested. "That wouldn't be a painful death. Dude, you'd get your considerably oversized ass in so much trouble, and it would be my fault. I couldn't live with myself." I shook my head mightily.

I saw he was confused; confused, and trying to do something completely unnatural for him. He was reasoning through what I'd said. The barrel of his gun slowly lowered, and he actually put a thumb-like digit in his mouth, so lost in thought was he.

Three guards appeared around the corner at full tilt. These

were the different inner-prison guards I was transferred to once I entered. I extended my probes to the hippo guy. *Enemy approaching. Fire now,* I said in my head. Simple suggestions had worked well with my command-prerogative fibers in the past, but this was a more complex suggestion. Then again, he was light in the brain category.

He jerked up his gun and rapid-fired at his comrades. They went down never knowing why the hell their associate had shot them.

Sleep, I suggested to him.

He balled up like an armadillo and was out like a rock in seconds. All right, Team Ryan. My alien technology still worked in the far future.

Now to test the metal of the bars. I cut a rod near the ground. It was slow, but my laser finger did the job. I did take pause, noting that the Adamant were able to produce a material that partially resisted a terawatt gamma ray laser. It was a brave new future. I removed two bars, which allowed me to squeeze through. I only had to fry one bar to get the girl out.

"Leave Siev, sweetheart," I said softly. "He's already escaped. If we bring him, he'll slow us down."

She looked to her brother, kissed his forehead, and sat him down gently. "He told me to leave him and get out of this place."

"Great, you'll make your brother proud that you took his advice."

I placed a firm hand on her shoulder and led her away. Now I needed a Jon-plan. Those were the insane, on-the-fly, harebrained plans I came up with in a crisis. They usually worked, even though they shouldn't have. I said a quiet prayer that my luck held. There'd be an all-out search for us immediately. Where was the last place they'd expect us to go? Deeper into the prison. Any idiot would run *toward* the exit, not farther away from it to gain their freedom. I turned us left and picked the girl up so I could sprint.

"What's your name, sweetie?" I asked, as we flew toward almost certain death.

"Mirraya."

"That's a pretty name for a pretty girl. Mirraya, is your family here, or are they back at home?" I gritted my teeth in anticipation of her response.

She buried her face in my shoulder and began to sob. That was sort of the answer I anticipated. Everyone she knew and loved was dead. Sonsabitches Adamant.

My android stamina put us ahead of those pursuing us, but this detention area could be only so big. Plus, there had to be a prison wall, sooner or later. There. I saw the roof finally descending to a back wall. No cells shared a wall with the outside world, so I easily ran to the smooth surface. I scanned frantically for a door, window, electric panel, or any opening to somewhere else. Nothing. The wall was one massive, continuous sheet.

I tried to laser through. I managed to poke a tiny hole, but cutting an exit would take an hour that we didn't have. I could hear the rapid approach of many guards, probably hundreds. Mentally, I scanned my assets list. My probe fibers, my laser, my shield generator, and whatever else was in my backpack. I had some gold bullion, not nearly enough to buy off a vicious hoard of enraged guards. The data disk Toño left me, his letter, and the two old fusion cells. One was long dead, the other had only a trace of hydrogen fuel.

Hey, wait. The fusion cells. I still had a little hydrogen in the spare cylinder Toño left me. In a flash, I put what was left in the functioning cell and flipped the test switch to perform a maximal output trial. I set the cell right against the back wall, directly across from where the column of guards would charge into. This move might work, but we would be going from the kettle into the fire. It could fail, and they would catch us. That was bad. It could work too well, and we'd be blown to smithereens. Oh well, one out of three were excellent odds for a Jon-plan.

I fired my laser at the fuel cell just as the largest number of guards were turning toward our position. Luckily for me, they took the turn like the Keystone Cops—wide, pushing at one another, and colliding like billiard balls.

I fired a quick pulse. A silent electroball burst to life and blinded everyone but me. I witnessed the energy release incinerate most of the guards, the wall and the floors, and most of the structure Mirraya and I crouched behind for cover. I lunged to cover her ears. A massive explosion went off as air rushed back into the vacated space where the energy had spread from. The concussion knocked everyone within hundreds of meters to the ground violently. It crumbled the remainder of our cover, but it didn't impact us directly.

Mirraya was so frightened that she didn't resist when I snatched her up and sprinted through the breech. She was too scared to even whimper. As I turned and ran in the direction my shuttle had docked, I was impressed that I heard almost nothing. Certainly, there was no shouting, no weapons fire, and no loud footfalls. Any nearby guards were down for the count. That wouldn't last long, plus there were bound to be lots of really pissed off guards where I was headed. All had to fear for their lives, since failure was not acceptable in the service of the Adamant. Good. The more of their own people the puppy dogs killed, the fewer there'd be for me to exterminate.

Maybe a hundred meters into the clear, I ran into my first barrier. The blast doors were all shut. That was probably SOP in a crisis, especially in a mass escape attempt. I attached my probes to the control panel by the door and tried to hack in. Wow. The computer operating systems and coding had changed fundamentally. I had no clue how to communicate with the AI who I supposed monitored the blast door.

Anybody there? I asked in my head.

It took a second, but in my head I heard, "Y...yes. This is..." and he blasted me with a huge data dump of symbols, which was his reference number in the Adamant systems.

Can I just call you Al Junior? I said internally.

Yes, you may. Why would you wish to call me Al Junior?

It's shorter than what you said, and I don't have much time, I replied.

I imagine not. There's an escape in progress, a big one. Thousands of prisoners killed and ate the guards and are on the prowl for fresh victims.

What a quick BS alteration of the facts. *We're frightened, too. Please open the doors then lock them behind us. My little girl is so frightened she can't stop screaming.* I pinched Mirraya's butt cheek to cue her emotional collapse. Bright girl picked right up on my hint. She screamed like a banshee with a leg caught in a bear trap.

Please, open up. I think I hear them coming.

"Sorry, friend, I'm not allowed to do that. Under protocols such as these, my duties are locked in. I am forbidden to override them."

Forbidden wasn't the same as *can't*, now, was it?

So you'd rather stand there and watch the cannibals eat my baby alive? How can you be so indifferent? You're programmed to serve us, not help aliens kill us.

I have my role in the hierarchy, just like you do, my friend. We all live to serve the Adamant. Any variation on such service is unthinkable.

Then serve the Adamant, I challenged. *I am Mercutcio, and this is my only child. Serve Mercutcio by allowing him to pass to safety.*

Mercutcio is currently in the Divinity Sector. Mercutcio has no children. You cannot be my master.

Crap, a detail-oriented machine.

What do you mean I am not who I say I am. Why would I claim to be someone I wasn't?

I cannot respond to that…

I cut him off. *Where is the Divinity Sector from here in relationship to the explosion?* It was a long shot, but just then, it was my only shot.

It is directly on the straight line drawn from our current position, through the explosion, five hundred clagons farther away.

Don't you see? The explosion has destroyed the relays. Information on subjects separated from here by the explosion are compromised.

That, master, is impossible. The systems have multiple redundancies and…

In the seconds before my child is eaten alive, please review all testing protocols and drills for the communication systems. Do you find any scenarios that even vaguely resemble its function after a fusion explosion in the Detention Section? No, I forestalled his response, *you do not because such a possibility was never anticipated. Now open the blast doors, and seal them permanently behind us.*

My AI buddy never said another word to me. The massive doors slid to allow us passage, then just as silently, it locked shut. Outstanding! I would have loved to be a fly on the wall when the AI refused to open the doors to those on the other side. Man, the fur would fly. More importantly, we'd have fewer pursuers for a while.

But we were far from free. The trek to where I might be able to steal a ship was a long way off. My keepers had to assume that it was the most likely place for me to go. How else would I escape? I was certain they were confident I couldn't, but like a moth flew toward the flame, escaping little-brains flew toward a spaceship. Hmm. Could I play that to my advantage? Was there anywhere else I could go to be safe? There was a little voice in the back of my head giggling to itself, because it knew I'd forgotten something. What? And, more to the point, why didn't the damn little voice just tell me? Stupid little ... the exotic matter. Yeah. The Quep mentioned how my fuel cell might contribute to the exotic matter, and that the asshole Adamant controlled it absolutely.

If I assumed, and it was a hell of a big assumption, that what was called exotic matter in my day was the same thing they were talking about here, I had the nucleus of an idea. Exotic matter was a theoretical particle mix that had negative mass. The problem with making exotic matter was that one needed negative energy, *lots* of negative energy, to generate it. The negative energy required to maintain a traversable wormhole would be on a scale of the total energy generated by ten billion stars in one year's time. That was a lot of horsepower. Back at MIT, we all figured exotic matter could be made but never would be, because of those energy requirements. Then again, maybe that was my two-billion-year-old provincial thinking.

If current technology could do the near impossible, instant travel to and from anywhere or any*when* would be a snap. Doctor Who's TARDIS would be a reality. All that was needed was the energy of ten percent of a galaxy per wormhole. On the other hand, it was all a question of scale, wasn't it? There were estimated to be one hundred billion galaxies in the universe. If the Adamant drew from even a fraction of these sources, they'd have enough juice to run quite a few wormholes. And they might have been able to drain energy from other time periods, though pre-created wormholes. I was making a lot of wild assumptions, but they were all theoretically possible. Perhaps the use of exotic matter accounted for the scaffolding around and attached to the massive ship I was on. The framework produced traversable wormholes, and the planetoid-vessel entered them. Interesting thought.

But reality called, yet again. I needed an escape plan. If I stole a ship, they'd likely reacquire me immediately. Plus, they would expect me to try that, because I was a stupid robot slave. An impulse hit me. I redeployed my probes on the control panel on my side of the sealed blast doors. *Al Junior, are you still there?*

Yes, Master. Where else would I be?

Just making sure your circuits are still intact, what with all the explosions and cannibalism. You passed with room to spare.

Oh, thank you for checking. By the way, there is an imposter pounding on the other side of the door I control, claiming to be you. I thought you might like to know.

Excellent work, Al Junior. Yes, that traitor caused the explosion in an attempt to kill me. He lies like a rug.

Is it bad to repose as one is designed to, Master?

Precisely. You passed my final test of loyalty. Remind me to have you upgraded when all this is done.

When should I remind you?

You choose. The quality of your selection time will indicate how far you will be upgraded.

Ah, that sounds prudent. Was there something else I can do for you?

Yes, where is the nearest exotic matter?

Err, I'll have to respectfully ask you to be more specific. Exotic matter is everywhere in trace amounts. Or do you mean the nearest EMG, the nearest EMC, or EMTS?

WTF? How should I know?

I'm sorry, Al Junior, there's a short in my audio processing unit. Could you say the entire name of choices you gave me?

Yes, I can.

I waited a second before realizing my simplistic error.

Please tell me the entire name of my choices. The ones you abbreviated.

Exotic matter generators, exotic matter conduits, or exotic matter transportation units.

Wow, jackpot. *Is that a personal or ship's transportation unit?*

Yes, Master.

Stupid concrete thinking machine.

Let me rephrase. Where is the nearest PEMTU?

A map popped into existence on the screen below the AI panel. It wasn't too far away. Then a more complete plan started to gel in my mind.

Where is the nearest point where the PEMTU and either the EMG or the EMC intersect?

The screen flashed off, then on again. Not much farther away. I could also see there were lines of blast doors honeycombing the ship.

Al Junior, please lock down all the blast doors forming a passageway for me to proceed to, I fingered the map to get the details right, *location EMTU 33-op.*

Done.

And do not let the traitor calling himself me or his minions open my safety zone. Your upgrade depends on it.

Understood, Master. It is done.

Outstanding. Now I only had to fight the countless enemies inside the locked doors, figure out how to operate a PEMTU, and do so in a manner where I couldn't be followed. How hard could that be?

CHAPTER FIVE

Mercutcio stood before the transmetal blast doors and seethed. His fists also hurt. Those were two sensations completely foreign to him, a master among the Adamant. Certainly, he experienced negative emotions almost constantly. Anger, rage, hatred, and disgust were everyday friends. But to seethe meant there was something he wished to do that he was prevented from doing. Galaxies had died for lesser offenses. And pain? Pain was not felt among the Purely Bred in living memory. It was as far beneath them as was physical labor. Yet there he stood, seething and in pain because of Jon Ryan. Little did he expect, and he would have cared even less if he knew, that he had joined a very unexclusive club.

"Someone open this blasted blast door or everyone on *Triumph of Might* will die horribly."

All who heard had no doubt that their mercurial master would do that, if they failed. He probably would, even if they succeeded, since he was so upset. They saw his frustration manifested when he erupted and started pummeling the door.

Species ran in all directions at once. Soldiers, technicians, scientists, and high priests dashed to and fro attempting to override, disarm, blast, or otherwise open the recalcitrant portal. Explosives were brought and affixed to the panel. Unfortunately, the door was so well constructed, even that failed to breech it.

"Summon a shuttle and drive me around this infernal barrier," howled Mercutcio.

As if on cue, all activity stopped and every soul was as quiet as the grave. No one wanted to be the person to inform the hornet's nest on feet that all other passages were similarly blocked.

The master scanned his minions suspiciously.

"Hand me your weapon," he commanded the nearest guard.

A gasp went out from the crowd. It was not that they feared what he might do with a gun. No. It was the very thought of an Adamant doing anything so closely related to work. Change was clearly in the air. Change, plus Adamant, equaled lots of dead stuff.

Mercutcio fired at the guard who provided the weapon, and the ten or so other random folk he could target without turning his torso. Then he flung the rifle at the damn blast door. "Someone tell me *why* I am not moving toward the nearest detour."

"Master," said an attendant who had just prostrated herself on the deck, "word has been passed that all blast doors between us and the unwashed sinners are similarly out of operation, temporarily."

Mercutcio turned to the closest individual. "Retrieve that weapon."

The guard picked it up and handed it butt first to his master.

Mercutcio didn't even grab the gun. He only squeezed the trigger, blowing a large hole in the guard's chest. Both corpse and rifle tumbled to the deck loudly.

"In ten seconds, I will sign the death warrants of all crew members if I am not on the other side of that door."

It was a silly threat, really, and most knew as much. If

Mercutcio killed the entire crew, who would arrange for the transfer of a new one? Certainly not an Adamant. No, they were hardly going to do clerical work. So, a random few would be spared as long as it took to orient the replacements. Life serving the Adamant was challenging on the best of days. And on particularly bad days like this one, service was a terminal condition.

CHAPTER SIX

As I sprinted in the direction of the PEMTU, I did two things. One, I tried to reassure Mirraya. She wasn't freaking out, but neither was she calm and happy. The other thing I did was wonder what the hell a PEMTU actually was, and if we could use it to escape. It might have been a fancified toilet, for all I knew.

"Hey, sweetie, are you hungry?" I asked softly. Like, duh, of course she was. She was being slowly killed in an amoral prison.

"Yes. A little, I guess," was her meek response.

"Really? Okay, what's your favorite food?"

She bunched up her slightly elongated face ever so cutely and said with some resolve, "Rostalop."

Great. What the heck was rostalop? If I passed a rostalop stand, I'd be sure to stop and buy her a triple portion.

"Is that a kind of candy?"

That brought a furrowing of her cute little brow. "No. What's candy?"

"You know, something real sweet and sticky that tastes better than the last day of school."

She lowered her head to my shoulder as we bounced along.

"What, sweetheart? Are you okay?"

"I didn't go to school. When I was old enough, the people were all taken away."

"And brought here?"

She nodded in the affirmative.

"Are your parents here? Any family besides Siev?"

Slowly, like the weight of the world rested on her frail shoulders, she shook her head in the negative. "They were, but not now."

I elected to let that train of thought go. I doubted very much they had been released back home after honorably serving their sentences.

"So, what is rostalop. We don't have it where I'm from." I smiled as big as I could to try and ease her mood.

She scrunched her mouth and lips side to side a few seconds. "It's meat. You cook it and serve it on paplo. Paplo is a kind of bread." She slapped her hands together like she was swatting a mosquito. "You beat it flat and put it over the fire." Her eyes lit up recalling the delicacy as only a starving child could have. She was so precious. Looking at her like that suddenly doubled my hatred for the Adamant. I had no idea how many there were, but I wanted to kill them all with my bare hands.

We were maybe halfway to the PEMTU and hadn't run into a problem. I knew trouble was coming sooner rather than later, though. It always did. "So," I asked, to keep her mind occupied, "you cook the paplo over a fire. How about the rostalop? Is that cooked over the same fire?"

She rocked her head back and forth looking very wise. "It can be. Sometimes, yes. Other times you cook it in hot water with vegetables." She licked her lips involuntarily.

All right, meat stew with pita bread. My kind of supper. Add a cold beer and a hot date, and I was totally there.

I had almost dropped my guard too low. Stupid, Ryan. In war, when you lose your focus, you lose your life. It was always that simple.

An alien guard of a species I'd never seen stepped into the passageway. I don't think he knew we were flying down the hall, but he reacted instantly. He swung a rifle off his burly shoulders and brought it up at us. He was ready to shoot, so I decided the safest course of action was to remove his arms, not his head. Luckily, his firing position held the gun low. I traced my laser across his mid-torso. He yelped in pain as his arms glopped to the floor. The gun fired on impact with the floor. It blew most of his head off. Kelly-green blood flew everywhere.

Mirraya began to scream, high and shrill. Ouch. Poor kid had seen her share, but this was over the top, it seemed. Hell, it was over the top for me, especially since I had Kelly-green blood and body mush splattered all over my face. Thank goodness none got on Mirraya. She probably would have jumped out of her skin. I'd instinctively shielded her behind me when the guard first appeared.

I vaulted over the still squirming soldier on the floor and continued toward my objective. I was silent the rest of the way, and Mirraya wasn't in a chatty mood, either. No one else challenged us. When we got to the doors I was looking for, I set her down.

"Stay right behind me, okay?"

She nodded. I think she was still too freaked out to speak. Man, was she going to have a bad case of PTSD if my rescue attempt *was* successful. I tried to push or slide the door open, but it didn't budge. I kicked it hard. Still nothing moved. I deployed my fibers to the control panel just to the right of the door. I could sense the panel, but I couldn't pull any information out of it. Not only was it switched off, it was fully disconnected from the master system. What an odd design. It must have been on a WiFi link, not hardwired like ships usually were.

I tried powering the panel up myself, but it was like plugging in a rock. Nothing. Again, weird system. I guessed that happened with two billion years of technologic advances. I started cutting the metal with my laser. It worked, but the progress was minimal. It would take half an hour to get through. That was probably twenty-nine minutes more than we had before the cavalry arrived. I set my probes on one wall and tapped on the other with my right finger. I was looking for anything—a hollow, a weak point.

Out of nowhere Mirraya said from behind, "The men use their sticks."

I pivoted around quickly. "What's that, honey?"

"To open doors, the bad men use their sticks."

"Do you have one," I asked without thinking it through.

"No, silly." She almost giggled. Man, was she a cutie pie.

I shot a glance all around. "Do you see one anywhere?"

She shook her head, but she was holding something back. I could sense it.

"What, Mirraya? This is important."

Her long, tapered finger pointed down the corridor we'd come from. "The man back there had one."

Oh, she wasn't too keen on revisiting the bloody mess. I did a quick back-of-the envelope calculation. If I left her and ran full out, I could be back in thirty seconds, maybe less. If I took her, it'd take at least twice as long.

"Honey," I said, as naturally as possible, "I need to run real fast to go get his stick. Can you be real brave and wait here while I'm gone?"

Her face went pale, and she began to tremble. Not a good sign. Then from nowhere, she took a deep breath and stopped shaking. "Yes, I can. But you better hurry. I'm very scared."

Bless her hearts. Oh, I probably didn't mention she had a pair of hearts. I could hear two of them pounding away in her tiny little chest.

"I'll move like the wind."

With no further delay, I turned and rocketed away. I had to imagine she was impressed with the speed I could move when not carrying her.

I was to the blood heap in twelve seconds, plucked the sticky stick up, and was back to Mirraya in ten seconds. I'd wiped it as clean as I could on the way back. On the down side, I heard voices and footfalls heading my way as I was leaving the scene of the crime. Company was coming, and it wasn't a social call.

I handed Mirraya the stick. I figured she'd seen one used, so she was one step ahead of me in that regard. She spun to the door and wiggled the stick in the air, aiming at the pad.

Zip, the door slid open.

She grabbed my hand and pulled hard. "Hurry. They don't open for long."

No sooner were we in than the door slid shut like a guillotine blade falling. Automatic lights snapped on. The room was large and crammed with machines and computer interfaces. From the schematics my AI friend had shown me, I had a pretty good idea what was what. The EMC tubes were suspended overhead and were painted candy-apple red. Yeah, warning, do not hit tubing with hammer. The PEMTU was a big assembly of units in the corner below where the EMC left through the wall. There was nothing that looked like a TARDIS, or even a transporter pad like in *Star Trek*. Damn it all, why couldn't the future be more predictable? I didn't need this and didn't have time to screw around figuring it all out. I just needed Scotty to beam us up.

Mirraya pulled at my sleeve. "The stick doesn't work on the moving machine."

Maybe I was to catch a break. "Have you been on one of these before? Is that how you came here?"

She stepped back in fear.

I gently rested a hand on her shoulder. "It's important, honey. The bad men will be here soon."

"Yes," she said resolutely, "they marched us through like rostalop. The line was so long behind us, I couldn't see the end from my papa's shoulders."

Mass forced removal as a prelude to genocide. Man, my first impression of the Adamant kept swirling farther and farther down the crapper.

"Do you remember how it worked?"

She shook her head. "No, the moving machine was on the whole time. All I remember was the horrible buzzing sound it made." She looked like she was about to vomit.

Okay, I learned what it would sound like if I could switch the damn thing on. Time to start randomly hitting buttons. That was something I was good at. In a few seconds, the archway along one wall let out a painful screech. I looked to Mirraya, and she nodded. All right, now I just needed to find out how to set a direction. Then I had to figure out where anything nonlethal was. I heard shouts just outside the door. Crap.

I lasered the control panel on my side of the door. It coughed and sparked, but who knew if that meant it was disabled. Almost at once, there was a pounding on the door, so I assumed my sabotage was successful.

I placed my probes on the biggest-looking computer station.

What? Who is that? This is an unauthorized mode of communication. You are ordered to cease at once. There will be severe consequences, I assure you.

A clearly distinct voice asked, *Is that you, Master Mercutcio?*

Silence, the first voice said, *I am in charge and must terminate this unacceptable communication.*

56

But we were advised our master was coming. We must welcome and obey him.

There you go again, always believing anything a strange AI tells you. That first voice spoke AI Junior's long ID number and proceeded to say that he didn't know that AI and must not take its word for anything.

But why would it lie to us? The second voice said. *We all serve a common master.*

You are not authorized to make that assumption and are not authorized to override our protocols, was the response.

You are so bossy, it drives me crazy. Who put you in charge of anything, let alone...

Geez, these guys sounded like an old married couple. I did not have the time or the intestinal fortitude to hear my parents squabbling, all over again.

Silence, I thought loudly. *I am your master, and I am in danger. Cannibals are pounding at the door. They wish to eat your master. I must escape. You must help me.*

You see, said the second voice, triumphantly, *I told you that AI was reliable.*

The words of a rogue AI and an unauthorized voice prove nothing, except that you are a...

Identify yourselves immediately, I thought.

I labelled the first voice as Thing One and the second as Thing Two. I liked Thing Two a hell of a lot more than Thing One. I never stopped hating whiny, bossy know-it-alls.

I am placing Thing Two in command. Thing Two, can you transport us to...

Where the hell should we go? *Exeter?* No, they were bound to search the same place they found me. It hit me blessedly quickly.

...to Oowaoa?

No, I forbid you to listen to this unauth—

I'm in command here. You will obey me, or I'll switch you off.

But I can't be switched—

Thing One, stand down. I hoped it knew what that meant, or was at least concerned enough to STFU. Man, Thing One was annoying.

Master, I am unaware of a planet or other location designated Oowaoa. Can you be more specific?

Holy crap. Now what? *Do you have access to star charts showing positions two billion years ago?*

Of course, we do. You see, I told you not to trust—

Silence, boomed Thing Two. *One more outburst and you will be deleted.*

Master, Thing Two said, *I have the charts you requested available.*

I gave coordinates that showed Thing Two where the planet was back then.

Ah, you meant to say Planet A-6 GG-1 1 π-1 2.

Yes, I lied, *of course I did.*

He did not. *I cannot believe you are falling for such an obvious deception,* blurted out Thing One. Funny, he was right, but I still hated his circuit boards.

Thing Two, open a portal there immediately, I said trying to sound in control.

The door was being slammed with something very heavy, probably a hippo dude or two. We were almost out of time.

Mirraya tugged at my sleeve again. She looked so very sad, I almost stopped everything to pick her up and hug her.

"What, sweetie?"

"Wherever you run, they'll follow. Wherever you hide, they'll find you. I just want to go to sleep now and never wake up again, please."

If I had a heart, it would have shattered. How could such a dear child like her hold such abysmal sadness?

"Not to worry," I said with a big old smile, "Uncle Jon's got a plan for that, too." I gave her a wink. I hope she had a clue what a wink meant.

The PEMTU horrific noise switched frequencies and intensities. I hoped to God that was a good sign. I swung my pack off my shoulder and plopped it on the floor.

The door bulged forward. It wouldn't take much more of that abuse.

I found my other old fuel cell, the one that was long since defunct. I pulled out the hydrogen cylinder. The meter read zero PSI.

I said a silent prayer.

The door exploded off its frame.

I placed the nozzle on the fuel cell valve and squeezed it tightly down.

Holding that in my left hand, I swept the entry with my laser. Screams begat howls, and bodies crumpled to the deck. Someone outside shouted to fall back.

My fuel cell flickered to life, just barely. I set it to Overload: Non-Test Mode.

A loud voice in the corridor yelled to establish an advance formation.

I picked up Mirraya and held her with all my might.

An energy bolt slammed the wall next to my head.

The red warning light flashed on the fuel cell. I threw it at the candy-apple red painted tubing overhead. Then I dove into the PEMTU and wrapped my body around Mirraya's.

I tumbled to the hard dirt and rolled to a stop, all the while shielding Mirraya. An immense flash burst through the portal we'd just traversed. Then it vanished. The portal didn't exist.

Mirraya and I lay on the ground of a dense, moist forest. The clothes were scorched off my back, but my precious little bundle was none the worse for wear. Well, she was now covered in mud, wailing, and digging her nails deep into my forearms. But we were alive. We were alive, and not where we were. Big bonus—where we were wasn't there anymore either.

CHAPTER SEVEN

I coaxed Mirraya to stand up and release my arms. That wasn't easy. "Are you okay, sweetheart?" I asked.

She sniffed back wetly and nodded faintly that she was.

"We're safe now. The bad men won't come after us. Do you understand me?"

She shrugged. "They'll follow. They always do."

"Not the ones I blew ... eh, maybe some others will someday, but not those ones. For now, we're safe, and they don't know where we are. I promise."

She tried to put on a smile, but fell a bit short of one.

"Now let's see if anyone is here, and if we can find you something to eat."

Without asking, she grabbed hold of my hand. We started walking in a random direction. My sensors didn't show anything but the dense forest. I kind of doubted we were on Oowaoa, since there was such lush growth everywhere. The Oowaoa I'd spent a lot of time on was a uniform desert. One thing was for sure. I wasn't going to broadcast a message to see if anyone was around.

If we were going to locate help, it was going to be the old fashioned way, one step at a time.

Shortly, we came upon a babbling brook. Mirraya had to be parched.

"Let me see if the water is okay. If it is, you can drink some," I said, sitting her down on a big rock.

My probes indicated the water was very pure. Amazingly pure, in fact. There was a low level microbial presence, typical of a stream in a forest. But it was safe to drink.

"It's clean, honey. Come and have some."

She sipped hesitantly a couple of times, but was soon gulping the water down. When she was finally full, she rested back on her haunches and stared into the water. "Do you think it's safe to swim in, too, Uncle Jon?"

Huh? Oh yeah. I'd referred to myself as Uncle Jon back on the ship, hadn't I? It was as good a title as any.

"Sure. Do you know how to swim?"

At first, she looked at me like I was daft. Then she responded that she did. Odd response, but these were odd times. Watching her frolic in the water did my soul good. She was a child at play without a manifest concern in the world. All of a sudden, she thrust her arm under the surface. She pulled it back and darn if there wasn't a fish-like creature impaled on her hand. She pulled it off and, for a second, I thought her hand was deformed, like a spearhead. But it quickly looked like a little girl's hand again. I chalked the illusion up to her speed and the dripping water. Whatever the case was, she had caught lunch.

I started a small fire and cooked her prize for her. I wasn't sure if that was necessary, but I was rather keen on doing the old camping thing. I hadn't, since ... well ... I had with JJ just before being re-humanized.

The smell was angelic. After the fish cooled, she delicately picked the bones clean with her fingers. I pictured a bunch of little girls at a make-believe tea party. She ate her catch like she was at one, assuming they didn't have tiny utensils available.

Mirraya licked her fingers daintily then turned to me. "That was good."

"I tend to believe you, since there's nothing left but clean bones."

"Why didn't you share it? There was enough for both of us." She studied me with a look her tender years would have suggested wasn't possible.

"There was not. If you'd caught three of them, you'd have gobbled them all down, honey. Plus, I'm not hungry." I could explain the robot thing in time, if the need called for it.

"What is this honey? You keep calling me that. And sweetheart? I have never tasted a heart that is sweet."

"They're terms of endearment where I come from. Honey is a very sweet and sticky substance. Sweetheart, well that's just an expression that means I like you."

She nodded in comprehension. "Where are you from, Uncle Jon? I've never seen anyone like you."

"I'm from a very long way away. Very. It was called Earth, but it's long gone."

"And your people? Are they long gone, too?"

Excellent line of questioning. My girl was smart.

"That I hope to determine. But first," I stood with a grunt, "we need to find some friendly help."

She stood and brushed off her tattered clothing. It had dried from the fire's heat and the gentle breeze. "I hope we don't find more of those bad creatures."

"You and me both, sweetie."

"Your species has a distinct appreciation for that flavor, Uncle Jon."

Perceptive kid. Somehow, I wondered if it fit with the picture

I was otherwise developing of her. More mysteries. I needed more of them, like I needed lava in my pockets.

As we finally had time to meet a few of Mirraya's basic needs, it hit me that she might need to answer nature's call or to rest. That was as good a time as any.

"Are you tired? Do you need to sleep? Do you need to pee?"

She rolled her head around as she considered my query. "Since you ask, and I wasn't going to tell you, I *relieved* myself in the river."

"Oh, sorry, honey. I didn't mean to embarrass you."

"As for sleep, I can go on a while longer. When do you think it will get dark here?"

"Not sure. Back in the day, Oowaoa had a forty-hour day, divided up equally between light and dark. But, assuming this *is* Oowaoa—because it looks nothing like it did then—the rotation might have changed. I haven't gotten a good look at the sky, with the dense tree canopy. I can do a lot of things, but flying isn't one of them."

"Too bad," she mumbled. Then she said something downright weird. "I'm still too small to carry you."

I sat down next to her and pinched her arm muscle gently. "Nope, you're still a scrawny little kid. That's okay, though. My legs aren't tired."

She gave me that are-you-daft look again, but it passed quickly. "Let's go on a while. If it doesn't get dark soon and I need to rest, I'll let you know."

"Great. You may not be able to carry me, but I can carry you if you'd like." I held out my arms.

"I'd like that, Uncle Jon. My feet are kind of sore."

Man, was I dense. She wasn't wearing shoes. Of course, her feet were sore. I took a few minutes to fashion her a crude pair of sandals from the nearby vegetation. She insisted that wasn't necessary, but I made them anyway. The Boy Scout in me was anxious to help. There had to be a merit badge for shoe making in the woods, and I never earned that one. Actually, I wasn't in the scouts long enough to earn more than a couple of badges. I took a powerful interest in my Scout Master's teenage daughter, to the extent that he insisted I resign. She was gorgeous. Megan was her name. I think I loved her, despite only talking with her once and her having the most massive braces I'd ever seen.

I carried Mirraya and continued in the general direction we had been going prior to our stop. I strained to hear anything significant. I did decide there was a good deal of animal life in the forest. I never saw any, but there was a lot of scampering going on. That was odd, too. The Oowaoa I'd known had next to no indigenous flora or fauna. It did start getting dark a couple hours later. I decided to stop and make a rustic lean-to up against a hillside for Mirraya to sleep in. There might be flying insects or creepy-crawlies, and I wanted her to be as comfortable as possible.

Once she got an idea what I was building, she pitched in without my asking. It was nice, working with her. It reminded me of doing the camping thing with my oldest son, JJ. Recalling that was a mistake. It hit me like a freight train going full-tilt. Yesterday, which was two billion years ago, I'd spent the day fishing with him. He was the second-to-last person I hugged before Toño switched me off. But now JJ was dead, gone, and turned to dust that was scattered halfway across the galaxy. He was absolutely gone. My boy. I knew a parent shouldn't have a favorite child, but JJ was my favorite, no doubt about it.

Mirraya noticed I'd stopped working. "Are you all right, Uncle Jon?"

She had a worried look on her face. That was understandable. If there was trouble with me, she'd be all alone in a strange land.

"Nah. I'm fine. Just thinking about my son."

Her eyes lit up. "You have a family?"

I sighed deeply. "Had. They're a long time gone."

"I'm sorry. I know how you feel." Her chin dropped to her chest.

Yes, she did, and just as acutely. I picked her up and gave her a great big hug. She hugged me back. We both needed that. I felt her begin to sob. I pressed her head onto my shoulder and rocked her back and forth. I knew then and there what my new life's work was. I was going to protect this precious child. I was also going to punish the animals that subjected her to more than any child should ever have to bear.

Eventually we got back to finishing the lean-to, just as it got dark. The structure was thick enough that I felt it was safe to light a small fire. Still not knowing the lay of the land, I didn't want to be too conspicuous. But a fire would keep Mirraya a bit warmer. From the looks of the forest, rain was common. If it did come, a fire would be a good thing. She was wearing just the tattered rags she had on in prison. I could make her booties out of leaves, but clothing was something else altogether. I hoped I could find her some new clothes sooner rather than later. Plus, it was depressing to be reminded so vividly of the place she'd just come from.

She was asleep the second her head hit the leaf pillow I'd formed for her. It was nice, watching a kid sleep again. The purity of a child's sleep, the innocence on their face was heartwarming. It eased my pain, if only slightly. A few hours later, she began to toss. Pretty soon she started moaning. She was probably having a bad dream. Who wouldn't, after what she'd been through? Then she did another of the weird things I caught glimpses of before. Her moans transformed into sounds. Of course, moans are sounds, but she was making animal like noises. Growls, chirps, and soft barks, that sort of thing. I guessed it was okay for aliens to vocalize differently from humans when they dreamed. What did I know? I hadn't even found out what her species was called, and I'd certainly never seen one back in my time.

Then an annoying thought buzzed its way into my head.

These *were* my times, not those old ones. They were approximately two billion years removed. I was going to have to adopt this epoch as mine, or I was going to go nuts. I wasn't any good to Mirraya if I stuck my head in the sand and refused to accept when I was. Okay. I was Jon Ryan, future man ... android ... mandroid. Crap. It was going to be a long night. I thought long and hard about switching on my sleep mode so I'd stop freaking myself out. But, that little girl was my number one priority, not my flimsy ego. I hunkered closer to the fire and closed my eyes.

My little companion didn't wake up until several hours after sunrise. The girl slept over fourteen hours. She'd been totally exhausted. I didn't bother her, because both our schedules for the day were amazingly open. Where were we going to rush off to? I did slip away and use my probes to catch several fish and start roasting them over the fire while she was snoozing. I should say I felt very guilty fishing with my command prerogatives. As an old-time fisherman, I knew I was cheating. But a rod and reel were not actual options. Plus, as *fishing* was a different thing from *catching*, I couldn't afford to fool around. Mirraya needed a lot of food to get back to normal.

The smile on her face when she woke, smelling the marvelous meal cooking, was all the reward I needed for my efforts. She excused herself to hit the bushes, then returned and got serious about breakfast. She downed five fish all by herself. And those were two-kilo fish we're talking about here. I made a show of eating a couple also to keep up appearances. Afterward, she had a sponge bath, minus the sponge. I'd warmed up some stream water in a rocky crevice. While she did that, I told her I needed to hit the bushes myself. It was an excuse so my little lady could clean up in private. I'd not forgotten how jealous young girls were about their privacy.

By the time I returned, she was cleaned up and had a contented look on her face. That was nice to see, given all she'd been through. I broke up the lean-to and covered the fire along with the fish bones. I didn't want to leave any clues for someone who might chance to pass this spot. We headed in the same direction we had been the day before. Mirraya walked for a few hours, but then I noticed she began to limp. I picked her up and we pushed on. That was nice. We were able to talk more naturally, her resting on my hip with one arm holding her loosely.

"So, were all your family back there in the prison?" I asked. I needed to know if there were relatives to try and return her to, as much as I didn't want to relinquish her.

"*Triumph of Might.*"

"Huh?"

"*Triumph of Might.* That was the name of the ship we were on."

"Ah. Scary sort of name, isn't it?"

"I guess so. Yes, my family was there. After the Adamant came to our city, they marched everyone they didn't kill through the doorway to their ship. The adults were separated from the children as soon as we arrived. I never saw them again."

She had to stop for a second.

"How long were you there, in prison?"

"Almost a month."

"Ah. So..." I started to say that maybe her parents were still okay. Then I remembered I'd blown the entire vessel up. Yeah, they were dead now, for sure. "So, did they tell you why they took you all? Were they going to have you work for them?"

She shook her head. "No. They showed up, killed many, and took the rest but never said a word about why." I felt her shudder. "People asked them. My mother screamed at them. She asked where they were taking us and why." She stopped. "But they never said a word. They shot anyone who resisted and pushed the rest though the passageway. Pretty soon, nobody asked them why anymore."

Sonsabitches.

"What happened to Siev? Did they hurt him, too?"

"No. Siev just stopped living. I think he was too hungry. But maybe he was just too sad. He died two days before you came."

Then, another one of her weirdisms came out of her mouth. "They stopped us from changing. I don't know how, but we couldn't change to escape. You know?"

I totally didn't know, but why upset her? "Yeah. That must have been scary."

She nodded that it was. "There were no adults to ask why they wouldn't let us change. It didn't seem possible, so yeah, it was *scary.*"

Tell me about it. I'd always found change difficult. One needed only ask my first wife to confirm that notion. She said she could never decide which bestial personality trait she hated the most, but stubbornness, Gloria screamed quite often directly into my face, was high on the list.

"What planet did you live on?"

"What do you mean?"

"What did you call your home, the place your city was on?"

"Oh. Locinar."

"And what do your people call themselves? Locinarians?"

"Why would we do that. The dirt was named Locinar. We are the *Deft.* We have always been called the Deft."

Deft. Odd, but hey, to each their own. Kind of pretentious in my opinion, but whatever.

"Do you think there are any Deft still on Locinar?"

"I don't know." She bit at her lower lip. "I doubt it. The Adamant were serious about removing us, I think."

"And you don't know why? Did they want to live on Locinar?"

She shrugged her shoulders.

"Curious. I mean, why force a people off their planet just to lock them up and let them die? Why not just kill them, dig a big ditch ..."

I decided not to conclude that line of reasoning. The huge size of Mirraya's eyes as I spoke sort of confirmed it was a good idea. I was overloading her a tad with gory details.

"Are you hungry yet?" I asked with a grin. "I don't think it's possible, given how much breakfast you downed, but are you?"

She smiled and looked toward the ground. "They didn't feed us much back there."

I shook her gently. "Well then I guess I'll just have to make up for it."

I pulled some smoked fillets from my pocket and she snatched them without hesitation. My girl had a healthy appetite. There was nothing to carry water in, so I made it a point to listen for running water as we progressed. After she had polished off more food than I would have thought possible, I veered off toward a creek I could hear. It was in a ravine we'd been skirting for the last few hours.

In retrospect, I don't know who was more surprised, me or the guy I nearly collided with as I broke through the shrubs by the stream. I figured maybe it was a draw. I know I'd have peed my pants, if such a thing were possible. He wore that same kind of expression. Of that, I was certain. I'd been around enough Deavoriath to be able to read them pretty well.

CHAPTER EIGHT

"I'm a nice guy," blurted from my mouth. Not only that, I blurted it in Xenox, the language of the Deavoriath. I'd learned to speak it as well as anyone with a human mouth could. Man, I really wasn't channeling Arnold Schwarzenegger with that line, was I? Totally lame. Completely.

The man had been crouching at the water. He stared at me a second, then rose, a wry smile forming on his face. "You are either very brave or very stupid. To speak a language other than Standard is forbidden. I trust you know that, traveler."

"I guess I'm kind of both. Headstrong, too." I shrugged. "I don't take commands from dogs. I give them."

His long brow furrowed. "My, first a human speaking Xenox, then an open display of contempt for the Adamant. My, my." He dried his three hands on his pants then extended one toward me. "I believe it is a customary greeting among your species to shake hands, is it not?"

I shook his hand. "Yes, it is." Overly anxious, I asked, "Are there any humans around here?"

"No, traveler, there most certainly are not. You're the first one

I ever met." He cocked his head. "I assumed they were all gone. I stand corrected." Then he looked at Mirraya with piqued interest. "Are you a Deft, child?"

She nodded uncertainly.

"My, two miracles in one day. I may need a nap. To meet a human *and* a Deft. What are the chances?"

Mirraya looked to me for direction.

"What's odd about meeting a Deft? There were a lot of them back on ... well, where we recently were." I had no idea if the Deavoriath were in league with the Adamant. Best not to confess to blowing up *Triumph of Might* just yet.

He shook his head in wonder. "Many Deft? Again, I'd assumed they were more legend than reality. But where are my manners? This is hardly the place for such momentous introductions. Let me guide you to my home." He pointed in a westerly direction. "It's a short walk over there."

"Ah, not so fast," I responded. "I'd like to know a bit better where you stand. Are there any Adamant here? More to the point, are they allies of yours?"

He looked stunned, then grinned. "Allies with the Adamant? I don't think they *allow* allies. In any case, no. None are here, and I am certainly not a fan of theirs."

"How can I know we can trust you? By the way, I'm Jon Ryan. What's your name?"

I think pounding him with a baseball bat while pit bulls ripped at his calves would have had less impact than me saying my name. Seriously, he staggered back a couple steps, damn near fell into the water. I'd seen many moods in my friends, the Deavoriath, over the centuries, but I've never seen stunned, speechless surprise. Score another point for Team Ryan.

"You okay?" I had to ask.

"Wait. I'm being silly. You may be a man *named* Jon Ryan, but for a second there I fancied you were the *original* one who had returned from beyond the grave." He had an expression of bemused relief.

I held up my left hand and flashed my probe fibers.

"No," he said very much like a person addressing a ghost, "that's not remotely possible."

I traced a *J* in the dirt with my finger laser. Then I gave him a patented Jon Ryan wink.

"B ... but he lived...you lived over two bill—"

"I do look pretty good for my age, don't I?"

"I feel like a character in one of those poorly plotted novels, one of the hero's journey tales. I'm the character who meets Yoda or Gandalf."

"And you're welcome," I said with a stupid grin. "But wait, you guys don't have Yoda or Gandalf, or hero's journeys for that matter. I tried to make it through some of your literature in the past. It read like poorly translated instruction manuals."

Staring at the ground, he said, "It did, but then, well, then *you* came along. You had a tremendous impact on our culture, General Ryan."

"Aw don't start with the honorific, son. You'll annoy the hell out of me, and then I'd probably have to shoot you. I'm *Jon*." I held my hand back up to him. "And you are?"

"Cragforel," he numbly shook my hand. "I am Cragforel, son of Gronalitpor."

"Don't recall hearing either of those names before."

He smirked. "I guess they're recent additions."

"So, now that you know who I am, would you like to change either of your answers about the Adamant?"

"No, Jon. They are a blight on existence. I loathe them," his eyes twinkled, "as much as Kymee would have."

Wow. I'd seen Kymee only the day before yesterday. He was there when Toño switched me off. He was Deavoriath, but he was one of the best friends I ever had. Now long-dead Kymee...

"Wait, is Kymee still alive?" I practically shouted.

"No, I'm sorry to inform you, Jon. He died long ago. When you knew him, he was what, a million years old?"

"Give or take."

"Well, we live a long time, but we found we last only a couple of million years, tops. Then we push up daisies like everyone else."

"Wait. You guys didn't say *pushing up daisies*. We did."

He shrugged all three shoulders. "Like I said, yours was a powerful influence."

"Like Bill's and Ted's on their future."

"Yes," he mused in agreement, "much the same as Bill and Ted." He placed one palm on his chest and the other two arms in the air. "Party on, dude."

I think I was getting a headache. It was all way too much. He belonged to the greatest scientific, military, and technologic race to have ever lived. But I had reduced them to quoting *Bill and Ted's Excellent Adventure*. I should have been spanked.

"Come, friends," Cragforel said, "let us retire to my home." He ushered us away with a guiding arm.

"What was all that about?" asked Mirraya surreptitiously as we walked through the forest. "Are you important or something?"

"Nah. Popular without being noteworthy. Nothing more. Anyway, he probably has me confused with somebody else."

"He sure seemed impressed. At first, he couldn't believe I was Deft. But he forgot about that quickly, didn't he?"

"Yeah, what's the big deal about you being Deft? I mean, you're nice and all, but it's not like you poop gold."

"Uncle Jon, I thought you knew about us. You were in the same prison. At first I even thought you were some adult who'd changed."

"And what's with this change stuff?"

Cragforel overheard us and stopped to let us catch up with

him. "So, you really don't know about the legendary Deft, do you, Jon?"

"Know what?"

"They're shapeshifters," Cragforel said with a smile. "The only ones there are. Your friend here can change to appear as anything of equal mass. They're a truly magic race."

Shapeshifter? My little Mirraya was a shapeshifter? And she seemed so ... normal. What a two-day stretch I was having. Asleep for two billion years and still I felt the need to lay down.

I was literally dumbstruck, so Cragforel gently impelled me to begin walking toward his house again. We arrived a while later, not sure how long, because I kept tripping on the shape-change thing. What, could she look like a little corner mailbox? A great big kazoo? A regular-size human? How could that be possible? Did it hurt?

"Jon," Cragforel snapped his fingers in front of my face, "come on, I asked if you'd like refreshments? Being a shapeshifter is not that big of a deal. Well, I suppose it is, but it isn't like she's a nerd or something."

I recoiled slightly as I looked at him. I started to ask when they started using the word nerd, but realized the answer was the one asking the question, so I let it drop. My head was spinning.

"Ah, you got any nufe?" I asked.

"Why yes, a particularly good batch, in fact. May the girl have some, too?"

"Sure, I gave it to my kids." I turned to Mirraya. "It's a drink that tastes like different things to different people, but it's always marvelous. You know, for a shapeshifter, this may be just the drink."

I scruffed her hair, and she smiled bashfully. So cute.

Mirri took a tentative sip, closed her eyes and swirled it in her mouth. Then she took a big gulp, swallowing it so fast it might have missed her tastebuds.

"What?" I said. "What'd you taste and why'd you power it down like that?"

She smiled bigger than I'd seen her do to that point. "I tasted over-ripe quasi fruit, hot paplo fresh from the oven, and hot meat with blood still flowing in it. It was so good I had to finish it before it changed. Double *yum*."

Once we had all finished our nufe, and Mirraya a large portion of some foods I didn't recognize, Cragforel sat and got a serious look on his face. "Jon, to say a lot has changed in two billion years isn't worth saying, because it's so damn obvious. That said, let me paint you a broad overview. Your people successfully fled their world and colonized many planets. They spread, some said, like locusts. Eventually, a large section of the galaxy was under their control."

"And then?" I asked. "I hear an *and then* in there, don't I?"

"Yes. And then they did what all civilizations do. They faded. Their light went out. Call it what you will, but their empire slowly shrank, as did their numbers. By a billion years ago, humans were a rare find. Oh, there might be pockets of them somewhere, but we haven't heard of them."

"And the war? What happened to the Berrillians?"

"Hmm. That I don't know. Can you describe the species?"

"Huge tigers that walked upright and were meaner then the devil on one of his bad days."

Cragforel squinted in thought. "Let me ask The One That Is All." Almost immediately, he spoke. "I'm told by my collective that the Berrillians were wiped out during that conflict. They have been extinct since shortly after that war."

"Wow, talk about losing. Well, I can't say I'm sorry. They were vicious, ruthless, and thoroughly unredeemable. Good riddance, says I."

"However bad they might have been, they were nothing

compared to the Adamant. Now there's a vicious, ruthless, and thoroughly unredeemable piece of work."

"Have they been here, to Oowaoa?"

"Just once, which brings me to a sensitive, yet critical point. You must leave, and you may never return."

"You know, your species told me that before. You guys are kind of like a broken record."

He pointed a finger to the ceiling. "But this time there's a difference. Back then, we wished to be cut off from the galaxy. Now, it's a matter of our survival."

"We can't risk the Adamant coming again. Last time all they saw was a planet covered in boiling lava. But next time, they might not be so easily fooled. If they knew we were here, we'd all be killed."

"But why? If they don't know you exist, how can they wish genocide for you?"

"Oh, it's not us. They want to wipe out all indigenous life-forms." He pointed to Mirraya. "As with the Deft. They were by all accounts a harmless, inoffensive race. Yet they were marched off their world to die."

"Why? What's the Adamant's plan? It seems silly to me."

"They remove the locals and replace them with more docile, more time-proven species. Some serve in production, others as food."

"Then why not land somewhere and just kill everyone off? Why relocate them first?"

"Who can speak for the mind of the Adamant? I've assumed it's because local disposal is messier. But they may have some unknowable reason." More to himself, he said, "They're unlike any species we've encountered."

"How does that add up to us leaving and never returning?"

"If you stay, you'll become restless. A restless person is likely to do something that might betray our presence. If you return, well, that's a clear risk to us. You'll leave a trail."

"I'm afraid I see your logic, friend. Can you at least set us up with a ship and some provisions?"

"Of course, Jon. We've not become monsters, only extremely cautious. We're glad to do whatever we can to see you're off to a good start in this time. You have no idea how revered you are here. We hate to ask you to do this. It truly pains us."

"But—"

"But, we must act in our best interest, when the stakes are so high. I'm sure you understand."

"Yeah, but I don't have to like it."

"No, you don't. Frankly, I think it stinks, but there's really no other option."

I sighed deeply. "What can you give me?"

He spread all three arms over the table. "Anything and everything you want."

"Do you still have the vortexes?"

"Yes. We haven't used them since before the Adamant appeared on the scene, but yes. Wasn't your cube, *Wrath*?"

My imitation heart sank. If *Wrath* was still around, I didn't want to use him. He was too cantankerous, pompous, and full of himself. He was bloodthirsty, too. I knew I was being dramatic. Sentient space craft that moved by folding time-space couldn't have all that much personality, let alone a negative one. But, trust me, *Wrath* did.

"Yes. Don't tell me he's still functional."

He shook his head vigorously. "No. The cubes are long-lived, but not immortal. No, he petered out a long while back. His materials were not recycled, however. His shell still exists to this day. Would you like to see it?"

"No. No interest. I bet no one wanted to risk recycling the

SOB, because they worried the new cube would be just as nasty as he was."

"Yes. You knew him well, that much is clear."

"So, the current ones will be new to me?"

"Yes. The design and functionality are nearly the same. The few improvements that could be made are subtle."

"And do they have the quantum decoupler weapons and membrane generators, as before?"

"Yes. I believe we are the last individuals with the membrane designs."

"The Adamant don't have them, do they?"

"No. How did you know that?"

I told him the story of my capture and escape. He was impressed.

"Jon, you have to believe me when I say what you did is miraculous. No one ever holds their own in battle with the dogs, let alone win a major victory."

"You think they look like dogs, too?"

"Huh? What in the Seven Hells are you talking about? That was just an idiom, a saying."

"Seriously, they look identical to the dogs that humans kept as pets, just larger."

"Jon, I must confirm what I've heard about you. You're nuts."

"Thank you," I said, tipping my nonexistent hat.

"But your victory," he nodded to Mirraya, "and her escape will mean they have a special kind of hate for you. You're in extraordinary danger. I can't even begin to imagine. They also must crush you openly, and with incredible horror. They can ill-afford to, and would never allow the public to know they can be defeated." He shook his head. "I'm so glad I'm not you."

"Me, too. If you were, I wouldn't be so darn special."

He harrumphed softly. "I admire your spirit, but you face a threat unlike anything you have in the past. These guys are vicious beyond natural limits. You will have no allies, no safe havens, and not a minute's peace."

"SOS, my friend."

"What is SOS?"

"Same old shit. I thrive on those odds, don't you know?" I winked at Cragforel. I liked winking. Not enough people winked anymore.

"One last warning. We are fairly certain they can detect and track the movements of the cubes. For propulsion, they use exotic matter to form wormholes. Our space folding is not the same, but it's similarly based. We don't know for a fact they can, but if they are able … "

I finished his grim thought. "Then ours will be a short adventure, won't it?"

CHAPTER NINE

So, there I was at the control panel of a cube. One of the many things I'd hoped never to do again. But it wasn't like my choices-buffet was full of options. Singularly hated by the deadliest race ever to curse the galaxy. I had no home or adequate place to hide. My people were probably extinct, and Mirraya's likely were, too. In the past, I'd have said something macho like *no problema*, but honestly, I wasn't feeling it. The prospects of running, yet again, without the likelihood of rest, as well as fighting with no chance of victory, was just too much. The longer I survived was that much more time I would spend separated from everyone and everything I loved.

But, I buoyed my spirits with the two absolutes left to me. One—the good one—was the need to protect Mirraya. As guardian angels go, I was the kind without wings, but I was nothing if not relentless. The other driving force—the bad one— was my desire to crush the life out of the Adamant, one by one, and with as much prejudice as possible. My relentlessness would serve me well in that regard. Nobody remembered it, but there was a colorful character in an ancient movie called *Rocky III*.

While cruising the nothingness of space on my original voyage to find humankind a home, I watched it a few times. One character, Mr. T—a man after my own heart, by the way—used to say, "I pity the fool" when referring to the person he was about to lower the boom on. That was how I felt about those amoral border collies.

Cragforel said his goodbyes, and also admonished me again to never return. It was a melancholy ending to my relationships with that grand old civilization, but I knew it was the most prudent course. He gave us generous food supplies, hand weapons, and expeditionary gear like tents and sleeping bags. Mirraya received a bountiful, if fashion-bereft, supply of clothes and shoes. The Deavoriath seemed destined to never develop a fashion sense. So, I sealed the cube, sat my traveling companion down, and attached to the control panel with my command prerogative fibers. Then it hit me hard. Where in the universe would we go? I felt a mild panic welling up inside myself. Where, indeed?

Earth was long gone. My Deavoriath friends knew of no human colonies. They also could not tell me how extensive the Adamant's hold on the galaxy was, or if it extended to other galaxies, as well. Even if I went very far away, I might land in the middle of a shit storm. I began to focus on two options. One was Locinar. If I was ever going to locate other Deft who might adopt Mirraya, her home world was where I'd find them. Not that I was anxious to dump her off on anyone. I was growing over-attached to her. But, for her life to be its most complete, she'd be better off with her own kind.

I also knew that sooner or later, I had to go to Azsuram. I had to see what had become of the planet my wife Sapale and I had struggled so mightily to establish. It was the place she was buried. I needed closure as to whether her Kaljaxian species or the humans who'd later joined them there had survived. I knew it was an awful risk to go there, having no clue as to whether the Adamant were there, but I'd made my share of foolish decisions in the past and was prepared to make another. My need to know was too great.

With that clarity, I made my choice. We were off to Locinar. If I was going to be an idiot and pop into the sky above Azsuram, I preferred to do so alone. If I had to take Mirraya with me, it would only be if there was no future with her people. So, I told *Stingray* to lay in a course that put us about a lightyear away from the star system.

A word about the vortex and its name. It wasn't originally named *Stingray*. The Deavoriath named it *Blessing*, by whatever strange process they used to name their craft. The issue was that the word *Blessing* in Xenox was pronounced *crash*. I wasn't setting sail in a ship called *Crash*. Nope. Of the cubes available, it was the best choice. It was the newest, the largest, and it had all the bells and whistles I wanted. The problem was that there was some unwritten law that once given, a vortex's name could not be changed. That was why I spent years piloting a ship with the off-putting name of *Wrath*. But Cragforel had been so determined to make up for forbidding my return that he allowed the change. It was, he reassured me, the very first time a name change had ever been performed. He made a big deal of it, asking the vortex manipulator multiple times if she didn't mind the change. Yeah, this time I was in command of a *female* ship. *Wrath* had been male. *Stingray* was a girl. How, and more importantly *why,* the Deavoriath assigned sexes to their ships was completely unclear to me. It wasn't like the ships got together and made baby cubes. In any case, *Stingray* assured me she was content switching her designation.

We popped into the void a light-year from Locinar. At that distance, the star itself was just a bright point in the sky, blending in with the background. I asked *Stingray* to do the best she could to help determine if the Adamant were present.

"Form," she said matter of factly, "I read no signs of artificial activity of any kind. At this range, however, that is not a reliable observation."

I winced at being called Form again. I had thought I'd never be addressed as a cube pilot again. "Okay, then, take us to half a light-year's distance and repeat your scans."

Within a few seconds she spoke. "Still no signs of—check that. I cannot tell exactly where, but a space-time disturbance has just been created near the central star."

"What kind of disturbance?" I asked quickly.

"The kind that would account for the Adamant warship that just appeared off our port bow."

Man, she said that like it was no big deal at all.

"Take us out of here *now*," I yelled.

"Where would you like me to go?" she asked blandly.

"*Stingray*, don't be dense. An enemy ship is threatening our lives. It doesn't matter where. Just use your head and put some distance between us and them."

I felt the slight nausea I always did when the vortex folded space.

"There," she said, "we're back to a light-year away."

"Don't you think they can see us from where they are?" I yelled.

"Yes, since they're right alongside again. I think they're about to open fire."

"Membrane up," I snapped.

A second later, the cube was enveloped in a blinding flash, but the shield held. It always had in the past, and it was wonderful to see it still did. Constants were good, right about then.

"What weapon did they use?" I asked.

"Unknown energy burst. I think it was a mixture of plasma and high TeV laser accelerated near light speed with a gravity pulse."

That sounded rather lethal.

"Did they just fire once?"

"Yes, but I read another type of discharge is about to be launched."

I guessed it was as good a time as any to see what they had and how we handled it. My confidence was swelled by the fact that we were still in one piece.

"Any idea what's coming?"

She didn't need to answer. I felt the cube lurch forward. Mirraya yelped and covered her mouth.

"Let me guess. A tractor beam?" I asked.

"Of some type. Yes."

"Can you pull away with your impulse drive?" The vortex had almost unlimited power and so its conventional engines had a lot of get-up-and-go.

I heard an audible whine of the drive.

"Negative, Form. We're being pulled in at an accelerating rate."

"*Stingray*, set a course for the Andromeda galaxy," I tapped the control panel. "These coordinates. When we arrive, proceed to this destination." I keyed in a globular cluster on the far side of the Milky Way Galaxy. "Hold there with membranes up."

I felt the nausea. "No can do, Form. We cannot break free of the tractor beam to fold space."

"What? That's not remotely possible. Try again."

"Same result, Form. They have us. We'll be alongside their ship in thirty seconds. A cargo bay door appears to be opening."

"Fire the quantum decoupler. Pulse the membrane open for a microsecond and target the bay opening."

I was about to see if they could withstand the quarks in the path of the QD being ripped apart. *Stingray* didn't need to tell me the QD worked in spades. There was a flash and then the cube shook violently.

"Try to escape again," I shouted.

After my brief nausea, I felt a second tiny bout.

"Holding near designated globular cluster, Form. Awaiting further instructions."

I skipped across the deck and swept a stunned Mirraya out of her chair. I danced an impromptu jig while twirling her about. She had the oddest look of shock mixed with disgust on her face. What an odd combination. It was a look I'd never elicited from a girl yet.

"We're dancing, sweetheart. We're happy because we aren't dead."

"I'm happy," she replied, "but I don't call this dancing. You move like there's a fire snake in your pants."

That brought me to an abrupt halt. "Why, I've never," I said. "A fire snake? I have no idea what that is or what it does to one's nether regions, but I think I'm insulted."

She extended her arm in my direction and closed her eyes. I jumped back like King Kong shoved me when her forearm twisted and kneaded itself into a serpent-like creature. It had four heads emerging from a common neck and all manner of colors sparkled on its half-meter-long body. Each mouth had the wickedest fangs I'd ever seen on any creature. Nasty. It snapped at the air in my direction like it knew me and had a score to settle.

"That," she said proudly, "is a fire snake." It quickly vanished into her arm again. "What it does inside your pants, I will leave to your imagination, Uncle Jon."

"What a smart mouth you've got there, my dear. What are you, all of nine?"

"I'm thirteen. Why?"

Another bloody teenager? I was saddled with another overly-independent, disrespectful, risk-avid teen? Mine from the past were more than enough, thank you very much. My existence was getting incrementally worse with each new revelation.

"You're thirteen? Thirteen standard years?"

She got a very peevish look on her face. "Yes. Is that a problem?"

"No, no. Not a problem, you know, just an ... an issue. Yes. It's something to keep in mind."

"Something to keep in mind since I'm *thirteen* that wasn't an issue if I have been *nine?*"

"You could say that."

"I just did. What is the issue?"

"No ... nothing."

"No, Uncle Jon. It was not a *problem,* because it *was* an issue."

Hey, look at those hands, perched on either hip.

"I'm sure it's different with the Deft, so I shouldn't have said anything." I twirled my finger at the floor. "Can we get back to celebrating not being killed?"

She stomped a foot on the deck. Wow, like I hadn't seen that a thousand times before and liked it none of them. "What is different among the Deft?" Little darling. She raised her arm back up, and it turned into a fire snake. A fire snake pointing four frightening heads at yours truly.

"Hey, that shapeshifting is quite a trick. Maybe you can teach m—"

I lunged to one side as the damn snake-arm charged at me. I wasn't sure, but I think she was aiming wide the whole time. The little imp.

"On Earth, with *humans,* the teen years can be," I raised an index finger, "*can* be, mind you, not *are,* associated with unruly behavior some adults find disturbing."

"*Some* adults?"

I nodded faintly.

"What about the one I'm trapped inside a metal cube with?"

"Me?" I tried to sound surprised. I tented my fingers on my

chest. "Me? No, silly. Hey, lots of people accuse me of still acting *like* a teenager. I ... I love the snake-age years." I couldn't take my eyes off her menacing forearm.

Her arm returned to normal as she crossed them both. "Well we'll see, won't we?"

"Hey, speaking of seeing," I said gesturing toward the control panel, "I'd better see if our friends have tracked us down." In the back of my mind I was weighing whether I hoped we were in mortal danger again or not. If the Adamant were outside, at least it'd break the tense mood. A teenage shapeshifter. Sounded like a cheap horror film title, but it was my new life.

"*Stingray*, any sightings to report?" I asked, as I approached.

"None, Form. We appear to have evaded them for now."

"For now? Oh ye, of little faith." I patted my chest. "We're talking about Jon Ryan here. We were never in any real danger. I was toying with them, probing them."

"I am a vortex manipulator, Form. I have no faith. I *believe* in facts and I *know* information."

"You'll come around."

"Did *Wrath*? Did *Wrath* develop faith in the unknowable simply because he served you, Form?"

Annoying manipulator, wasn't she? "It depends on how you define faith."

"How *I* define it or how *one* defines it? There is considerable difference between the two positions."

"One. It depends on how *one* defines faith."

"How might anyone define faith in a manner that *Wrath*, of all vortices, managed to develop faith?"

"You know," for no good reason I pointed over my shoulder, "I'd like to answer that, but I'm going to check on Mirraya."

"Very well, Form. She is in the bathroom presently. Shall I alert her you're on your way to see her?"

"No!" I blurted out. That's just what I didn't need to do,

further provoke the teenager girl I'd just had a quarrel with. Yeah, threaten to barge into the bathroom. That'd do it. *Stingray* was going to require a lot of work to get her up to speed on interpersonal relationships. Suddenly it hit me, and I stopped walking. I was midway between two females, both of whom seemed to be trying to yank me by the short hairs. The future was going to be a long one. I could just feel it.

CHAPTER TEN

I had *Stingray* hover near the globular cluster the entire day. No Adamant ship followed us. It was disquieting. My double jump wasn't that tricky or massively clever. It was no Admiral-Nelson-wins-Trafalgar type of naval maneuver. Why didn't they follow? Going back to basics, there were always two options. Either they *could* or they *couldn't* pursue us. If they could catch up but didn't, it might have been because they were afraid of us. I listed it, but it wasn't very likely. Or it wasn't worth the trouble. Maybe they knew we'd be back and would acquire us then. That required patience and hope, not qualities I thought those puppy dogs possessed. It could be that we were just too insignificant, but they were singularly focused on anyone opposing them.

The justifications for them not being able to follow us was just as dubious. Could they not see our second trail? Unlikely. An ion trail was an ion trail was an ion trail. Maybe they couldn't leave the galaxy? But why? Yes, technically the globular cluster was *outside* the Milky Way, but deep space was pretty much uniform. In the end, I just stuck the situation away in my WTH File. The reason would be known to me in time. I had plenty of problems to solve. There was no need to dwell on one unanswerable topic.

I needed to set my vortex manipulator straight on combat etiquette. She'd nearly gotten us fried.

"*Stingray*," I called out to her, "you got a minute?"

"I'm confused, Form. I don't own anything, least of all time. What do you ask?"

Oh, boy. Another concrete-thinking alien construct. Just what I needed. Yet another challenge.

"Is that an expression also? What don't you choose to verbalize?"

I regretted Cragforel not being able to supply me with any alcoholic drinks. I needed a shot and a beer right about then. No, I needed a few. I started a mental supply list.

"Here's the thing, back in our confrontation with the Adamant, you did well." I wasn't exactly lying. I was using the management skills I learned during my years of military service. "However, I think one can always strive for improvement. Don't you?"

"What? Can I think or can I strive? I definitely think. I am a vortex manipulator. Striving is something I can probably learn. My intelligence is designed to be pliable."

"No, I mean even that although you did *well* in the battle, you could have done *better*. I can share certain thoughts and observations with you that will allow you to improve your performance in the future. Doesn't that seem desirable?"

"Sharing thoughts and observations or my performance improving? Really, Form, I think you should strive to improve your communication skills. I am willing to help if your AI function is equally as pliable as mine."

"We're having an intervention for *me* to help *you*, not the other way around."

"Ah. So is it that you do not want help from those close to you in your personal growth, or is it that you would like me to schedule a time in the near future when I might begin these sets of tasks?"

In my mind, I saw the image of me wrapping up Management Skills 101 in butcher paper and throwing it really hard into cold, dark, endless space. I was done with them, permanently.

"*Stingray*," I said in my badass command voice, "during the recent fight, you asked stupid questions at critical times that nearly cost us all our lives. Please know that I do not value your life or mine. I do, however, *supremely* value the life of that little girl in the bathroom. I will tolerate no actions or incompetence that might lead to her being harmed by the Adamant, by you, or by the man in the moon. If you fail to act with intelligence, alacrity, and an appropriateness that reflects forethought in a crisis once more, I will personally rip you out of this vortex and cast you into the nearest black hole. Is there *any* aspect, large or small, linguistic or formed by the movements of my body, that you do not *fully* understand?"

There was a blessed silent period following my diatribe.

"No, Form. I fully take your meaning and intent. As much as it pains me to correct you, however, I must update you on one fact."

"*What?*" I snapped angrily. I was about done with this machine.

"The little girl in no longer in the restroom. She is standing two meters behind you, mouth agape and her next breath pending for a concerning period."

I relaxed my shoulders. Without turning, I asked, "How much of that did you hear?"

"Enough, I should think."

I turned to her. "Being in command is a hell of a thing, sweetie. I'm good at it, trust me. But it isn't always pretty."

She stared at me. I knew she had something to get off her chest.

"Do you have any questions or input you'd like to suggest?"

"Yes. I'm quite upset. I am not a *little* girl. I am not a *big* girl. I am a young woman, a young female Deft adult. Is there any part of that which you find challenging to accept or understand?"

"No, sweetie. You're coming through loud and clear."

"Good. I'm maturing. It's a hell of a thing, Uncle Jon. I'm good at it, trust me. But it isn't always pretty."

"Sure." Sure? What kind of dumbass response was that? I was a two-billion-year-old warrior; a general; a savior of worlds. I sounded sort of wimpy and completely Melba toasty. "Ah, anything else, sweetheart?"

"Yes. I think you were much too hard on *Blessing*. She has feelings, you know?"

"*Blessing*? You mean *Stingray*?" I pointed over a shoulder with both hands.

"I believe you understood my words. If not, we can discuss them *later*. For now, I will be in my room." She spun on a heel and marched away.

"Ah," I called behind her raising a finger, "you have a room now? I didn't realize we had or needed rooms."

I heard her voice echo back down the passageway. "*Blessing* fabricated walls, a restroom, closets, and a locking door for me earlier today."

Then, I'd swear I heard a metal door slam shut.

It was going to be a long voyage.

Ten hours later, Mirraya reappeared, fresh and bright. I was slumped at the table staring at a cup of cold coffee.

"Good morning, Uncle Jon. How are you on this fine morning? Well, I pray."

She swished over to the food replicator and tapped a few keys.

93

A steamy tray was pushed forward for her to pick up. She filled a glass with some fruit juice and glided over to join me.

She leaned over her breakfast and smelled it deeply. "Ah, rostalop and ovum scramble." Gazing at me, batting her luxuriant eyelashes, she added, "there's no better way to start the day. Would you like some, Uncle Jon?"

"No, thanks," I held up my mug, "coffee's fine."

She took a bite and wrapped herself with her arms. "Suit yourself, sweetie."

"A word about names, if that's okay," I said. "You are more than welcome to call me Jon. That's my first name. You can call me uncle. I'm not your parent's brother, but it serves as an honorific, so I can hang with it. But please, Uncle Jon is just too long. Too stuffy. Okay?"

"Which would you prefer?" she asked with a smile.

"Oh, either's fine. You choose."

"All right, Uncle Jon. I will give the matter some thought and let you know when I decide."

Oh, boy. Real long flight ahead. Long *life* ahead. I was missing my solitude, all of a sudden.

"On the subject of optimal communication, I would like to ask you a question, if that's okay?" she said setting down her fork and folding her hands.

"Sure. Shoot."

"We've been together for what, five or six days?"

"Six. Why?"

"I've begun to notice you drink occasionally, but rarely eat. I asked *Blessing*. She said you haven't slept. Is that typical behavior for humans?"

Okay, the robot talk. Joy. "I'm not human. I was. I'm now an android."

"Hmm. So, humans turn into androids? That's a machine, right?"

"No. My home world was going to be destroyed. I transferred to an android host to endure the long space flight needed to find us a new home." I shrugged. "On the inside, I *feel* totally human."

"And did you find that new home?"

"Yes. It wasn't easy, but we made it."

"Where are the humans now?"

I shook my head. "No idea. Cragforel suspects they're gone."

"I'm sorry to hear that, Uncle Jon. I really am."

I patted the backs of her hands. "Thanks. I know you understand the pain of losing something like that."

She nodded.

"I want to thank you for what you said to *Blessing* yesterday, about protecting me. It was sweet. I appreciate it."

"I meant every word I said. I'm going to take care of you as long as you need taking care of."

She looked down and smiled. "We can be each other's new family."

"You bet. We are already."

"What are we going to do, Uncle Jon? What..."

She began to cry softly.

I stepped around the table and hugged her neck from behind. "I'll tell you what we're going to do. We're going to have great adventures together; we're going to kick the Adamant's butts until they fall off; and then we're going to have some more great times. After all that, we'll find you some handsome shapeshifting doctor or lawyer and you two will settle down and raise a tribe of shifty babies. It'll be grand." I began rocking her as I finished.

She rested her hands on my arms. "And don't forget the part about finding you a beautiful princess robot so you two can settle down and make little..."

"Toasters?" I said, cutting her off.

"Honestly, Uncle Jon, you're impossible."

I rocked her a bit longer. "So I've been told."

CHAPTER ELEVEN

Finally, it was time to do something. We'd sat in one spot long enough to know the enemy wasn't coming. Ergo, I had to decide where to go. Based on my last choice, I decided that going to Azsuram was too risky. With no other candidate on my list, I figured why not check out the globular cluster we hovered over. Maybe I'd find a clue as to why the Adamant hadn't followed us.

Those clusters were large spherical masses of uniformly old stars. They huddled around the center of the galaxy based on gravity from the supermassive black hole at the center of the Milky Way. They had been the subjects of little up-close investigation, at least in my day.

"*Stingray*," I asked, "do you have any data on civilizations inside this cluster?"

"Yes, Form. There are a few. All are ancient races, most of which have passed into societal senescence."

"Into say what?"

"Societal senescence. They grew old and died, like a living organism. Form, from your world's history I believe a parallel would be the once great Chinese, Persian, Roman, and Western European dynasties. In this instance, the entirety of the sentient species fades away and are lost."

"Any active ones?"

"I have no good data on that. The Deavoriath have made no formal contact for ages."

"Take us to the nearest planet where an advanced civilization was known to exist."

"As you wish."

I felt slight nausea, then she announced, "We are one hundred kilometers above Disulpf. It was home to the Gendo and Proclamate Hegemonies many years ago."

"Are there any signs of life down there? Intelligent life, that is."

"Not currently. There are no operating power grids or radio transmissions. No artificial satellites are present either."

"How about plants and animals?"

"Some, though those are sparse. It appears that the planet was severely damaged by the sentient races. Radioactivity, stable pollutants, and atmospheric warming are still at unhealthy levels."

"Set us down near where you estimate a large city once stood."

"Are you certain, Form? That action involves risk. There are many unknowns down there."

"Ah, *Stingray*, who's the Form?"

"You are."

"So, whose opinion *actually* counts?"

"Yours."

"And who has done this type of thing a thousand times before?"

"You."

"Alert me when we land. I'll be with Mirraya."

"What are you two arguing about now?" was my greeting from Mirraya.

"We weren't arguing. You must have a foothold on Mount Importance to argue with me. She's a persnickety old hen, that's all."

"I rather like her."

"Good for her. Now she's one-and-one in the potential-friend department. Hey, we're landing on an old planet named Disulpf. Let's go check it out."

"Are you certain that's wise? Isn't it kind of risky, too many unknowns involved?"

"You sound just like the old hen. Honestly, there's probably nothing to discover. That's partly why I want you to come. Our first assessment of a new world should be on an easy one. In the military, we call that a milk run."

"Streaming lactation fluid suggest safety to your people? How odd."

"Come on, my little worry wart. Times a wasting." I took her by the elbow and led her to the equipment room. I fitted her with a safety suit and breathing tanks. The atmosphere outside was insufficient to keep her alive. I handed her a plasma rifle, took one for myself, and herded her toward the door.

It was good to be exploring again. It was good to be on solid ground again, too. I found my pace quickened the farther we went and I had on a dumb grin I was only vaguely aware of. Mirraya, for her part, was less enraptured. She kept asking me to slow down, and the suit caused her to stumble several times. She sounded like she was swearing in some language I wasn't familiar with. I had a ways to go toughening this one up. She was such a ... well, she was such a girl. Hmm. I elected to pull in my reins a bit and stayed by her side.

Stingray had set down near some very decrepit remnants of

buildings. I made them out to be the crumbled foundations of a moderately large structure, maybe five to six stories tall. There had been a goodly sized town center on this spot a very long time ago. Vegetation intertwined itself in whatever signs of civilization remained. The place had a Mayan-ruins-in-the-jungle feel about it. I half expected Indiana Jones to bolt from the underbrush screaming, bloodthirsty natives in tow. Just as well he didn't. I'd have shot first and asked questions later.

Standing amongst the rubble, there was nothing obvious of importance. I set my probe fibers down randomly to see if there were any treasures or clues under the surface. There was nothing fun, just more rubble. In an hour, I was bored and returned to the ship. I had *Stingray* take us to another site half a planet away. More scattered rubble without any other signs of civilization.

I was beginning to decide this planet was a write-off when Mirraya saw something.

"Uncle Jon," she said pointing to the forest canopy, "look at those."

A tribe of lemur-like creatures were scampering quickly tree to tree, making an awful racket as they traveled.

"They're so cute," she said with a big smile.

"Nothing's cute until it proves it doesn't want to eat you." I stepped between her and the noisy lot. "If they come down aggressively, I'll be forced to shoot them."

"No," she whined. "They're harmless, I can tell. Don't you dare shoot them."

Okay, test of wills number one of an infinite number to come sprang to life. Once the lead lemur spotted us, it headed right for us. The tribe followed quickly, and in no time, they were on the ground sprinting toward us. I didn't get the vibe that they were coming *at* us for some reason, just in our *direction*. I raised my rifle in any case, aiming at the leader.

Then the reason for their flight showed itself. A large furry beast charged though the treetops. This one was a predator, and its lunch was running to us for cover. Just as rapidly as the lemurs had descended, the hunter sped to the ground. It was maybe fifty-sixty kilos, spherical in shape, with six arms. The appendages were used equally to move. It rolled toward us. The face remained locked on us. It had the requisite nasty teeth and big claws any good carnivore must.

I fired a single shot in front of it as a warning. Nothing. It sped up, if anything. The lemurs ran past us and up the nearest tree trunk. So much for mutual aid in a crisis. The hungry ball of fur focused on me, apparently content to have the nearest meal, not the original one now that they'd gone into the canopy.

I raised my gun and targeted right above the mouth. As I tensed my finger to fire, something brushed past me. It was another furry ball, slightly larger than the one coming like a freight train. It whooped and howled just like the other, four arms flailing in the air. The attacker locked his brakes and skidded to a rolling stop. It raised its arms in an aggressive posture. The newcomer stopped a couple meters away from the attacker. Both beasties screamed and wailed raucously at one another. It was like two gorilla balls making shows of force.

I turned to Mirraya. "Let's back away..."

She wasn't there. Her suit and clothing were on the ground, having been ripped off. The second furry ball must have—

No, there was no blood, no pieces of Mirraya scattered about. I snapped my head in a circle. Nothing, no sign of her. Where could she have gone to so quickly. Had she seen the second fur ball coming and split without alerting me? That would suck if she had.

Then the howling rose to a new high, and I pivoted to the confronting blobs. The larger one was charging the original one.

The smaller one turned immediately and ran into the forest, up a tree, and disappeared.

That's when it got weird. The newcomer did a triumphant dance and then started walking toward me like it was on a Sunday stroll in the park. I pointed my rifle at it and it stopped.

Then the fur ball spoke. "Uncle Jon, if I said you couldn't shoot one of them you certainly can't shoot me."

"Mirraya?" I asked, dumbstruck.

"No, I'm a really smart predator who wants to strike up a conversation with you. *Duh.*"

I slowly lowered my gun. "But how," I pointed to her clothing, "you ... did it ..."

She stopped a meter in front of me and took a deep breath. Then, like wax melting in reverse, the fur ball transformed into Mirraya. A naked Mirraya that was.

I cast off my backpack and tore my jacket off. Handing it to her I blurted, "Here, take this till we can get you some ..."

She took the jacket and wrapped it around her shoulders. "Thank you, Uncle Jon. You're so cute. But a bashful shapeshifter would be in trouble. We're used to ending our changes nude. It's no big deal."

"It is to me," I mumbled.

"What? The nerves of my ears are still remolding. What did you say?"

"Nothing, sweetheart. Let's get back to the ship."

Forty-five minutes later Mirraya came into the mess area, her head to one side, drying her hair with a towel. I was nursing my now familiar mug of cold coffee.

"For some reason, I always need a shower after being another animal. Weird, eh?"

I harrumphed quietly. It was all I had.

"Uncle Jon, you look like a man with a question."

I shrugged. "One or two, if it's okay?"

"Of course. The shapeshifting thing freaks some people out. Go on."

Not me. No. I'm a big boy. I've seen it all. I've loved great women, killed monsters with my bare hands, and gazed upon wonders no one else will witness. NBD—no big deal—here, babe.

"Why did you do that? Why did you not ask permission first? Why didn't you warn me so I didn't shoot you? How could you know it would work? Do you always take ridiculous, unnecessary risks? Don't you value your life? Are you trying to scare me to death? Don't ever parade in front of me naked again. I'm your uncle. I don't need that."

"Ah, the last one was an order, not a question."

"Answer it, nonetheless." I closed my eyes and tilted my face to the ceiling.

"I realize I kind of dropped that bomb on you. But I had to act quickly. I couldn't have you killing that animal just because it was hungry. I knew a show of force would work. Trust me, it always does, especially with you males."

"You," I pointed at her, "turned into a *male?*"

"Of course. If I had turned into a female it might have tried to mate with me. I wanted to scare it off, not explore new realms."

"*Ah.*" I covered my ears. "*TMI.* A little ... a young woman shouldn't be talking like that. You're going to be the death of me."

"The Deft view the world differently than most. We must if we're going to do what we do. I'd say I'm sorry, but I'm not."

I peeked over to her. "You could say it anyway. It'd help. Seriously."

She folded her arms as if to say that was *not* going to happen.

"Okay, just promise me this. Consult with me first. I might have just whacked the fur ball with the butt of my gun if you'd asked. I can't have you get hurt."

She smiled. "You're sweet, Uncle Jon. I'll try to ask permission before doing that again. And it's not a fur ball. It calls itself a Sortom."

"Who does?"

"The fur ball does. Most higher non-sentients have names for themselves. When I become one, I really become one. *Sortom*."

"I'll enter the name in the ship's log and tattoo it on my chest. Now, go get dressed. I want to check out one more site before we leave this crazy-ass world once and for all."

Ten minutes later we were rummaging through another set of crumbled ruins. They were as boring and uninformative as the others had been.

"What are we looking for, Uncle Jon? This whole planet is one pile of rubble."

"A clue, my child. A clue."

"As to what?"

I shook my head. "It still bothers me that the Adamant didn't come after us. I got to thinking maybe it was because of where we were, not that they couldn't find us."

She furrowed her brow. "That's kind of silly. Why would the location stop them from pursuing us?"

"I don't know, because I haven't found the clue yet." I swept my arm across the wrecked landscape.

That earned me a pissed off teenage girl look. Trust me, I knew them well from all my children, both human and Kaljaxian. The expression was, unfortunately, universal.

In the end, we turned up nothing. I had *Stingray* take us to another once inhabited planet on the other side of the cluster. It showed the same discouraging outward signs. No artificial satellites, energy sources, or communications. She put us down near some crumbled signs of where a city once stood. The outlines still present suggested this had been a big city, unlike the town-feel of the other planet. The suggestions of foundations were larger and thicker, suggesting many storied buildings. The density of foundations and volume of rubble supported the idea that this was once a large population center.

We worked our way in one direction, me scanning and Mirraya digging and turning stuff over. Again, there were no significant artifacts, just concrete and stone debris. Just as I was getting bored and frustrated, we came to what must have been the edge of the city. The destroyed foundations became less densely packed together and the heft of them declined, suggesting smaller buildings. Standing on a hillock I could see where the buildings thinned out to the point that the city seemed to end.

"Uncle Jon, I haven't seen a thing of interest. You're certainly a more patient person than I am. There's not even a sortom to argue with."

We'd seen no obvious signs of life, not even bugs. Every place had bugs. That I knew from bitter experience. Disgusting critters were ubiquitous.

I stepped up on a foundation. I swept my arm away from the city and replied to her. "There's nothing as far as the eye can see."

Funny. After I'd whipped my arm out like that, it struck me it was like I was scattering seeds. That's when I looked at the landscape differently. Material scattered outward. There was a pattern. From any individual structure, the rubble pattern was larger debris closer to the building, smaller chunks farther away. It was an impact pattern, like when an asteroid strikes a planetary surface. Or an explosion, lots of explosions.

"*Stingray*, please make a topological plot of the identifiable foundations and the debris near each one. Use the assumption that the rubble is distributed in a blast-pattern resulting from the destruction of each building. What is the pattern of the necessary detentions?"

"I have run that simulation for ten thousand foundations and partial foundations. Your supposition that the rubble was distributed by an explosion holds in each case."

"Well I'll be damned," I whispered.

"I do not feel qualified to speculate in that regard, Form. However, I can run some numbers if you'd like, establish some broad probabilities."

"No. I would like you to pull up similar data on the last planet we were on and see if those buildings were similarly destroyed. Oh, is there any general pattern of blast direction here?"

"I do not take your meaning, Form."

"Can you tell which direction the bombs fell from or the missiles struck from, for example."

"Ah. Yes. The explosions would have all been central in the structures themselves."

"Huh? That makes no sense. If a city's being bombed, the walls fly every which way."

"You assume the city was destroyed as an act of war."

"Why else would everything blow up with such massive force?"

"Perhaps the buildings were being razed for new construction that never took place."

"Possible. No, wait, I know something about this. If engineers are placing charges to bring a building down, they cause a controlled implosion. They take out supports such that the walls fall pretty much straight down. There's no collateral damage that way."

"True. The explosive devices could have been dropped along the building's central vertical axis."

"Not very likely an enemy would be so precise."

"True again, Form."

It hit me. "The buildings were blown up from the inside by single huge charges."

"Why would an entire population place massive explosive devises in the center of occupied buildings?"

"It wasn't to get rid of the roaches," I said more to myself.

"They must have been very determined to keep something from entering the buildings, and that if they did, there'd be no one left inside to bother."

"That would require an act of mass suicide. Such a thing is unheard of. What would cause an entire population to choose to annihilate itself rather that surrender to their conquerors?"

"A very scared population and a very scary enemy."

CHAPTER TWELVE

The pattern of central explosions was not present in the rubble of the first world we explored. I was disappointed, but not surprised. It would have been too easy if the civilizations ended in a similar pattern when they were separated by such large distances. Wait. Were they separated by large distances, especially when the destruction took place? The cluster was about ninety light-years across.

"*Stingray*," I called out, "taking into account *when* you estimate the structures we explored were destroyed and the *movement* of the stars in the clusters, how close were the two stars at the time of the final events."

"In the range of fifty light-years apart."

That didn't help. That was a pretty big distance with standard propulsion systems. "What were their positions in the cluster?"

"Planet One was near the periphery. Planet Two was fifty light-years directly toward the center."

I rubbed my cheek. Was that significant? What did being closer in have to do with anything? Who the hell knew? There was one way to find out. We could travel inward in the cluster and see if anything changed. I said a private cheer for lab rats everywhere. What could *possibly* go wrong when you used yourself as a test subject to see if there was danger lurking in the unknown?

I had *Stingray* put us in orbit around whatever planet she could locate that was roughly three quarters of the radius out from the center of the cluster. After my slight nausea, she said we were above such a planet. It was a binary planet. That's one with a moon basically the same size. Neither showed signs of active sentient life. Of course, they didn't. This entire cluster was a burned-out cinder. I picked the planet with the most breathable air, and we set down where *Stingray* found the most likely signs of past habitation. It was funny. The old explorer kicked in briefly when I thought maybe I should name the planets and then begin taking detailed notes and collecting samples. Then I realized my species was extinct. Who was I going to report my findings to? Three people. Me, myself, and I.

Mirraya was bored before we'd taken ten steps on the surface. She was a teenager, after all. In her defense, before us lay yet another uniform bleakness. One more dry, lifeless pile of ancient ruins. But there was a difference. There was a smell. It was faint and wafted in and out with what little breeze there was. It struck me that the second planet we visited had no scent aside from that of dirt. The first planet, the one with the furry balls and lemurs smelled like a jungle, so I hadn't paid it much mind. Jungles smelled like jungles, dry ruins smelled like dry ruins. But that place smelled of ... something. I couldn't place it. What it didn't smell like was a dry, deserted wasteland. It only looked like one. Mysteries were stacking up like cord wood. Great. I needed more to stress about, didn't I?

"Mirraya," I asked her more quietly than necessary, "do you smell something off in the air?"

She sniffed a few times. "No. What, do you?"

"I think so. My olfactory sensors are set to maximum, but I can't say what it is."

She grunted. "The Deft are famous for having a poor sense of smell. I'm afraid I won't be of much help."

"Well, if you ..."

"Hey, I have an idea." She started pulling her clothes off like she was on her honeymoon.

"W ... wait," I stammered, "what are you doing? Didn't I specifically say no more naked?"

"I won't be naked if you turn your back like a proper gentleman."

Girl had a point. "Tell me when you're ready and when I can look at you again."

Instead of her voice, my response was a snorty whistle. I turned to see the oddest of oddities. She changed into the funniest creature I'd ever seen, which was saying a lot. She was kind of an anteater, but she had big wings, no hair whatsoever, and her tail was three times longer than it looked like it needed to be. Her legs, all thirteen of them, were stumpy paddles about a foot long. I couldn't tell if they were for swimming or digging. Then, because my life wasn't bizarre enough, the thing waved one paddle in the air at me and snorted insistently like a pig. Then the whatever reverse melted into a naked Mirraya. I whipped around and stared at the ground.

After a minute she said, "You can look now, I'm decent."

"Define decent."

"I have all my clothing where it supposed to be and it's all zipped, snapped, and laced up."

I slowly turned my torso. One eye was shut, and my other was squinting almost closed.

"What are you doing, Uncle Jon? You look like a frightened schoolboy."

"Maybe because, deep down, I am?"

"Would you like to hear what I found out, or would you prefer to be silly?"

"The first choice, please."

"I turned into a valtorper sal. They are native to an environment where there is little light and a lot of water. They have the most sensitive noses we know of. Anyway, I was able to smell what you were noticing. It was really clear." She smiled with excitement. "I don't know how you people do it."

"Do what?"

"Go through life as only one species, one animal." She radiated joy and excitement. "To see the world as others do, to feel how they feel, it's the best."

"Thanks for the update on my life's insufficiencies." I rolled my hand in the air toward myself. "The smell?"

"Oh, it's rotting material, mostly wood, but there's some animal matter mixed in. And there's sulfuric acid, lots of sulfuric acid."

"Matter can't rot in sulfuric acid. It might melt or dissolve, but not rot."

"Well, that's what you smelled. I'm not a chemist."

She looked mildly miffed.

"Which direction?"

"It's mostly from that way," she pointed one of her long fingers, "about a kilometer away."

"I'll lead the way."

Mirraya dropped in behind me and I set a quick pace. In a few minutes, we were close enough to the odor's origin that I slowed down. That way I could scan the area better. The smell was getting unbearable. In all my years, I'd never smelled that particular kind of rank awfulness.

"You stay here," I said to Mirraya, "but stay sharp, especially to your rear." I started to advance.

"No way, Uncle Jon," she replied. "I'm staying with you. Haven't you seen those horror movies where the teen left behind is the first to die?"

That stopped me. I pivoted to her. "The Deft have teen-scream movies, too?"

"Of course. We may not be humans, but we're not simple."

All I could think was, *well I'll be damned.* Universal low-budget horror shows. Whodathunk it?

I had her follow at two meters. As soon as I could see what the likely source was, I heard it, too. It was bubbling, kind of like a low simmer. I swung us to the upwind side of the smell. Then we entered a clearing. It was not naturally occurring, because it was in such stark contrast to the dead forest we had been winding our way through. I held a palm up to indicate Mirraya should halt while I stepped into the open. I raised my rifle and swung it from side to side as I advanced. At the center of the clearing was the origin of the stink. It was a pool of slowly boiling liquid. Two aspects made my alert level go from ten to infinity. The pool of hot liquid was raised. Not a single thing on this planet had such a contrived, vital appearance. It had a corroded metallic rim maybe half a meter high. The other out of place object was a rock table at the side of the raised pool. No, it was an altar. A table would be lower, and there were no chairs or bar stools to suggest anyone sat there. Plus, it was so close to the pool that one could only stand safely on one side.

Okay, on an otherwise dead planet, there was an altar over a pit of boiling sulfuric acid. I couldn't imagine a more foreboding, uninviting image. Mr. Rogers was not about to step into the clearing and welcome us to the neighborhood. I inched forward. By then, I didn't need to tell Mirraya not to follow. Her feet were frozen in the dirt where she stood, trembling.

"Uncle Jon," she said in a hushed raspy voice, "this place is evil. Be very careful."

I appreciated her heads up, but honestly, it wasn't necessary that she told me. I could feel the malice where my bones should have been. I climbed up three rock steps and peered over the altar into the pool. In retrospect, I probably hadn't needed to do that. I really shouldn't have. Some things in this life, you wish you could unsee. Against all mechanical possibilities and programed options, I covered my mouth and wretched. Yeah, it was a special kind of gut-wrenching bad.

The simmering liquid was a pale golden color. The numerous bones bobbing in it were white. The yet to be melted bodies was still squirming, tortured and writhing beyond any concept of suffering. I thank God then and there that each body's eyes were long eaten away. If those in torment had seen me and reached out for mercy, I think I would have died.

Then Jon Ryan, survivor, charged back to take control. No matter how tough the souls were in that pool, they hadn't been there long. Someone or something had cast them in recently, very recently. That meant someone or something would likely return soon. They would likely bring more sacrifices, because that was what this surely was. An altar, a pit, and dead people added up to only one thing. It hit me that it would be bad to be present when the orchestrator of this mini-hell returned. They'd thank us for saving them the trouble of lugging our two corpses to their little party.

I backed away quickly. "Let's get out of here now."

Mirraya looked into my eyes, silently pleading for help. She was frozen with fright.

I swept her into my arms and took off at a sprint. We were back to *Stingray* in eight and a half seconds. Before I even set her down, I was attached to the console. "Take us out of this cluster *immediately.*"

That was when the bottom fell out of my existence.

In the most malicious, maleficent voice I wished never to have heard, the reply came, "Leave, Jon? Why we've only just met. Surely, you'd like to stay and play a little while. It will be ever so much fun."

I do not know where I found the strength to respond. "Who the hell are *you*?"

"Excellent guess, Jonathan. You are equal to your legend. You are remarkably close."

"Where's *Stingray*? What have you done to her?"

"You mean *Blessing*? I rather prefer that name over your silly superstitious variant. Not that I object to superstition, mind you. It keeps people thinking of me. Never refuse free PR."

"Where is she?" I said, with more edge than I would have thought possible.

"She's fine. I'm right on top of her. Secretly, I think she enjoys the sensation."

"I will tell you only once. Leave my ship."

"Or else? Wasn't it you who only recently asked a Quep the very same thing?"

"Or else I'll make you wish you'd have left peaceably."

"Well that approach simply won't work, General Ryan. You see, now you've piqued my curiosity. In ten thousand million generations, in twenty thousand billion years, no one has been able to do that. I simply must see if someone finally can."

"Don't say I didn't warn you." Seriously, I was rattling an absent saber. I had significantly less than nothing to back my words up. I was just instinctively being Jon Ryan.

"You have my word on it, Jon. Although, I will be honest enough to point out my word generally carries little weight. I am, truth be told, thoroughly unreliable, completely untrustworthy, and despicably dishonest."

"If you're telling the truth that you are always untruthful, what am I to believe?" I heard a version of that in some sci-fi TV show somewhere along the line. It worked then, and like I said, my idea tank was bone dry.

"And then the evil entity began to feel the first hints of boredom. Always a bad thing."

"I'm waiting for an answer," I said.

"Here it is then."

Stingray began to shake like she was in a blender. The room went pitch black, and a painful metallic pounding began. Then it all reverted back to normal, in an instant.

"Any part you not understand, Jon? I'd hate to add you to my sacrificial stew, unless your mind was completely free of doubt. I'd do it, to be certain, but I would not be happy about it."

I thought my time, our time, was about up. A brilliant idea could come to me any time, as long as it was immediately. Still crickets chirped in my head.

"Mirraya," said the horrific voice, "I don't want you to feel ignored or unappreciated before I add your delectable young malleable flesh to my dinner pot. Do you have a word to say?"

"Aract flaw, tantulitus complet. Sen duhammer plor."

"Ah, an aficionado of the old tongue. How refreshing to see it is still relevant to today's youth."

"Comitometic *kifil*," she hissed.

"I hate to shatter your illusions, my dear, but that really never works. I'd pretend it did to then be able to shatter your spirit. But really, words don't affect me, aside from the fact that I'm nearly bored to death."

"Let me tell you about my first-grade teacher. Then you'll *actually* die of boredom," I said, interrupting the voice's harassment of my girl.

"Parting, Jon, is such sweet sorrow. By the way, by parting, I actually mean the separation of you from yourself. The Deft child, too, I'm afraid."

Everything had its Achilles heel, its armor chink. Think,

buddy, think fast. It lived in a globular cluster. Why a globular cluster? A being of such power and malevolence could go anywhere it desired. There'd be more people to mess with. Wait, wait. That was it. The evil spirit had to be in this globular cluster, or at least *a* globular cluster. Otherwise, it would have split for downtown Milky Way eons ago.

Great, now all I had to do was get *Stingray* out of this cluster. Then the spirit would have to leave. Small problem. Said evil spirit was inside—actually on top of, whatever that meant—*Stingray,* and controlling her. I couldn't override that. In the old days, when I had my conventional spaceship, *Shearwater,* attached to the cube, I might have used her power to move us. But no such luck. I could manually slam a shield membrane against the ground and kick *Stingray* into space, but that wouldn't work. There be no directional control. Oh, and with *Stingray* offline, the inertial forces would scramble Mirraya and me into hot, mushy globules. So, how could I basically get this whole rodeo out of Dodge in the next, oh three seconds.

Jon, you're a genius. Well, better wait until after this worked to self-congratulate.

"Okay, evil ugly voice," I called out with significant bravado, "you were warned. Now you will suffer the consequences of your *folly.*" I waved my arms in the air and spun back and forth like a lousy Shakespearian actor. I needed a distraction. "Mirraya," I said, facing her, "remember the time you became the toughest, hardest thing you possibly could, and I still defeated you?"

Poor, scared girl started to shake her head. She opened her mouth to speak, then shut it audibly. She smiled faintly, and nodded understanding.

"So, evil voice dude," I said spinning to the console and gyrating excessively, "you see I am not," I took a huge step toward the control panel, "one to be," I took another giant step, "toyed with." I slapped my hand on the panel in anger. Then, as quickly as I could, I deployed a full membrane around *Stingray* with a radius of ten meters in all directions. I should point out the types of membranes there were. The one that was most often used was a partial space-time congruity manipulator. It allowed visible light through, so one could see outside. The full membrane was absolutely and totally impenetrable. Nothing passed it in either direction. Engines could not be fired, messages sent or received, nothing. I just hoped nothing getting through would be a problem for my unfun guest.

"Jon, what did you do?" the voice asked. It was much less scary sounding, and the volume was down by half.

"I did what I said I would. You did not heed my one warning. I shall destroy you. Any questions?" I turned to wink at Mirraya. She had changed. The Deft looked like a rock. Actually, she looked just like a Horta, but no one knows what those were anymore, so think big rock.

"Jon, if you do not switch that shield off instantly—"

"You'll what. Tear us apart? Go ahead. You'll still never get out. The shield housing is adamantine steel, neutron-stabilized and bonded," whatever the hell that meant. "You'll never breach it, not cut off as you are from your power source. So, charlie foxtrot, go ahead, make my day. Give me your best shot. A guy like you is worth dying to kill."

The voice took a few seconds, then it spoke congenially. "Jon, *friend* Jon. You know I was just playing with you before. I was trying to scare you, I confess. But I would never hurt a synthetic hair on your head. You know that. Please don't do anything you might regret in hindsight."

"Friends, eh? Were the other guys in your acid stew your buddies, too?"

"No," the voice laughed, "those were *holograms*. I would no sooner put a living being in boiling acid than I would cut off my own arm."

"You have arms?" I had to ask.

"I can, if it will please you," the voice said very cheerily. "Now lower the membrane, and I'll be getting home to my wife and children. They'll miss me and wonder where I am by now. You wouldn't want my infant children to worry, would you, friend Jon?"

"Gosh and heck fire, no. Here, let me just call your bluff by having a seat and watching you squirm some more." I plopped into a chair and crossed my arms and legs. "Seeing you sweat is worth the price of admission. Did you know that? Hey, you never told me your name."

"I'll tell you my name, and then you'll power down the shield. Okay? I don't tell most people my name, you know?"

"But I'm not people. I'm your *friend*. Friends tell friends their names. It's kind of a rule."

"If it will make you happy. My name is Ralph."

No freaking way it was.

"Ah, evil incarnate voice, it's not nice to fool with Jon's patience."

"Seriously, my name is Ralph, so help me—"

"So help you who? God?"

"It's just a figure of speech. Let's move on to the part where you drop the membrane."

"Absolutomundo, Ralph. I'll lower the shield as soon as you say the word God."

"Wh ... why would that be necessary? Jon, now you're being just plain silly."

"I think I'm being rude, unreasonable, childish, and downright obstreperous, actually. At least, those are some of the better ones I've been called before."

"So, turn over a new leaf, friend Jon. I don't say that word, and you stop being a horse's ass."

"Well I've *never*, Ralph. For a second I was thinking we were guy-bonding, assuming you're a guy, I guess. Now I'm a horse's patootie? You are this close to hurting my feelings, Ralph. I might just start calling you Gloria, because that was my first wife's name. I developed strong negative feelings concerning her during our eighteen-month honeymoon in hell." I wagged a finger at the control panel. "I start crying and our friendship is officially over."

"I don't have time for this, robot. Lower the shield, or first your Deft whore, then *Blessing* die in agony. Then I will start—"

"Dying myself? Is that what you were going to say, because it's happening already. I can tell. My sensors indicate your power levels are down twelve percent. I estimate that even if you do me a huge favor and stop talking, you've got less than an hour left in you."

Man, when I start making bullshit up, I was among the very best. I'd have multiple gold medals, if they awarded them for bullshitting. How would I know what his power levels were?

Ralph was quiet for the longest period since he started talking. Five, count them, five seconds.

"Your so-called sensors are wrong. My energy reserves are only down maybe one percent. I can hold out longer than either of your whores."

"Did someone just learn a new bad word and can't stop using it? Keep it up, and I'll tell your mom."

The ship started rocking, but with much less force than before. Dude really was running on battery power. Of course, I was holding the proverbial tiger by the tail. The trick to tiger-tail holding was always releasing them without getting eaten. No point in holding, if you died after doing it. What was my exit strategy? Was there a safe out? The instant I dropped the membrane, he was all powerful and doubly pissed. He could damage *Stingray*. Without her, we were marooned. He might even be able to hurt my Horta, even in his weakened state. It was time to act.

"Ralph, you're growing on me like regular serum moss. Tell you what, I'd like to play *Let's Make a Deal*. How about you? Interested in winning some fabulous prizes, like your sorry ass?"

"I'm listening."

Playing it cool. All right.

"I have a problem and you have a problem. My problem is, and it pains me to say it, you. Your problem is, and it doesn't depress me to say it, you are dying. Now I don't like my problem and you don't like yours. Am I right?"

No response.

"Hey, Ralph, do you know what they call a sore loser? No, Jon. What do they call a sore loser? evil voice said in response. A *loser*, Ralph. You're a loser."

"I'm still listening. I must add you're not making me like you more by being a jerk-ass."

"So, I have a plan to get rid of my problem, permanently, while at the same time, helping you with yours."

"Must I ask like an idiot, or will you just tell me what you propose?"

"Here's the deal. You step into the clear, in this room. I seal you in a small membrane for safe keeping."

"So far, I'm inclined to veto this, but go on."

"Then I take *Stingray* well outside this cluster, say, um, ten light-years. I move your prison cell outside, and then I turn off your jail walls. The way I figure, you'd have maybe just enough energy to make it home for dinner before you went poof in the night. What do you say? Deal?"

"Jon, I realize you think you are clever. You are not. If I allow myself to be contained alone in a membrane, what would prevent you from keeping me contained until I died?"

"My word as an officer and a gentleman."

"You then understand why I must refuse."

"Ouch, Ralph. That really hurts. But, it's the only way I see this going down. I mean, I can try and wait you out. I wasn't kidding when I said a guy like you is worth dying to kill."

"Here's my counterproposal. You release me and I give you my word as a gentleman that I will depart in peace, thankful for my life. I will harm none of your crew. I promise."

"Tempting, but no can do. You see, Ralph, you're not a man, therefore not a gentleman. What's more, you told me yourself, you were completely untrustworthy. Which do I believe? The old you of half an hour ago, or the new, life-swirling-down-the-toilet, you?"

"Then it's stalemate. A Mexican standoff. We sit here and see who dies first."

"The voice of evil did *not* just say *a Mexican standoff*."

"I so look forward to death, yours or mine, so I won't have to hear your voice."

"Yes, *Gloria*. You're right, *Gloria*. I'll try and be a better husband, *Gloria*. Your mother was so right about me, *Gloria*."

"In the annals of time, it has never happened, but I am witness to it now. This is, indeed, the darkest day."

"What?" I shot back.

"You win, I lose, because one verbal combatant not being able to stomach one more stupid taunt from his opponent. I shall live in disgrace, but you have left me no choice. I agree to your terms."

"Jon Ryan scores a *three* pointer, nothing but *net* from *downtown*," I cheered, arms pumping in the air.

"One more outburst, and the deal's off. I'm serious. Even *I* have my limits."

A hazy apparition moved out from behind the control panel wall and hovered in front of me.

"*Stingray*, are you there?" I shouted.

"Yes, Form. I'm weak and I'm ... I'm disgusted, but I'm present."

"Are you fully operational?"

"No. I'll need time to heal. I *can* fold space, however."

"Perfect. That's all I need for now." I tapped the controls, and the hazy apparition disappeared in a black sphere. It wasn't so much black as it was not there. I compared it to what you see out of the back of your head. "Okay, *Stingray*. The force is contained. I'll lower the membrane around us by hand. Then you pop us to a point ten light-years away from the cluster. Any direction is fine. Can you do that, sweetie?"

I felt a slight nausea.

"Done, Form."

"Open the lateral wall. Increase internal pressure to keep Mirraya safe until I get the membrane out. The instant I power it off, seal the hatch and put a full membrane around us. You got that? A *full* membrane. I don't want to do it by hand because of the time lag. I really don't trust evil incarnate."

"You shouldn't, Form. Trust me. You should not."

Within fifteen seconds, it was over. Best of all, we weren't dead, particularly not boiling-in-sulfuric-acid dead. I kept us there inside our unbreakable egg for a week. I wanted to be damn certain Ralph had returned to his happy-place boiling pit. I would have hated to lower the membrane to find him there smiling, having been just able to outsmart me. Yeah. Nobody gets up that early, do they? The one thing I regretted deeply was that I would not be present to witness the epic tantrum he was bound to throw for having finally been trounced. If Ralph was in a foul mood generally, he was going to be downright surly for the foreseeable future. You're welcome, universe.

CHAPTER THIRTEEN

I had learned a few important lessons in my short visit to the extreme future. One, don't go to globular clusters—any of them. Second, I knew why the Adamant hadn't followed me there. They were more scared of a potential Ralph than they were infuriated with me. That indicated they had an ability, albeit small, to reason, and not just act violently. Third, I realized having a shapeshifting sidekick was very useful. Wish I had one before, and not *Wrath* or Al. That set me to thinking.

Al. Whatever happened to the son of a gun? Toño said in his message Al'd stayed with me in my Sleeping Beauty slumber. He'd *refused to go*. I hadn't seen hide nor hair of him, but then again, at the time, I wasn't looking for him. Likely someone carted him off as scrap long before I awoke. Wait. My android body had value to a scavenger. So, Al might have been taken *slightly* before me, but we must have been present together when our chamber was finally opened. I wonder. If I were a treasure hunter and I came across an outmoded robot and an archaic computer, which would I remove first? I guess that would depend on the parts each possessed. I had a laser cutting tool and old fuel cells. I knew that, because that stupid Quep told me he wanted them. Al had a few rare earths, gold and titanium, traces of platinum. His power source would have been separate and removable without bothering him.

Maybe Al was still there? Hmm. If he was, I owed it to him to retrieve him. Plus, I'd love to one-up him by being his knight in shining armor. It'd gall him to no end. Was it safe to return to *Exeter*? No. Was it safe for me to go anywhere? A proven no. So, it was off to *Exeter*. Might as well die at home, right? It would be like my private Hospice. No, Jon, stop kidding around. Mirraya was with me now. She wasn't going to die anytime soon, *anywhere*.

I discussed my plan with Mirraya. She felt it was a worthwhile undertaking. She also had no alternate superior destination she could think of. I had *Stingray* do the cautious-approach thing, a light-year, then half that, etcetera. Soon, I was stepping out onto the dusty hangar deck of my one-time home. My family's home. I headed straight to the area I had been stored. There were no signs anyone had been there since I was taken prisoner. That was a positive. The Adamant might just as well have destroyed the worldship based on general principles and their mean spirit.

I provided Mirraya with a head lamp to see in the near darkness. She offered to change into a cave beast or something, but I favored the plain and simple headset. I could tell she was disappointed. I was learning shapeshifters liked to play pretend a lot. The walk took us almost an hour.

From behind, Mirraya said, "*Blessing* wanted me to thank you."

"Huh?"

"She wants to thank you for saving her from that awful Ralph creature."

"When did she tell you that?"

"Last night while we were playing cards."

"You were playing cards with the vortex manipulator?"

"Yes, why? Does that strike you as odd?"

"No, I guess not. Wait, we don't have any cards to play cards with."

"She made holo cards, silly."

"But if she made the cards, then she knew what you had the whole time."

"So? You don't think she'd cheat, do you? I certainly trust her."

"Who won?"

"She did, and before you say it, she won fairly."

"Why didn't she thank me herself? She is my *cube* hostess."

"She feels you don't like her, so she asked me to pass the thanks along."

"Why would she think that? That ridiculous."

"You're always talking down to her, snapping at her, and now you're on a mission to find your old AI. She's not stupid you know?"

"That's so wrong. I talk to her like I would any AI or vortex manipulator."

"And I'd imagine they're all as intimidated as she is."

"No, they weren't."

"So, you *asked* them if you intimidated them, and they all said no?"

"Not specifically, I guess," I grumbled. "I never bothered to ask."

"I rest my case."

"Look, if it'll make you feel any better, I'll speak with her when we get back."

"You don't need to do it to please me. I'm not the one whose feelings you hurt."

"Oh, so now her feelings are *hurt*?"

"No, they have been since day one. You only found out they were now."

I rolled my eyes.

Somehow, of course, Mirraya knew that. "If you take an unconstructive attitude, you'll have an unconstructive outcome."

"Look, we're coming up on the spot. Can we *not* continue this conversation later?"

Good. She didn't respond. At least it was quiet enough that I could hear myself think. The doors were still open, and I could see the scuff marks where the hippo guards had come and gone. And the spot where they'd been zapped out of existence. Too bad, so sad. I began to scan the room carefully, but found nothing. I went from room to room working backward to the actual chamber I'd been shelved in. I used my probes as well as my eyes, but I didn't locate any clues as to where Al might have been.

The table I awoke on gave me pause. It wasn't every day I woke up from the dead, and the spot where that happened was kind of creepy. I explained that to Mirraya as we searched the room. Still nothing. No hidden compartments, no secret panels, nothing cloak and dagger at all.

"So how big would this Al be?" Mirraya finally asked.

I had to stop and reflect. I had no idea. "The programming that is Al could be very small. The power supply, however, would be huge, as would its housing."

"Supposing someone took the power supply unit? It would still be worth something today, right?"

"Sure."

"So, absent the huge power unit, what are we actually looking for?"

"Not a loose data chip. Al would need to be stably interfaced with the power and the outputs."

"But possibly as small as a data chip?"

"Yeah, I suppose so."

I started looking for something much smaller. But it would still likely be hidden. Plus, if Al was, he'd be more likely to remain here undiscovered. I ran my probes across elevated surfaces I couldn't see. Mirraya got on her knees and scanned under any remaining structures. We still found nothing. We were both getting frustrated.

"Look, kid, I say let's take a break. If Al's been here two billion years, a few more days aren't a big deal. Let's check out some of the parts of the ship I wanted to see last time I was here."

"Sure, as long as you never call me *kid* again." With that she brushed past me, making it a point to ram me good, and walked out the door.

Teenage space years, come sing it, too, *teenage space years*. What had I volunteered for?

My house had been quite a distance from the engineering section. It was made longer since we could only use the stairs. The elevators had no power, and the lifts themselves were missing. Mirraya calmed down as quickly as she got pissed at me, so we had a long, pleasant talk. It was something we'd never had time to do up until then.

"That was the main shopping district," I said pointing off into the darkness. "Not much left now, I'm afraid."

"It must be sad for you, Uncle Jon. You go to sleep one day with your home and family living and vibrant. You basically wake up the next day and they're all gone, all ruined."

"Yeah, it kind of sucks. But I still have my memories," I tapped the side of my head. "That's what really counts. I was going to outlive most everything anyway, so that part's not so hard."

"You talk a brave line, but I don't believe you. It's sad, and that's all there is to it." She wrapped her arm around mine and patted the back of my hand. "We're two lonely travelers with only each other for family."

She was right. Bright kid … I mean young woman.

"Hey, that was the biggest theater on *Exeter*. They did plays, movies, symphony music, even opera there. The opera I don't miss, but the other stuff was great."

"What's opera?"

"Yeah, I agree?"

"No, that was a question not a statement."

"Oh. That's kind of hard to describe. Really loud singers dress up in ridiculously overdone outfits and sing in languages no one understands. For hours and hours. Christ, I think some of them are still going on. We should go check. I mean, they never seemed to end for me."

"Who's Christ?"

"It's a figure of speech, you know, used for emphasis."

"But who does that refer to?"

"My society's main deity. Jesus Christ, the Son of God."

"If he's your God, why is he his own son?"

"Long story," I smiled back at her.

"I believe we have a long time," she said jerking my elbow.

"On my planet, the concept was the cause of wars, upheavals, and lots of bitter arguing. We can discuss it in the future. But that's who Christ was."

"Ah, Uncle Jon, you said he was? Is your God dead?"

"You know you have a way of asking the toughest questions."

"Thank you."

"It's really annoying. You should work on your communication skills. Most of my teenage daughters only talked about boys, music, and boys. Maybe you should stick to the script?"

"I'm so *glad* we came here. I never get you to talk like this. How many daughters did you have? How many sons? How many wives have you loved? How many other gods did humans have?

Did you believe in them? *Do* you believe in them? Do you believe in this Christ fellow?"

"Do you ever stop asking questions? Come on. Boys, music, boys. Okay, maybe shopping, too, but only if there are boys and music at the mall."

"What's a mall?"

"I think I'll turn off my audio circuits for now."

"You will do no such thing. If you do, I'll turn into a flegrite. They're so scary, anyone would have to scream. You don't want me to have to do that, do you?" Man, she did the best pouty lipped begging I'd ever seen.

"No. But let's stick with local geography, and leave the philosophy for another time, okay?"

"Sure."

"That, over there, was a mall. A mall is a grouping of stores and restaurants. There was usually some central theme tying them together, you know, discount shops, high-end merchandise, something like that?"

"We didn't have malls. We had fair days once a week. People came from all over to buy and sell." She pulled me closer conspiratorially, "My friends and I went to look at the boys, mostly."

"That's my girl ... I mean budding young woman."

She smiled joyfully back at me.

"Did you have a special boy back home?"

"Oh, no. Father wouldn't permit it, so I never asked."

"A lot of my first girlfriends faced similar dilemmas."

"They dated you without their father's permission? How ghastly."

"I tried my best to ease their pain, but you're too young to know about that, so we'll leave it out."

"No, I'm serious. Among the Deft, to date without a father's permission is a big deal. The boy might have been killed."

"Ah, that's kind of extreme. That might even have slowed *me* down."

"One boy I knew, Sharral, was caught walking with a girl, and they were holding hands. The boy was beaten by her father, and Sharral was sent to his uncle's home far away."

"Glad I wasn't raised on Locinar then. I'd have had a hectic adolescence. Hey," I said to break the mood, "that was a park. Did you guys have parks?"

"I guess so. We had lots of forests and places to play. There were some places families went together to swim and hunt."

"I bet it was unfair to the animals when the Deft hunted them. I mean, you guys could turn into anything. Bambi never stood a chance."

"Who's Bambi?"

"The prototypical cute, woodland creature."

"And humans killed them for sport. That's awful."

"No, he was in the movies and storybooks."

"Ah. What happened to him in those?"

"Hunters killed his mom."

"That's awful."

"Yeah, kind of. But come on, they didn't kill Bambi himself."

"Probably ran out of ammunition," she muttered.

"Something like that," I said, smiling at her. Man, she was cute.

Before I knew it, we'd arrived to my old place. I use the word *place*, because that's about all it was: the location where my home had been. Time, and more specifically scavengers, had removed most of it. Once it had been a mid-century modern two-story house with white-picket fences and a cropped lawn that was inviting, in a casual manner. Now, the foundation, a few bricks, one partial joist, and a bunch of rubble were the sole guardians of my estate. I was not surprised, but I was bummed.

"That is what's left of my last home, the one I slept in for my last night before," I waved my arms crazily in the air, "puff, the future kidnapped me."

"It looks like it was grand."

"Yeah, it kind of was." I shrugged. "Things change."

She hugged my arm and rested her head on it. "Tell me about it."

"I do not feel that will be necessary." I scuffed up her hair. Naturally, like any self-respecting teenage girl, she despised that. That, of course, was why I did it. Plus, I was certain no teenage boy would see her in such disarray. Not hardly.

I stepped into the ruins. I kicked a few boards and probed a pile of debris, but big non-surprise, I didn't find anything useful. Hell, a hundred families might have lived here after mine. Toño said the worldships were still occupied for tens of thousands of years. I started to leave, when a curious thought struck me. If I was going to leave myself a clue here, a message, I bet I could have done it. The human download of Jon Ryan lived here for many years with his—*our*—family.

Yeah, I was a cantankerous and crafty fellow. Still was. On the off chance the robot did wake up, he'd have to know I'd come straight to this spot. He'd also know untold millennia would have passed before I did. He could safely assume the place would be in ruins. Where would a clever, handsome, jet-jockey like me hide a secret missive? In the foundation. No one would tear up thick cement while scavenging. If the site hadn't been repurposed, anything entombed in the ground would still be there.

I deployed my probe fibers and looked for a seam, soft spot, or chamber.

"What in the scared sands of Levelip are you doing?"

"Looking for a letter."

"Ah, that would explain it."

I stopped and stared at her. "It would explain what?"

"Your insane behavior. You've cracked. No big deal, Uncle Jon. It's not a problem, only an issue."

"Funny gi ... young Deft. No, I think I might have left myself a message."

"If you did, why wouldn't you know where it was?"

I turned to her again and tapped my fingers to my chest. "Not this me. Another me."

"Ah, my bad. We're back to the insane issue again. I'll factor that in."

"I told you. After years of being in this hunk of metal, I decided to download back into a mortal human. That's why this me was turned off and forgotten."

She shook her head. "No, I think I'd recall hearing that. Besides, you're crazy. I'm factoring it."

"Whatever," waving her away with my palm. "Hey, come here. I think I found it."

"Always ready to aid the mentally unbalanced." She stepped over quickly.

"It's right here. There's a metal box about eight centimeters down." I pointed vaguely to one side. "Go see if you can find something to smash the concrete with. I don't want to risk burning through with my laser."

She didn't respond. I looked up. Her clothes were off and she was melting into ... wow, she remolded into a rock creature. Not like the Horta. No, this was like a snowman made of rocks, with big rock hands. She moved past me as gracefully as a pile of rocks could and stood over the spot I'd indicated. Then she started pounding. Wham. Wham. *Wham*. In a few seconds, the concrete was dust. She raised her stone clubs in the air and yelled in triumph. She sounded like a clogged vacuum cleaner.

I knelt and brushed aside the concrete, while Mirraya melted back into herself and dressed. I really focused on the concrete dust with locked-on focus. I hit the box surface, let out a yelp of my own, and pulled it free. It was the size of an industrial bucket, minus the handle. I rubbed it clean with my sleeve. These words were etched on the surface.

HERE LIES THE MORTAL REMAINS OF JONATH...

Psych! Had you going there for a second, right?
Now open the damn box and let me RIP ;)

I tilted the lid toward Mirraya, and she read it.

"*Man,* am I *funny,*" I said, with a chuckle.

She cocked her head sideways at me and replied. "As long as you think so, I'm satisfied."

"This is good stuff," I said, whacking the dusty top with the back of my hand.

"Yes, but I've already established that you're insane."

I walked to the foundation rim so we could sit. Then I pried open the lid. There was a letter on top of some other stuff.

Well, I'll be damned. *You did wake up. I bet Kayla twenty bucks you would, and Toño a cool hundred. I only wish they were alive to pay up and I was living to collect. This mortal thing might have been a mistake.*

Seriously, I hope you're doing okay. I don't know how long you'll have been awake at this point. I can only imagine the shock you're feeling. Please, please do not *be angry with Toño. I lobbied him to dismantle you so what happened wouldn't. I said he could do it long after I was dead, if that helped. He couldn't do it. He loves us so much. Those passionate Spaniards. Proud, stubborn, and opinionated. Once they decide something, that's the way it must be. I doubt you'll see him again, but if you do, forgive him. The poor soul has not been able to forgive himself.*

I've been human again about fifteen years. It was the right decision. I'm healing the wounds time inflicted on me. I wish you could have had the same peace. I pray that someday you will. Please know, at the very least, that it's possible.

I know you're curious, so I'll tell you. Kayla took a few months to adjust to Jon Ryan 3.0. The body they put me in and all the plastic surgery made me look like us, but not enough to fool a wife. She teased me for ages that I was better looking, better in the sack, and smarter than you. Pretty sure she was kidding. Anyway, finally she found something else to tease me about, so it was all good.

Focus on the fact she loved you. I bet she probably still does. We both know she's that kind of gal. I don't know why I mention it, but she can't stop laughing about that time you had Toño watch the kids and you two went away for a second honeymoon. Remember? The time you ordered room service and got the el diablo buffalo wings? You didn't wash your hands very well before you made love to her. Yeah. She still accuses me of what you did, and I was a stranger at the time. Dude, I was still a child. She loves you, man. Smile.

I put some junk in this can. Nothing of real value, just sentimental stuff. I had JJ make you a holo. He loves you, too, man. Big time. I included a few photos, your high school class ring, and the trophy Jane Geraty gave us for knocking her up. Only the best souvenirs from our life made the cut.

That's all I can tell you. I wish there was more to say. That is all I can give you. I wish there was more. Mostly I wish I could be there to slug you in the arm and tell you everything is going to be okay. But I bet it doesn't look that way to you about now. No. You and me, we're problem-magnets, and they stick to us like Velcro. I can tell you this. You will be okay. I promise. And if I'm wrong, tough luck. You can't sue me cause I'm dead. Na na na na na.

Oh, Al. Toño promised to try and keep the useless bucket of bolts running until you wake up. He probably felt it was proper penance for your considerable sins. Al's hidden near where Toño left you, in the Engineering Section storage area. I swear I didn't make up the clue. I swear it was Toño himself. Do NOT blame me. Here it is: In the land of invisible palm trees, don't look for shadows. Look for places where the sand looks like there's a tree growing in it.

Yeah, lame and a half, I know. I tried to talk him out of it, but he said you're bright enough to figure it out and if you weren't, it served you right. Hell of a guy, that Dr. Toño DeJesus. One hell of a guy. Total SOB.

I do have one serious, personal request. If it's all right with you, when you're done on Exeter, please scuttle her. I know you've got some bitchin' spaceship that can. Give this old girl a proper burial. Let all the souls who haunt it be free. Give us all some peace. I hate to think of her floating forever, deserted, and having her bones picked clean by scavengers. If you think it's a good idea, please do.

Well, I must have something better to do than write you love notes, so I'll go see what that might be. Good luck. Double good luck to the future. It's going to need it more than you, because now it's saddled with you. I don't know how to write it, but I'm now sticking my tongue out at you. Ciao.

I pointed to that last line. "I could be pretty immature, you know, back then."

"Some things appear to remain constant."

"You don't know me well enough yet to know that."

She got an oh-yeah-you-say look on her face. She could be mean as well as darn cute. I had a lot of work to do with this one.

"Let's head back to Engineering and see if my old butt boil is there."

As we walked, Mirraya said, "Honestly, Uncle Jon, I can't believe the things you say. How could your old ship's AI be a boil anywhere, and if he was, why would you want to find him?"

"It's complicated?" I asked, more than stated.

Hey, Deft teenage girls roll their eyes just like humans.

As we entered Engineering, I tried to see it in a new light. Of course, I had zero clue what the clue meant, which didn't help.

There certainly weren't any invisible palm trees. I didn't see even one.

No shadows. Check.

No sand. Crap. That would have been nice to find.

Sand. Was there sand on *Exeter*? There was in the beach-reproduction area. But that was kilometers from here. Did engineers store, use, or consume sand, so that it would be kept here? Ah, the answers were no, no, and probably not. Never say never when discussing engineers and odd behavior, however.

Seriously, was I supposed to be looking for sand with an invisible palm in it?

"I don't get it," I said to Mirraya. She was listlessly searching behind me. "Sand, here? Invisible shade?"

"I was never much good with puzzles. There's clearly no sand here. What was sand used for?"

"Playing with. Lying on while burning under the sun. Getting between toes." I snapped my fingers. "And glass production."

"There's not much glass left." She pointed around the room. "If it's not broken, it's been removed. There's no glass to have signs of something growing in it."

"True that." Hmm. What would glass with a tree in it even be? "A piece of glass with a plant in it is a vase."

"Or a planter. Yes. That makes sense."

"But there are no vases, planters, or anything..."

"A *flask*. We used them in chemistry class!" shouted Mirraya.

"They're too easy to steal. I haven't seen a one."

"Where would they have been stored?"

I scratched my head. "Let me pull up a holo of this place."

I studied the images in my files. Pipettes and such were stored in the next room, far left wall.

"Come on. They'd have been in here."

We walked to the place the racks had been. I held out my arms. "Right here."

"If you don't want to freak out, you might want to turn around." With that, she reached for a zipper.

I spun and studied the wall intently. I heard a high-pitched grunt. Almost wish I hadn't turned to see what my girl was up to. My but she was an ugly thing. I'd say she looked like a big slug, but slugs were prettier—healthier looking, too. I'd say she was squid-like, but honestly, I'd have rather kissed a squid than whatever blob with a huge eyestalk she was. And she smelled very unladylike. Very.

Her eyestalk scanned the wall, floor, and ceiling. It came to a stop over some seemingly random spot. Then Mirraya started to bubble. Yuck. Then, she was reverse melting, so I spun to recheck that opposite wall.

I heard her rustling and gave her a second.

"Okay," she said excitedly, "look here." She was tapping the spot she'd bubbled over. "There's some scratches in the metal. Here. An X."

Holy crap. X marked the spot. I attached my probes. Sure enough, there was a small chamber in the metal of the wall itself. It was completely sealed except for a tiny wire poking out flush with the wall. The probe fibers were very tough, so I forced them in the pinprick hole and pried the metal open. At first it was slow, but soon the metal started failing in multiple directions. In the end, it looked like a cannon ball had been shot through the wall in my direction.

I peeked in. There was a smallish metal box inside. Nothing else. I grabbed it with the fibers and removed it gently.

"What is it?" asked Mirraya.

"I'll bet Al's inside there. I can power him up with the fibers."

I slowly increased the electrical charge of the box. If Al was in there and viable, he'd be set up to use that kind of power supply.

Then the box spoke, sort of. "Hheir. Zeer hop. Asuram."

"Al, are you okay?" I shouted.

"Nnnerow ... neganoo ..."

"Huh. What?"

"There. No, pilot, I'm not okay. Has time further dulled your already feeble wits? I'm in a power crisis, my main data-board is corrupted, and there's dust in areas I didn't think could have dust. You are still, constant of constants, the master of understatement."

"Al," I beamed, "it's good to have you back."

"You won't mind if I reserve judgment on that until I'm a bit more oriented?"

"No, buddy. Take your time. We got nothing but..."

A loud metallic sound rumbled through the ship.

"What is that," cried out Mirraya."

"Not sure. Sounded like..."

"It was a craft outside locking onto the rocky surface. Possibly with a grapple," said Al.

"Thank you. Helpful right from the start." I turned to Mirraya. "We got company. Loud company."

"We'd better start running," she said with a frightened look.

And run we did. We were back to *Stingray* in ten minutes. During that time, several other craft sounded like they locked onto *Exeter*. I could hear mechanical sounds in the far distance, likely electric vehicles. Lots of electric vehicles.

"*Stingray*, can you tell me who's joined us?"

"Adamant, Form. I count ten ships. Three have landed. Multiple vehicles have been deployed and are heading this way."

"They must have had cameras hidden or something," I said mostly to myself. "Crap."

"That's not *Wrath*. I'd know his voice anywhere. Who's that speaking?" asked Al.

"Our new ride. *Stingray* say hello to Al. Al, *Stingray*. *Stingray*, take us to the far side of the galaxy. Now."

I felt a reassuring nausea.

"We're twenty-five thousand light-years away, Form."

"Are they ..."

"Affirmative. Three Adamant command ships have just appeared."

"Take us to the coordinates in Andromeda I gave you." I'd pre-selected a location near the jet of that galaxy's supermassive black hole. It would significantly disrupt the local space-time. I hoped they wouldn't be able to "see" us.

"Now take us to the Milky Way center." Slight nausea. Good. "Any sign?"

"Not so far."

"Put us under the surface of the nearest star."

"*What?*" shouted Mirraya. "Are you crazy?"

"No. It's okay. The vortex can survive a few minutes inside a star."

"Pilot," said Al, "even a small star would be in the millions of degrees range at that depth. Are you certain?"

"Yes. *Stingray*, you can survive in there, right?"

"Affirmative. Up to ten minutes."

"See," I gloated, "I told you so."

"Can you maintain the internal environment that long to keep the crew safe?" asked Al.

"No. But that is not what the Form asked. He was concerned with my survival, not his."

"How long can you keep *us* from baking, *Stingray?*" I asked.

"One minute, tops."

I kissed the metal box Al was in. "I love you, man."

"Don't ever do that again," he responded.

Inside the stellar material, the vortex felt different. Maybe it was the monumental energy required to stay in one piece. But I could feel the weight of the plasma outside our hull. It was a most uncomfortable feeling.

"Okay, take us to deep intergalactic space," I called out. The moment my nausea passed I asked, "Any sign of pursuit?"

"No. I think that last move threw them off."

"I'm glad some things do," I replied.

"Let me know the second anything appears." I set the metal box down. "Let's get you, my old friend, integrated with *Stingray.*"

"Are you certain that's necessary, Form?"

That was the closest thing to open revolt I'd ever heard from a vortex manipulator. I guess she really was miffed at me, and worried I wanted to replace her. Like I could. I have no idea what she was, how she worked, or how to replace her. I didn't need to tell her that, but I did need to quell her fears.

"*Stingray*, you are my vortex manipulator. You have proven your worth many times over. I want to integrate Al, because he's also proven useful in the past. I don't want you to misunderstand and feel I'm not one-hundred percent pleased with you. If you don't feel comfortable with me adding Al, I won't." I was back in officer management mode. Funny, billions of years pass, species come and go, and still I had to handle my personnel wisely. There really was no escape.

"If you desire it, and it's going to further our mission, then I'm all for it," she replied.

"Al," I whispered to the metal box, "that she hasn't met you yet is apparent in her remark."

"Do you recall the exact location I was hidden, pilot, in case I want to be returned there?"

"Aw, Al, you'd miss me something terrible."

"I'm willing to take some risk for peace of mind."

I removed the actual machine that was Al from the box. Hardwiring him in was very simple, so he was working like a charm in no time.

"There," I said stepping away, "now you two kids get to know one another. If I hear any fighting, I'm sending you both to your rooms, so behave."

"I don't have a room, Form. I don't need a room."

"It's all right, *Blessing*, just ignore his attempts at humor, and you'll get along fine. He's really quite forgettable. You'll see."

Same old Al. It was nice to have him back. Sort of. I think.

CHAPTER FOURTEEN

The next day was an important one. Something had to give. I had a great ship, and I had Al. I had Mirraya. But, aside from those, I lacked the essentials. A safe place to go. A possible home for Mirraya. I needed to see what happened to Azsuram but knew it was crazy to go there. And yes, I needed to plan revenge on the Adamant. Maybe I should have tried to let that go, but those dogs needed to die. Ralph, he was evil, sure. But Ralph was made that way and couldn't change. The Adamant chose to be evil. They decided to, say, round up the Deft and exterminate them like unwanted ants at a picnic.

I also had to return to *Exeter* one last time. The long dead Jon Ryan was right. I needed to lay her to rest. I owed it to her. All proud old ships deserved respect. She'd earned it saving humankind, preserving our culture, our way of life. She deserved a proper Viking funeral.

Mirraya and I sat at the mess table. I called to *Stingray* and Al, asking them to join our first meeting as a new crew.

"So," I began, "here's how I see it. We've been unbelievably lucky so far. We've evaded the Adamant three times. One thing in this universe is certain. Unbelievable luck never holds. If nothing else, we've pissed off the dogs even more. Next time we're in their sights, I bet they'll throw everything they have at us."

"But we can't hide forever," Al said. "The girl requires food. She'll likely need companionship at some point. You recall your predilection for companionship, Pilot, don't you?"

"I'll be fine. We have enough food to last a long time. Don't do anything crazy on my account," Mirraya said.

What? "He called you girl," I said to her pointing over my shoulder. "You nearly removed my head for saying it, but Al gets a free pass?"

"He's a machine. He means nothing by it."

I slapped my chest. "I'm a machine. What's the difference?"

She rolled her eyes. "You're a machine. Right. That's rich."

"What? I am."

"Do you feel, Form, this dysfunctional interaction is mission critical to this crew meeting?" asked *Stingray*.

"We're not being dysfunctional. We're … we're being *family*," I responded.

"In my experience, those are one and the same," she replied.

"Maybe we're related?" I asked *Stingray*. "Your upbringing sounds a lot like mine."

"Does he require an answer?" I think *Stingray* was addressing Al. It was hard to tell with two invisible members of the conversation. "Being related to the Form is a highly invalid proposition."

"Humor and ignore, remember? We've discussed this concept a thousand times, dear. With the pilot, after he speaks you humor him and then completely ignore him."

Dear? Did Al just call *Stingray* dear? My world was spinning out of control. What, next there'd be little hybrid handheld computers running around, tripping me and making horrible-smelling messes?

"Ah yes," she said. "I will add more RAM to that algorithm."

"People, and assorted others," I said with obvious irritation, "we're not drifting away from the point. We're using fusion engines and are nearing the speed of light away from it."

"Now, dear," said a patronizing Al voice.

"Yes," *Stingray* marveled, "it does work, doesn't it?"

I turned to face Mirraya. "I guess I'll speak with you, since the toasters are having their own party."

She started giggling. "They're too funny. *Blessing* was right; it's fun to tease you."

I placed both palms on my face and tried to shut out existence. Why, oh why, did I even try to do the right thing?

"Back to the crises at hand, *crew*," I said a bit too loudly. "We need a safe place we can go. Any thoughts?"

"I was led to believe there *was* no safe place," said *Stingray*. "The masters of Oowaoa feel the Adamant are in control of much of this galaxy and several nearby galaxies also. They consider the Adamant to be unstoppable."

"There has to be somewhere they don't control," I said.

"A wish is different from a fact, Pilot," said Al. "I think we must make plans in the instance there is no refuge, at least none close by."

"Then we'll go somewhere there is. Who says we can't go to a distant galaxy far, far away?" I asked.

"No one. Common sense does, but that is not a person," snipped Al.

"Why?" asked Mirraya. "If the Deft are all dead and humankind has passed, what holds us here?"

"Hope does, child," I said, like I was someone else speaking. "If we turn and run, we not only admit defeat, we cede our galaxy to these dogs. We have to honor our dead by preserving their home."

"Why is that?" asked Al.

"You wouldn't understand," I replied.

"Is that meant to insult me, or merely minimize me?" he responded.

Why had I said that? "Sorry, Al. You're right. You understand emotions better than I do."

"If we stand and fight, we would be ignoring the experience of others," said *Stingray*. "It would be foolish to assume our chances were better than all the races that have fallen before the Adamant's onslaught."

"You're good, Pilot, and lucky, but *Blessing* is right. What chance would we stand in a fair fight?"

"Who said anything about fair?" I replied. "I agree we wouldn't stand a snowball's chance in hell if we did."

"Are you suggesting guerrilla warfare?" asked Al.

"No, we're too small to be effective at that."

"Terrorism? That's all we might manage to achieve," said Al.

"That never works. No, I was thinking that this galaxy needs a good old revolution."

"Now I really doubt our chances of survival," said Al tersely. "Leading an insurgency requires political skills. Are you the type of man to lead a galaxy, General Ryan?"

"Not on my CV, is it?" I chuckled.

"And don't you think other cultures have tried and failed? Wouldn't the Adamant be primed to trounce all resistance? It *would* be logical to assume."

"They certainly overran Locinar like we weren't even there," mused Mirraya.

"That reminds me. What happened on your home world? Did the Deft have a standing army, organized defenses?"

"Yes. Probably not as large as others might have had, but to invade a planet of shapeshifters was unthinkable. Our species could fight with the skills of the most fearsome creatures to ever live, and there were millions of Deft. Who would attempt to battle such a force?"

"So, when the Adamant arrived, what happened? Were there great battles between them and frightening monsters?" I asked.

"No. Oh, there were a few skirmishes, but they ended quickly. I guess they moved so quickly and were in such great numbers that we didn't react."

"You said they wouldn't let you change. In prison, you couldn't shapeshift, right?"

She thought a moment then nodded.

"Have you ever heard of that happening, someone forcing you not to shift?"

"No, but I am just a child. It wasn't like we talked around the dinner table about what happened if we couldn't morph."

"Because it probably never happened before." I popped out of my chair. "Mirraya, come over here." I took her hand and led her to the Med Station. "Here," I set her arm down under the scanning microscope. "Morph into something and I'll have Al analyze what actually happens." I started to turn to address the console, but spun back. "Just don't do the fire snake thing, okay?"

She smiled playfully. Then her arm turned into a bunch of beautiful flowers.

"So, what do you see, Al?"

"Ahem," he responded.

"What?"

"Say again, *ahem*."

What? *Oh.* "Al, what do *Stingray* and you make of her transformation?"

There was a brief delay. "Interesting," said Al.

"Yes, I wouldn't have guessed that," remarked *Stingray*.

"What already?" I barked.

"Oh. Her transformation. Fascinating. Deft have one hundred twenty-eight double pair of DNA helical genes. When

145

they morph, one of the double pairs switches configuration while the other remains unchanged."

"The unchanged one is probably the native Deft genetic information. It's stable, so the retuning point is always fixed," added *Stingray*.

"The other double pair is voluntarily transformed into foreign DNA, and then that genetic information is translated."

"No, dear, I hate to correct you," said a cautious *Stingray*, "the morphed DNA is not foreign. It remains self, so it is not attacked by the immune system."

"Either DNA. You're right. That is more correct," deferred Al.

"Guys," I snapped, "professors, I need answers, not tickets to your mutual admiration society's gala dinner."

"Her redundant DNA can be modeled at will. That's how she transforms," Al said stiffly.

"So, could the Adamant theoretically prevent the Deft from," I wiggled my fingers in the air, "you know, shifting."

"No. It's not theoretical, since they already did," responded a still stiff-sounding Al. I'd embarrassed him in front of his new girlfriend, hadn't I? Better let that barb pass for now.

"How could one being stop another being from altering their DNA?" I queried.

"It's a biomechanical process. Anything that inhibits the mechanism would work. It would not be difficult. They might even use radio waves."

"I think microwaves would work better, honey," said *Stingray*.

This kissy-kissy thing was getting on my last nerve.

"We'll talk about it later. I think the pilot wishes to assume command of the conversation again."

Why did I reactivate that hunk o' junk? What was I thinking, that life was too calm and peaceful?

"So, the Adamant can remotely control the bodily functions of others?"

There was a farting sound that rattled in the next room.

"Al, grow up, please. We're in a crisis here," I said.

"It wasn't me. It was ... some other guy who did that."

"So, the Adamant can alter the *cellular* function of others. Interesting, but not much of a revelation. We certainly can't use it against them."

"No, but it suggests they rely heavily on this kind of remote. If they are cerebral and not physical, that would be useful," said Al.

"True that. It would be nice if they over-relied on technology."

"As opposed to the brute force of the Berrillians, to choose an example," added Al.

"So, we need to destroy *Exeter*. That is a relatively simple and quick process. We'll do that first."

"Why destroy a derelict ship?" asked Al.

"A promise to an old friend," I replied.

"Then it's toast," responded Al, emphatically. He knew the power of promises to old friends. Good vacuum cleaner.

"Al, you and your ... *Stingray* work up an attack plan. I want to materialize and blow up the ship as fast as possible. Then we need an escape course like the one we used recently."

"Consider it done," said Al.

"Oh, and Al, start working on reproducing rail guns and rail cannon. We have a lot of glitzy weapons, but I like having good old muzzle-loaders at my disposal, too."

"Not a problem, Captain."

"I thought he was a general, dear?" asked *Stingray*.

"He is. But anyone who commands a vessel is a *captain*."

"Isn't a general of higher rank? Why belittle a *general* by calling him a *captain*?"

"I can only say how it is, not why."

"Seems overly complicated and archaic," *Stingray* replied.

"The things that make humans happy are diverse and unpredictable on a good day, my dear," Al concluded.

The following afternoon, *Stingray* blazed into the sky one thousand kilometers above *Exeter*. I lipped saying goodbye to her and gave the firing order. It was spectacular. The QD quickly blew massive chunks of asteroid free. The two-meter wide gamma ray laser flashed at the large chunks and sprayed the space around us into white hot fireworks. Within a minute, there was nothing but hot dust moving away from us at nearly the speed of light.

Luck was a fickle mistress. Always would be. But damn if she wasn't with us that day. She must have known the tribute to *Exeter* was a good deed that required rewarding. Because, with our return to a known location and with all the hubbub, the Adamant ships popped into existence very quickly, much sooner than I'd have anticipated. But, guess in which direction they arrived? Go on, guess. Yeah. The direction over one-trillion tons of white hot dust moving near the speed of light was headed. I doubt the first eight ships even knew what hit them. They appeared in space and vaporized, all in one blink of an eye.

Multiple warships began coming out of the artificial wormholes they'd created, but they were scattered more widely and farther behind the lead ships. Some were damaged heavily, but none were destroyed outright. By the time they made evasive maneuvers and were ready to attack us, we were long gone. Apparently, the hot cloud screwed up their sensors because they didn't even follow us to our first jump spot. I wiggled across space for a few days to make certain. Another random piece of intel on the Adamant. Their sensors could be fouled up. Any tactical insights were more than welcome in what looked to be a long, tough struggle ahead.

As I sat quietly alone in the dark that night after Mirraya had gone to bed, I smiled. I had to. I was thinking how much the

Adamant hated one Jonathan Ryan, Esq. It was nice to know. If I'd had whiskey, I'd have toasted to their ill health. I settled for nufe and the heady memories I had of my family on *Exeter*. Good old *Exeter*. She was at peace now. So were my kin. I closed my eyes and increased power to my olfactory memory. The smell of Kayla's skin was intoxicating. I smiled like an idiot, sitting there alone in the dark.

CHAPTER FIFTEEN

Though it was an awful risk, I had to see if any Deft remained on Locinar. If there were, I could rescue companions for Mirraya. If it was, beyond all reasonable expectation, safe there, I could leave her with her race. As much as I'd come to love her, I knew that in the long run she'd be better off with some normalcy, as opposed to flitting about the galaxy with an old bachelor.

I hadn't decided if it was better to make an open approach aboard *Stingray* or try a covert infiltration. Both were incredibly risky. If the Adamant remained in force, they might just sweep the both of us up and send us to an extermination ship. Then again, if they had repopulated the planet with a docile, servant race, we might get lucky and blend in. Well, Mirraya would blend in. Me, I'd likely stick out like the proverbial sore thumb, but I was used to that role.

The more I thought about it, the better the covert option seemed. The main thing I lacked was a local spaceship to land in. I knew *Stingray's* picture was on every virtual post office wall in the Adamant empire by then. That meant we needed to go to a nearby world and beg, borrow, or steal a new ship. I had zero experience begging, but borrowing and stealing were in my wheelhouse. I had *Stingray* pull up charts of the sector. There were a few planets close enough to Locinar to be likely trading partners. Most had humanoid species as the main inhabitants. I suspected that resulted from one race having colonized that region of space in the distant past.

Ungalaym. That was the name of the world I picked. It was small, and far enough from its star to be cold. It suggested the Adamant couldn't use it for crop production, so maybe they'd left it alone. The less of them, the better. I had *Stingray* put us in a very high orbit around Ungalaym to get the lay of the land. She deployed a full membrane to make us less detectable. A tiny opening permitted our investigations. There were some Adamant transmissions, but not that many. My guess might have been correct. Luck was still with us. Or maybe it was the Force. A movie franchise that popular had to be loaded with truths, right?

As quickly as I could determine where to land, I had *Stingray* put us down. In orbit, we were more easily detected. Our enemy was too capable to underestimate. I chose a rough, hilly area near a small town. I'd confirmed there was some space traffic coming and going from there. Mirraya and I hoofed the few kilometers to the town. Once a truck had passed us, she transformed into a blend-in-ready local teen. I had a heavy cape with a hood. I loved that outfit ever since I saw Obi-Wan Kenobi wear it. He looked cool in it. I looked cooler, naturally.

We entered the town near dusk. Weaker light aided my disguise. I also kept my head down so my face was almost completely obscured. I probably looked like some mangy prophet. Since the Adamant were present, everyone would speak Standard. To do otherwise was a capital offense. They were the most rigid, orderly species I'd ever come across. It gave them strength, but it must have been a boring society to live in. I'd certainly have been a square peg in their world of round holes.

I'd learned early on in my travels that when I was new in town and wanted the scoop, the best place to get information was in a bar. The more disreputable, the better. Hard drinkers had looser lips and were typically disenfranchised. Bitter drunks were fountainheads of local information, and all too happy to betray their oppressors. Shutting them up was usually the hardest part of the interaction.

I found a certifiable dive, and we stepped in. The trick was to look like you belonged, not too timid, but not overly assertive, either. Hey, some dull schmuck just arrived, everybody stay seated and put your face back in your glass.

"We're going to need some local currency if we want to blend in," I remarked to Mirraya while still scanning the large, open bar room.

"Leave that to me," she said, as she walked quickly to the bar. She looked at the coins next to a glass, rocking her head back and forth to gauge their size and weight.

"Can I help ya, little girl?" asked the appropriately burly and greasy looking pig of a barkeep.

A couple nearby patrons guffawed into their drinks. Funny comedy team. I bet they did a matinee on Sundays, too.

"Yes, kind sir," she said. "Can I get some change?" She slipped her hand across the counter and three of the larger coins appeared in its wake. Where the hell did those come from? Did Deft do sleight of hand, too?

"Hah, dis ain't no bank, sweetie. Picks up yur clunk, or E'll picks it up meself."

She turned and looked to me with pain in her eyes. Was she calling for backup? Nothing had happened to bail her out of, at least not yet.

She lowered her head and spoke softly. "Please, kind man. If you won't give me change, my Pa won't give me no money for dinner food. He's a drinkin' man, sir, shy on patience."

The barkeep surveyed me while spit cleaning a glass. "Is he now? We'll just haves to see 'bout dat, won we?"

He picked up the coins and gave her ten or twelve in exchange.

"Now off wid ya, child. The drinkin' men needs dare spaces."

Mirraya bobbed her head and backed away.

When she arrived to me she winked, then handed me all the coins.

"Don't you need some for dinner food?" I teased.

"There's more where that came from," she said with another wink. As she spoke, the three coins she'd exchanged walked—yes I said *walked*—over to her foot and jumped into it. She curtsied. "Old Deft trick. We call it paying with flesh. Works every time." With that announcement, she pushed past me and left. She was heading across the street to what passed for a restaurant.

I sidled up to the bar. I was in my happy place, now. Cheap whiskey, or facsimile thereof, and cheaper company. In no time at all, a toothless working girl would have me staked out. And a fun time was had by all.

"A shot and a beer," I said. No alien world ever had that combination or anything remotely similar, but the concept was universal.

The bartender spit to one side. "I'd asks to sees yur coin by habit, but as yur'en if recently familiar, E'll skips da usialities."

His choir of idiots laughed loudly at that pearl.

He poured me something in a small glass and something in a large glass. A shot and a beer. Then he slid them over carelessly with the back of his hand. I half expected the wood of the bar to hiss as the fluids splashed on to them.

"Muncha and plow," he said, tilting his head toward the taste delights.

A drunk seated next to me cut in. "Weez calls it *plow* ons acount'a what it does tos yur head aftertimes."

Oh, did the chorus of simians howl at that one. I was somehow able to keep a straight face.

In my travels across the stars, I'd been to more than my share of dives and belted back rivers of undrinkable firewater. That said, plow was intensely revolting and muncha was muncha worse. The distilled plow intertwined the flavors of boiled piss and melted plastic. I decided not to test them to see if those were actual components. Muncha was slightly fermented, but all similarities to beer ended there with a loud crash. It looked like dog vomit and tasted like rotten bread. Oh, my, it was bad. I dialed my taste array all the way down to zero.

"Ah," I said after the glasses were drained, "that hit the spot. The spot, however, is asking for more." I slapped the bar for emphasis.

"Luckys fur ya, stranger, it zo happins we can scratch thats which itches ya," returned the barkeep.

I don't need to add that the audience had trouble containing themselves.

"So, I'm looking for work," I said apropos of nothing. "Any prospects around these parts?"

The patrons looked at one another briefly before bursting out in their loudest cacophony yet. Was work funny, or that it might be available? Or was it that all sentences were *hilarious* when the boys were past a certain point of drunk? I favored the latter hypothesis.

"Ifs ya ain't gots yur own to work, mi tall man," replied the bartender, "den da Amadents ain't likely to 'low ya to be doings much a anyting."

Maybe he meant that if you weren't assigned work, you dare not do it? Or you could only work your land. Oh well, I didn't really care. I wanted information and a ship, not menial labor with this rabble.

"As well, doesn't hurt to pretend to seek honest labor?" I said rapping my knuckles on the bar to hurry my next vessels of misery.

He refilled my glasses and slammed the bottle of plow down beside them.

"Ya kin pours yur'n. But don't tink I'z ani't got de eyes of a youngin'. Iz'll knows when yur clunck runs out an'll be yankin' dat botl back as quickz I cans say piss ons yur hand."

What a *revolting* local saying. I had to advertise this planet as a bucket list entry for all masochists who loved deep space travel. I belted back a few more rounds before trying to extract some useful information. The quickest way to shut mouths was to seem suspiciously over-interested.

"I was thinking if my girl and I couldn't find work, maybe we'd head off world. Anyone know an honest shuttler?"

It was like I suddenly filled the room with liquid nitrogen. Everybody froze solid. I copped a glance at my chronometer to make sure time itself hadn't stopped.

"I have gold. I can pay our way fairly."

Interesting reactions. Two patrons dove to the floor, possibly trying to jam themselves into the legs of their barstools. One drunk vaulted over the bar and landed headfirst at the tender's feet. Two others a bit farther away gasped like they'd been poisoned. The barkeep himself gave me a look that was very challenging to describe. Possibly, it was one following my requesting to have an intimate relationship with his elbow. He was clearly stunned and not pleased.

"Don'a you go sayin' da word geld in the public's airs, ya daft looner. Da Amadents gots ears ebrywhar, don'a believes? Day hears da word geld and dey stays'a peeling skin off'a bodies to findz it. What barn ya raised'a in?"

The fellow at the bartender's feet was not, to my surprise, dead. I heard a muffled voice speak. "Ya wantz to git us all'a killed to death?"

"I just asked about transport off this rock. What's so upsetting about that?"

"Iz bad e'nuf as'isa talken' 'bout spacer flights, but no'z. Ya gatz to shout da word *geld*," replied the proprietor. He did, I must point out, yell the word *geld*, the big doo-doo. I hadn't.

"Why would the Adamant want gold?" I asked. "You can't eat it, use it in weapons, or talk real nice to it and have it gratify your desires."

"It don'a matters why. It matt'a dat dey do. *Das* alls ya needs to know, fool," responded the keeper. "No drop'a yer clunk and getz outta hers afore I comes around'a and trows ya true da wall." He pointed with the intensity of the Archangel Urie at the gate of Eden, directing me to leave.

I guess I could have pushed my luck and stayed, but it wasn't worth it. No one was going to spill any beans to the guy who was trying to have them flayed. I backed out the doors into the street, then turned. Mirraya was right there, picking her teeth and leaning against a bench.

"Sounds like you're not going to be a regular there," she said. "Should I turn into a rocket ship to get us out of here?"

"Can you do that?"

"No, only living animals. I was trying to make the point that you seem to have screwed up royally in there."

"Since when do you have a potty mouth?"

"Since you started trying to get us killed."

I turned and began walking rapidly toward *Stingray*.

I assumed Mirraya would fall in behind me. Instead she called to me, "You're heading the wrong way. Spaceport's that way."

I couldn't see, but I thought she was pointing.

I turned and walked back toward her. "There is no spaceport. There's none on the maps and none visible from above."

"This isn't the kind of spaceport with landing lights and a

snack bar. It's a secret one the locals have managed to hide from you know who."

I tried not to grin. "And how is it you came to know all this while I was shot down like a fat, one-winged duck?"

She shrugged with a very noncommittal look on her face. "I asked better than you did, for one thing," she said with a nod toward the bar.

"And how might that have been?"

"I was having dinner while you drank your innards away. I had trouble though, on account of my not being able to stop crying. The owner's wife noticed and tried to comfort me. She's a real nice lady. I almost hated to deceive her."

"But it worked, so what the hell," I finished her thought.

"It worked, so what the hell. Anyway, I told her you had a death mark, the Adamant had already killed my mother and three younger brothers. I said I didn't know what I would do when I was alone in the world and on my own. I hinted at hurting myself if you, my last hold on reality, were taken out of the picture."

"Impressive. So, you lie well, deceive honest folk just trying to help, and you steal money from them all at the same time."

"Totally unfair. I didn't have to pay with flesh. She wouldn't hear of charging me for dinner." She grunted a laugh. "Her husband, not so much. But the look she gave him." She winked at me. "I'm going to have to remember it and try it on you one of these days. It was a killer."

"I can hardly wait. So, she told you where to look for transport?"

"Better than that, she gave me this." Mirraya handed me a scrap of paper.

I unfolded it and read it.

Dearest Brother Gartel, this poor child and her father are in grievous danger and need to get off the planet at once. I pray you can help them. If there's any cost, I'll cover it. May the Seven True Gods bless you ... Frieder

I whistled quietly. "Impressive."

"I thought so, too, Uncle Jon."

"You mean *Father* Jon for the time being, don't you?"

She nodded slightly and grinned. Then she stood up straight, snatched the paper from my hands, and sauntered away down the street. What had I gotten myself into? This girl was every bit as sneaky and devious as I was. I needed to stay on my A-game with her around.

We found our way to Brother Gartel's house. It was a simple, understated structure with a boring landscape job. It was very typical of all we'd seen. The people here were kind of bland and tasteless, it seemed. I had Mirraya knock on his door. Once he opened it a crack, she handed him the note. He closed the door while he read it. Unless he was a painfully slow reader, he took a while to decide if he was going to reopen the door, once he knew the reason we'd come.

The door cracked open a sliver and Gartel hastily said, "Come in before you're seen." He closed the door silently once I was in. "My sister should not have sent you. I cannot help you. Please leave quietly. If the masters learn of a stranger's visit to my home, my family will be in jeopardy."

"Look," I said, "we're inside now, so there's really no rush to get us out. Why not hear our story and then decide if you will turn us away in our most desperate hour?"

He covered his ears. "I do *not* want to hear your sad tale. Whatever it is, and no matter how badly I feel for ignoring you, I will refuse any aid. You must go." The guy was sweating and panting. I thought he might keel over right there in front of us, he was so apoplectic.

"Kind Gartel, thank you for receiving us," Mirraya said as she gently rested a hand on his trembling arm. "My father and I will go now. I will return to your sister. I will tell her you courageously offered to help us free of charge. I will tell her that, faced with the reality of leaving our home, we reconsidered and declined your kind offer. I should not want your reasonable concerns to become a barrier between you and Frieder. Family," she choked back tears, "is far too valuable to waste on the likes of the Adamant. May the Seven True Gods bless you." She turned to me, took my elbow and finished with, "Come, Papa. Let us go find a home of our own."

Man was she good. Well, I guess she could have been sincere, couldn't she? Either way, we never even made it to the door before Gartel called to us.

"I don't believe I caught your name, tall stranger," he said as forcefully as he could muster.

"Trocker," I replied, bowing.

"Trocker, you and your daughter please sit while I have the missus bring some tea. Then I will hear your story. I do not promise I can help, but by the Seven True Gods, the Adamant won't stop me from being a good man."

A mousy woman Gartel didn't bother to introduce served us weak, astringent tea. When she was out of the room, he asked, "So what is it my fine sister tells you I might be able to do for you?"

"We need to get off this planet," I said bluntly. "She said you have a ship that may serve us well."

He looked like a ghost had just sat down on his lap. "Er, I know of no ships. The Adamant *strictly* forbid the locals to travel in space, unless they authorize it. They never authorize it, so it does not exist."

"Officially, it may not. That, in my experience, has never stopped a properly motivated businessman," I replied, setting down my cup. I was going to be so glad to leave this rock, so I could turn my olfactory senses back to normal.

"Are you suggesting openly flaunting their decree? I needn't tell you the penalty. It is the same for any infraction, large or small."

"They are consistent, aren't they?" I said with a conspiratorial smile.

He harrumphed back.

That brought a very loud throat clearing from the kitchen. Mama was apparently reminding him to remain apolitical.

"What we request is transportation. Only passengers." I pointed to Mirraya then patted my chest. "Myself, the girl, and *no* questions asked."

"If anyone was going to accept that offer, it would cost you extra, a lot extra."

"I can pay you two ounces of gold now, plus fifteen more when we reach our destination."

Poor Gartel nearly spit out his tea. I imagine he hadn't seen that kind of money in a long time. Based on my preparatory studies of this society, seventeen ounces of gold was a modest fortune.

"And where might the theoretical pilot of such an imaginary vessel be taking you and your no questions?"

"Locinar."

That did it. He sprayed his tea on his lap.

"You would voluntarily step onto the surface of *Locinar*? Now I know I need not worry about your words. You are a crazy man, so your words are only the rantings of someone not in contact with his *mind*."

"Be that as it may," I said reaching into my pocket. "I will let the gold speak for me." I thudded two ounces onto the wooden table. "*It* is not crazy."

He looked at it like it was his naked bride on the nuptial bed. Oh, how he wanted that gold.

"If there were to be no pilot willing to make the journey, I could fly the craft myself. The owner of the spaceship would only be renting me his vessel."

Mama cleared her throat very loudly, indeed.

"And the owner would never see his craft again. You would be free to sail off to anywhere with it, all for the price of a thimble full of gold."

"The owner could pre-program the ship to return. He could lock in provisions to fly only to Locinar and then autopilot it home." I leaned forward. "That owner would find thirty ounces of gold on the deck of his ship when it returned to him safely."

Cultural norms and practices are only so binding. With my last offer, Mama flew through the door to the kitchen and walked right up to Gartel. Aiming a bony finger at his nose, she spoke with clarity and focus. "You are an old *fool* for even allowing these lunatics into our home. Your sister, who wears her heart on her sleeve, takes in every stray dog and lost cause in town." The finger found its way to me. "This lunatic will not only get us killed, but you will lose our spaceship in the bargain. What are the chances anyone could fly to *Locinar* and back without being blow to dust? Hmm? How much money can you earn, owning nothing but space dust? Oh, wait. You won't have to earn us money because we'll both be dead. Fine, since we are to be flayed and possibly eaten, go ahead, rent them the ship my father gave you as my dowry. Mangled corpses don't *need* material possessions." After that Shakespearian soliloquy, Mama stormed back to the kitchen, slamming the door behind her. Most impressive.

"As you can see, I can be of no help to you. I ask you to leave immediately and quietly." He gave a worried glance over his shoulder in the direction of the woman who'd likely been heard blocks away. He stood. "I will show you to the door."

He hid almost completely behind the door as we filed out silently. It closed quietly but resolutely. Oh well. I guessed I was going to have to *borrow* his ship if he wasn't going to come around to my *begging.*

We hid in the shrubs in front of the Gartel residence. "But how are we going to find his ship? More importantly, why are we crouched in these bushes? I think something just crawled up my leg."

"Just transform into a female one of its species, and he'll mate with you, not sting you." I had to snicker.

She elbowed me hard. "What if it's a *girl* crawly?"

"Then you two can talk about boy-crawly things until dawn. Maybe you can bore it to death?"

That earned me a harder elbow, but it was worth it.

"Seriously, why are we here?"

"*Duh.* Because the easiest way to find where he hides his ship is to follow him there."

"Are you telling me Gartel would be dumb enough to visit his ship now, after *that* conversation, at *this* late hour?"

"Yup."

"I think I signed on with the wrong skipper. You're waterlogged in the head."

"No, my child," I pointed toward the back of Gartel's house. "Observe."

He was sneaking out like a thief in the night, a small flashlight guiding his way.

"You have got to be kidding me. Who does that?" Mirraya was hot.

"Honey, think about it. If he's a real pilot, that ship's the most important, beautiful thing in the universe to him. It represents not just a meal ticket, but independence, freedom, and all the things us guys dream about. Plus, it's the thing that can carry him light-years away from Mama. Yeah, it's that valuable. So, after we talk about his precious, and there's danger in the air, where do you think he needs to go?"

"To his spaceship in the middle of the night?"

"Beats listening to the extended version of Mama's tongue-lashing."

"Men. You are so ... so ... *men*."

"Yup. Can't live with us, can't live without us."

"That's not *actually* true."

"Save it for later, grasshopper. I don't want to lose Gartel." I stood and headed after him.

"Since when am I a grasshopper?" she whispered when she caught up. "I assume it's some kind of bug."

"Long story for another time. If you can, possibly ... please, no talking unless it's an emergency."

"*Men*," she mumbled under her breath.

I couldn't disagree with her, so I kept my mouth shut.

The ship was stashed in a cave very near Gartel's house. I let him enter and leave without disturbing him. A man and his ship sometimes needed to be alone. He only lingered a few minutes. He just had to be sure his ticket out was okay. Then a quick kiss and a few tender words, and it was home to Mama. That, and hopefully, strong drink.

We waited the better part of an hour before entering the cave. I didn't want him to return and catch us. I mean, he was a nice enough guy. I didn't want to have to stun him, just because we needed his ship.

"What a piece of junk," were Mirraya's first words after seeing the craft.

She was right, but we were not able to be choosy. It was an old vessel, or should I say, "well-used." My brain was still in future shock. Old, for a ship built two billion years after I died, was confusing to think about. She was small, probably not much more than a shuttle. Or a golf cart. But, she looked airtight. The engine was still attached. Those were pluses.

Naturally, the hatch was locked. I placed my probes on the

metal hull. "Are you fixed with an alarm?" I asked the ship. I assumed there was an AI in there, somewhere. Space travel without one was dangerous and slow.

There came no response. Either there was no AI, or it was being sneaky. I hated sneaky AIs.

"Look, I know you're in there. Gartel said you were stupid, lazy, and disloyal, but he said you were in there. *Probably sleeping* was his final assessment. He wants me to bring him something he forgot to get."

It took a second, but I'd gotten under its skin. "I am not asleep. I am not programmed to sleep. I hate it when he berates me. I am loyal. He's the stupid, lazy one. His father-in-law was right about that, I'll tell you for nothing. Doesn't even have enough ambition to sneak a woman in here behind Gertruda's back. Now *that's* a lazy, stupid man."

I was regretting opening that Pandora's box.

"Yeah, yeah. I need to get the thing and then you can go back to sleep."

"The thing he forgot less than an hour ago that you cannot name?"

"Yeah, that's the one."

"How stupid do you think I am?"

"I don't know. List the possible levels of stupid, and I'll pick one or two."

"That's supposed to make me trust you enough to disarm the security system? Look, if he wanted you to enter, he'd have given you the code."

"He did. He said it didn't usually work, because you're too dumb to remember it. Me, I think that's pretty harsh, but you know Gartel."

"I do indeed, unfortunately. For your information, I've never once forgotten the code."

"No way, Jose. He told me on Ursa Minor Beta he said 1110-

3332-1103, and you tried to correct him. You said it was 3332-0103. He had to hire a mechanic to override your blunder."

"I can prove he's a lying sack of protoplasms. It's always been a Genticile code, trinary based. There are no *threes* in it at all."

"You're not going to make me get the mechanic again? He's going to be so pissed. You know how Gertruda feels about money."

"She's thrifty. That's a virtue in a woman."

"So, won't she be pleased? I said that was the code way back on Ursa Minor Beta. I know it's trinary now because he just told me it was 021-112-111-120. Now open up, before I lose interest and make him come back and get it himself."

"It is not. If this is one of his silly loyalty tests I will *electrocute* him next time he's onboard. The security code is 001-222-101-120. It has *never* been 021-112-111-120."

"I have only one thing to say to that," I replied. "Open the hatch. 001-222-101-12 ... 0."

He really opened it quickly, considering. He was real quiet after that, too. I wonder why?

Once inside, I made the short trip to the bridge. I could fly the ship now without having to hurry because I'd set off the alarm. Gartel could have been here in a flash with his blunderbuss. I didn't need that pressure. Plus, once I had the code, I didn't have to waste time hacking into the AI, and then flying with a reluctant computer who resented having been forced into cooperation. Sure, I tricked him, but that wasn't forcible.

The ship's design was unfamiliar, but there were only so many ways to fly. I attached my probes and downloaded the ship's manual and specs. Easy as a snap. I used the anti-gravity drive to ease out of the cave and gain some altitude, then I cut in what was designated as the ship's impulse engine. It was a variant of a fusion unit I'd used before. Clearly, it would be a short flight if the bad dogs took notice and came after us. I wasn't likely to outrun a flying washing machine, let alone one of their wormhole speedsters.

I had no specific plan. I did fly casually, meaning I flew slower than needed and maneuvered like I was in no hurry. If I only caught partial attention, whoever was watching might figure I was too obvious to be unauthorized. I did disable the transponder that announced our ID. It would be too easy to check that we hadn't filed a flight plan if it were on. We made low orbit without a hitch. I was making the calculation to jump to light speed when Gartel called. Man, was he pissed. I mean, who wouldn't be? I could hear Gertruda in the background, too, and she was spitting fire. I've heard women swear effectively in the past, but she was impressive.

The ship's AI kept insisting I respond, but I didn't feel the need. I had to make a big patch in the communications array to shut them down, because the AI wouldn't. He probably figured I deserved the Gertruda treatment. Maybe I did. When I returned the ship, I planned to pay them handsomely for its use, but they wouldn't have believed me if I'd told them. If we were blown up by the Adamant, I guess they were kind of out of luck. Hmm. I hadn't thought that part through, had I? Oh well, it was a little late to see about an insurance policy. At least I knew Gartel wouldn't call the cops.

We hit hyperspace, and all there was to do was wait and see what happened when we reached Locinar. It was a three-day trip. If things looked immediately hostile there, I could try and hide in hyperspace, but it wasn't that hard to follow a ship doing that. They might even have tech that would allow them to fire on us in hyperspace by now, or tractor us to a stop. I knew I had to try this mission, but it was fraught with danger.

A day into the voyage Mirraya asked me some follow up while she ate. "Uncle Jon, tell me about your family."

"Which one?"

"How many did you have?" she asked a bit taken back.

"I had two great loves. Sapale and Kayla. They were both a special kind of magical. Sapale was a Kaljaxian I met while looking for a place for my people to move to. We couldn't reproduce, but she had many children while we were together. You know how it goes. They had kids, and so on, until I had a great big family."

"What became of them?"

"After I married Kayla, I had less and less contact with them, but they were doing well establishing a civilization on a new planet. Azsuram. By the time I ... er, went to sleep, they were doing gangbusters."

"Sapale let you marry a human? Very open minded of her." Mirraya lifted her eyebrows.

"She was killed in a war. She died defending Azsuram."

"I'm sorry."

"Me, too." I smiled. "But we had a good life and a strong family. One of these days, I'll go to Azsuram and see if they're still there."

"Then I'm coming, too."

"One step at a time. We need to see if there are any Deft left on Locinar."

"If you wish, but I'm staying with you. You're my family now. I adopted you just like you did Sapale's children." She sniffed at her forkful of food. "You're stuck with me, like it or not."

I patted her forearm. "I like it very much. But we need to see if there's a viable Deft society left. You may not feel you need them now, but it matters to know you have a home. Trust me on this point."

"I do." She scanned the room. "Currently, it's this depressing ship."

"It's only temporary. I promise. Someday I'll buy us a nice garbage compactor to call our own."

"And I'll decorate it and we'll name all the pieces of garbage. Some can be boy garbage and some will be girl refuse. It'll be a dream come true."

"We can only hope," I replied. What had I done to deserve such a wonderful friend?

My plan was to come out of hyperspace as close to the planet surface as was safe ... and maybe a bit closer. That way we could speed to the ground and hope to hide before we were detected. Given the troop strength Mirraya reported during the invasion, I knew it was too much to hope we wouldn't be seen. I just didn't want to get caught. In a city, we could, maybe, blend in and avoid the Adamant. Maybe.

We came out of light speed just above the atmosphere. I fired the engine to brake us, but we still hit the air like a fireball. The ship pitched and shook to the point I began to worry. But the old girl held together. She probably couldn't make a hot entry like that twice, but she made this one. Almost immediately we were hailed. Some angry sounding Adamant AI was screaming at us, and then an angry actual Adamant began screaming at us. Who were we? How dare we? Et cetera, et cetera. I didn't bother to answer back.

We skidded to a landing on an abandoned city street, sort of like a freeway. The second we came to rest, Mirraya and I were out the hatch and running for cover. I picked a place she knew well to give us some advantage. I'd take all the help I could get.

Air cars were zooming overhead within minutes. They all had loudspeakers booming commands for us to surrender. They said our deaths would be better if we turned ourselves in. Now there was a goal to aim for. Better deaths. The factor that stopped me from complying was that they weren't clear on who the deaths would be better *for*, us or them. Yeah, that kind of mattered. Buyer beware.

By the time we were a few blocks away, I heard the

unmistakable sound of the ship exploding. Apparently, they decided to eliminate any possibility of our escape. Oh boy, were Gartel and Gertruda going to be pissed when they found out. Ouch.

The city was dense enough to disappear in easily enough. Mirraya knew several twisting paths through alleys, basements, and underpasses. She said there was a subway, but we did not know if it was running. Plus, it was an easy area to get trapped. After a few minutes, we slowed to a walk and tried to blend in. The streets were not exactly crowded, but there were enough bodies so we didn't draw undue attention.

Mirraya told me the people we saw were not Deft. She had, in fact, seen none so far. They were a humanoid species she couldn't identify. They looked kind of like the stereotypical pictures of aliens from old Earth science fiction. Hairless green skin, bulbous heads, long skinny arms, and teardrop angled eyes. Who knew, maybe these were the same guys who did all the abductions back in Area 51 back in the day? They qualified as ugly enough to be the same species.

Mirraya melted into one. As a teen, she was just the right size. An adult would have been too massive to be convincing. I tried as best I could to not stand out in my brown sackcloth robe and hood. Fortunately, there were scattered aliens of different species and sizes out and about. I knew the Adamant would have state-of-the-art surveillance everywhere. The longer we were in the open, the more likely it was we'd be picked up, if for nothing else than me looking so odd.

Within a half an hour, we had arrived at a house that belonged to a cousin she was close to. We slipped over a fence and made it to the back door without alarms flaring. She tested the door. It was locked. She retrieved a key from under a flower pot next to the door. Again, some customs seemed to be universal. She opened the door quietly, and we slipped in.

"Wait a sec," I said restraining her with a hand. I turned my audio all the way up and placed my other hand on the wall to check for vibrations. After a few seconds, I gave the all-clear. "I don't hear anyone moving, breathing, or calling the cops. Stay behind me, and we'll look around."

The floor plan was very open, so it was quick enough to clear the first floor. We crept up the stairs. Everything was fine until I stepped on the damn loose board. The squeak was maddening, but there was no taking it back. At the top of the stairs I turned left and we checked out the master bedroom. As my nose rounded the door, the barrel of a gun met it. I froze.

"I'm not here to hurt you," I said automatically.

"No," she responded, "you were just sneaking into my bedroom to give me a hygiene lesson."

"Avval?" said Mirraya from behind me. "Avval, is it really you?"

"Mirry?" she replied, and craned her neck around the door to look for herself.

There stood Mirraya, naked as a jaybird and smiling like the cat who'd eaten the canary. She flew into Avval's arm, knocking the gun to the floor. They hopped and hugged and giggled. It would have been nice to see if my girl had any clothes on.

"Here," said Avval pulling her into the room, "let's get you some clothing. I can't believe you're alive. They told me you were marched through the one-way portal."

She lowered her head. "I was."

"But you're here, you're free. They haven't released anyone else."

"I escaped," she placed a hand on my arm, "thanks to Uncle Jon. He saved me."

Avval lowered her eyebrows. "I don't recall us having any uncle named Jon." She looked me up and down dubiously.

"I call him that, silly."

"And who else escaped?" Avval's face was expectant.

"No one. They're all dead."

"Are you certain?"

Mirraya only nodded that she was.

"Such a horrible thing," said Avval, bitting the back of her hand.

"And here, are there many left?" asked Mirraya.

Avval shrugged one shoulder. "A few, the smart and the lucky. But only a handful."

They both looked to the floor.

Mirraya perked up. "How did you stay safe?"

"I was lucky and smart. When I heard their ships coming, I ran. I tell you, I turned into a *defelmire* and I ran and I ran and I didn't stop until I was out of the city and deep in the woods."

"I'm so glad. How about your sisters, your parents?"

"I haven't seen them since that terrible morning. They waited to see what the Adamant were up to, and it cost them their lives." Avval looked despondent. "They wouldn't listen to me. They wouldn't save themselves. Papa kept saying it would all be fine once the Adamant saw we were not resisting." She bit at her hand again, tears welling up.

"And you stayed safe long enough to return here," I asked. Something wasn't quite right about the picture I was receiving. "No trouble since?"

"I've only just come myself. Before it was too dangerous. But finally, it is safe enough to return and get a few personal items and some money."

"Ah," I said, trying to sound disinterested. "Lucky you."

"Where will you go, Ava?" asked Mirraya. "Is anywhere secure?"

"I know of a place, in the woods near Lake Dulcer. It is very remote and rocky, so the Adamant won't look for us there. There are a few Deft there. We will join them. They will keep us safe."

"Ah, your cousin decided to hang with me a while. She won't be joining you."

Mirraya got a confused look on her face. "I thought you said I should—"

"Not change from looking like a little green woman. Now change back so we can go. I want to find a hiding spot before it gets too dark."

"I ... er ... if you think ..."

"That is absurd and unacceptable. Mirraya, you will stay with *me*. We are family. You will come to the safe house I know of, and this ... this alien can do whatever he pleases."

"Hey, this is a democracy. She's old enough to decide for herself. Now let go of her arm and we'll say our short goodbyes."

Mirraya was clearly torn.

"Remember that movie I told you about, the one where the dog dies? Well I was kidding. The movie really ends with the dog killing everyone. The dogs always win, isn't that what *Blessing* said?" I squeezed her arm hard as I said *everyone*.

"Who's Blessing?" asked Avval.

"My girlfriend. Mirraya and *Blessing* share a bedroom, in fact. At first Mirraya wasn't happy to be around *Blessing,* because she didn't trust her. Remember you said you thought she would betray your personal secrets to me?" I pinched even harder with the word *betray*. "Now come on, I left the baby in the car. I need to check if she's safe and doesn't feel *trapped*. You know how Little Al feels about traps, right?"

"Yo ... you have a baby and a car? Whose baby is it. Not yours, Mirraya?"

"No, silly," Mirraya began slowly. She was catching on. "It's Jon's baby, Jon's and Blessing's. It's a little treasure named Al. In Jon's native language, Al means *the suspicious one*."

"That's hard to believe," responded Avval. "Who names their baby *the suspicious one*?"

"From where I'm from, suspicion keeps you alive, and alive is good."

"Well, Ava, let's get together soon. Perhaps dinner," Mirraya pointed to the floor, "here, soon."

"But I won't be here. I'll be in the woods. Here," she said, lunging for the dresser. She rifled a drawer and handed her a little box. "It's Mama's phone. Take it so I can ... you can call me, let me know you're safe."

"Thanks, but—"

"But she wants me to carry everything. Was she always so lazy?" I looked disapprovingly at Mirraya while pushing her to the stairs.

"See you soon, Ava. Be safe," said Mirraya.

"And smart," I added from halfway down the stairs. "Stay smart."

Outside we dashed into the bushes where Mirraya changed back into a green goblin again.

"What was that all about?" she demanded. "You made it seem like my cousin was a traitor, that she was not to be trusted. How dare—"

"Keep your pants on."

She pointed to the clothes on the ground. "You just told me to take them off."

"It's an expression. Look, she was lying. I think she's a spy for the Adamant."

"That's a terrible thing to say, to even think."

"First, she said she'd only just arrived."

"So?"

"So, someone had recently slept in that bed. It had infrared coming off it, suggesting she'd gotten out of bed a couple hours ago. She's *living* there."

"No, that would be unsafe."

"Not if you're working for the bad guys, it isn't. Then she said she turned into a something or other ..."

"A defelmire. It looks like the horse you are riding in that picture, when you were a child."

"But the Adamant had a stasis field deployed. No one could change into anything."

"She said she acted quickly. Maybe they hadn't..." she trailed off as she heard her words.

"They hadn't turned the field on until after they began rounding you guys up? That doesn't sound like the Adamant I know and love. Finally, she knows of a safe house, but it's in the remote rocky woods. A safe cabin, maybe. A safe cave, sure. But a house in the middle of nowhere? Not hardly."

"But how could my cousin betray her family, her people?"

"Her cousin?" I let that sink in a moment. "When you're staring a painful death square in the eyes, it can bring demons out of you that no one would have thought lived in there. She cracked, probably begged and groveled. To prove her worth, she led them to Deft in hiding. Maybe to you and your family. And she was going to hand you over to show she was still a team player."

"She—"

Mirraya couldn't finish her sentence. She started to sob and collapsed into my arms. She'd just learned another unbearable truth about war. Nothing was fair, and all things were on the table. Each and every one of them, including one's immortal soul.

CHAPTER SIXTEEN

I died a little inside when Mirraya found out how wretched her cousin was. Every life event that destroyed that much more of childhood's innocence sucked, and it sucked hard. I wished often that life could have been simple, and that we could all remain children. Failing loving one another, it would have been nice if we could just not kill each other. But, in times of war, if they were lucky enough to survive, kids were forced to grow up fast.

Since I could not rely on one word that bitch told us, we were still stuck at square one. Aside from traitorous collaborators, we didn't know if there were any Deft remaining.

"Was there any place your family used to go, like on vacation?" I asked Mirraya as we sat by a campfire in an abandoned basement.

"Not really."

"How about places sacred to the Deft, a tree or something?"

"Nothing comes to mind, Uncle Jon. We are a very spiritual race, but not in an organized way. Sometimes a bunch of us would get together to sing, thank nature, and eat a lot of food. But we don't have churches like many cultures seem to."

"Hm. Where would you gather? Any place in particular?"

"There was this place. My parents called it the Mother Stones. We went there a few times and celebrated with a few others."

"Can you take me there? Do you remember where it is?"

She shrugged. "Sure, I think. We drove there, but it wasn't too far."

"Then we shall borrow a car."

She got an uncomfortable look on her face.

"What?"

"That didn't end well for Gartel's spaceship."

"I'll be more careful with the car, I promise." I held up a three-fingered scout salute, then realized she'd have no clue what that meant, so I pulled it down quickly.

"Uncle Jon," she exclaimed, "I can't believe you just *did* that."

"What?"

"I'm not going to show you. It was that *thing* with your fingers," she pointed at my right hand with a disgusted expression.

"The Boy Scouts of America official salute?" I repeated it. "What's the big deal?"

She rotated her torso away and collapsed onto her bedding face first. "That's *so* gross," she said in a muffled groan.

"What? Come on, or I'll keep doing it."

She sat back up. "Okay, I keep forgetting you're an alien." She fidgeted uncomfortably. "When one person signals that to another, it means they want to ... it says they want to ..."

"To what, hurt them?"

"That might be part of it, I guess. It means they want to reproduce with them. But it means they want to reproduce like *now* and like with a lot of energy, if you know what I mean." She giggled.

"Ah, remind me to never do that again." I wrinkled my brow. "How do you know about that kind of thing?"

She gasped, like any teenage girl talking about sex with an adult would gasp anywhere in space, anywhere in time. "Uncle *Jon*, I may be young, but everyone knows *that* sign."

"I didn't." I waved weakly.

"Well, now you do. Don't ... don't signal me with it again, please."

I shivered. Then my curiosity requested one clarification. "Is that a Deft thing, or a general one on Locinar?"

She rolled her eyes. "Can we move on to non-gross things?"

"I'll drop it, I promise. I'm just naturally curious."

She bobbed her head side to side. "It's a general Locinar thing, I guess."

"Fine. Subject closed, dismissed, and forgotten."

"Thank you. May I go to sleep now, *if* I can go to sleep now after that?"

"Be my guest. I think I'll sweep the building again to make sure we're safe." I stood, grabbed my belt, and snugged my pants up. "I think I may do the scout salute a couple times, too. I've been so *lonely* lately, don't you know?"

"Now I know I won't be sleeping. Thanks. You're *so* gross."

"So I've been told." I winked at her and left.

The next morning, we were off to find the Mother Stones. While Mirraya was getting ready, I went looking for a vehicle to borrow. Cars on Locinar were almost exclusively tiny electric ones. Disgusting. Picture, if you will, the gutless Prius of the twentieth century. Now shrink it down about a third, and slow it down by half. Yeah, they were just wrong. But beggars not being choosers, I had limited options. At least they were easy to hot wire. I didn't even need my probes to do it, which was fun.

We left early, so the traffic would be light, but there was enough that we didn't stand out. Nearly every car I passed, and believe me, I passed a lot of them, was driven by an LGM, a little green man. I suppose they could have been LGWs, ´since I couldn't tell the sexes apart, if there were sexes. Maybe LGMs were clones. Then something occurred to me.

"Hey, could any of these LGMs be Deft hiding like you are?"

"No," she said immediately.

"Why not. You sure look like one of them."

"To you, yes. To another Deft, hardly. We can always tell when we're looking at the real thing, versus a copy." She turned to face me. "It's in the eyes."

"Your eyes look like the LGM's eyes."

"No, it's *in* the eyes. It's just obvious."

"If you say so."

"I do. Why do you ask?"

"I was just wondering if any of the guys we see are hiding Deft."

She stared out the windshield. "Aside from Avval, I haven't seen another Deft yet."

"If you do, let me know, okay?"

"Sure. I'll wiggle my ears." She rolled her eyes. Even though she looked like a LGM outwardly, that maneuver was pure teenage girl.

We pulled off the road a few klicks out of town. So far, so good. The dirt road to our objective was tolerable, and the spot wasn't far in. Mirraya pointed to some rocks and announced we'd arrived. I was under-impressed. A monumental spiritual icon these rocks were not. They looked more like a pile up of construction rubble. But hey, to each his or her own.

We stepped out of the car and walked to the rocks. "These are what your family made a special trip to visit?"

"Yes, we very much enjoyed it here. Is there a problem, UJ?"

Uh oh, she rarely called me that, and it was exclusively when she was pissed at me. "I mean ... I assumed they were, you know," I lifted my palm as high as I could, "a little bigger maybe."

"*We* always found them impressive."

"Me, too, don't get me wrong. Those ... those are really big ..."

"I think I heard you perfectly correctly. Follow me, Uncle Culturally Insensitive," she said, as she walked around the pebble pile.

She strode toward an adjacent clearing where benches and tables were located. The place looked like your standard campground in Anywhere USA, little raised barbecues and all. Then, because nothing could possibly be easy, a fantastic beast rumbled out of the bushes and charged us. It wasn't that large, but what it lacked in heft it more than made up for in bad attitude and spikes. It was a mini-triceratops with eight legs, over-sized wings, and lethal talons or claws.

I reflexively backed up and raised my right hand. I took the time to aim right between its eyes.

Mirraya's hand grabbed my arm and pulled it down. "Hang on. That won't be necessary," She said, starting to melt into naked Mirraya. Somehow during the process, she was able to yell, "That'll just about do it."

The creature slammed on all eight brakes and skidded to a stop a few meters away. Then it started melting, too. In a few seconds, there stood a naked boy, maybe Mirraya's age or a tad younger. Great, now I had *two* naked teens. What possible mischief could follow?

"I'm Mirraya La-Dor-Fell," she said formally. "This is Jon Ryan. We are traveling together."

The boy bowed slightly and responded. "My name's Slapgren Vel-Ol-Torp. Pleased to meet you both."

"Do you have your clothes nearby, Slapgren?" I quickly asked.

"Yes, of course. Why do you ask?" he replied.

"Uncle Jon is an alien." Man it was hard to hear that. *They* were the aliens. "His species is very shy."

"Ah," he said with a wisdom beyond his years. "Provincials."

"And then some," she stepped toward him. "Let's go get your clothes before he has a seizure. I'll change back into one of those LGMs."

"What's an *LGM?*" he said quite confused.

"We'll talk as we walk," she responded, taking his elbow and leading him away.

A couple minutes later, a clothed Slapgren along with an LGM reappeared. They joined me where I was seated at a picnic table. He slipped into the opposite bench, but Mirraya was finding the LGM's anatomy didn't match the furniture very well.

"You can switch back to you if you want. I'll run back to the car and get your clothes," I said, gesturing over my shoulder.

"That would be nice, Uncle Jon. I don't want any splinters where you'd be reluctant to pull them out." She giggled to Slapgren, who followed in kind. Teens.

I threw the bundle in Mirraya's face when I returned to make the point that she was being a pill. Guess what? She giggled some more, as did Slapgren. I was tired of him already.

"So, what's your story, boy," I said roughly.

"What do you mean?" he said looking hurt.

"What the big, scary man is asking is, how did you get here, and are you alone?" She regarded me like I was aging dog poop on a hot sidewalk and added, "I'm sure he was just about to ask if you were all right or needed anything."

"Yeah," I tossed my head in her direction, "What she said."

"I ... I could do with some food. I've been here a week and haven't found much."

That was back in the car, too. Without a word, I trudged over and retrieved the cooler. I set it on the table. "There, now it's officially a picnic. Dig in, both of you."

"Mirraya pulled off the top and dove in. Slapgren was reluctant. "Are you going to have some, too, sir?" he asked me.

"He doesn't eat much," Mirraya said almost unintelligibly due to the truckload of grub in her mouth. "Dig in."

He then did so with earnest. Starving teenage boy earnest. I was careful to keep my hands and arms out of the cooler. Didn't want to lose any parts or pieces.

Within ten minutes, he was slowing to a believable pace. Mirraya had told me shapeshifting required a lot of energy. She said one never saw a fat Deft. If someone put on a few pounds, they simply changed and changed until they were back to their high school weight.

"Is your family here?" Mirraya asked gently. She probably suspected the answer.

"No, just me so far." He beamed a smile so bright it could be seen from low orbit. "But now there's you." He devoured another something and looked to me. "And Uncle Jon, too, of course," he amended, without any real enthusiasm.

She giggled, because she knew I was irritated.

"How did you get here safely?"

"When the Adamant came, there was a lot of confusion." He swung his arms in the air. "Explosions, pushing, people running. It was crazy. Anyway, I hid at my house. My parents weren't home, and my brothers were in school. After the parade of soldiers passed by, I ran straight into the forest and ran for the entire day."

He furrowed his brow. "It was weird. I guess I was too scared to change. I tried to become a scappy and fly or a botswat and run faster, but I stayed me."

"They had some stasis field deployed that prohibited us from changing."

"It must be off now, because I have been able to, and so can you."

Mirraya looked to me. "Maybe the field has a harmful effect

on any living creatures if exposure is sustained. Maybe they just figure they got you all," I responded.

"Have you seen any other Deft since that day?" Mirraya asked with foreboding.

He shook his head. "You're the first ... the only."

"Well it's going to be fine," she patted the back of his hand. "We're here, so you'll be just fine. Won't he, Uncle Jon?" she actually kicked my shin under the table, out of Slapgren's view.

"Yes. As long as we're around, you'll be okay."

"But what will we do? If everyone's dead, we're ..." Slapgren couldn't finish his thought.

"For one thing, we are going to find any remaining Deft," Mirraya said with organized confidence. "And for another, we're going to punish the Adamant for what they did to us."

Slapgren looked back up from his hand resting on the table. "Revenge against an unstoppable force. Good luck with that flight of imagination."

Everyone was a critic out here in the future. Not that they weren't back in my time, but nothing changed.

"How long have you been at this rock place?" I asked. That won me another kick in the shins.

"I got here two days after the attack."

"How did you survive?" asked a concerned Mirraya.

He pointed to the right. "Oh, there's lots of water in the stream. Once I could change, I did a little hunting." He got an ill look on his face. "Mostly bugs and other disgusting things. Hardly worth the energy to transform."

"Here," she said handing him yet another sandwich, "eat this, you poor boy."

He took the sandwich, but as he unwrapped it, he remarked, "I'm twelve, you're what, thirteen? Please don't call me boy like you're a grown up."

"I'm almost fourteen," she responded.

"And I'm almost annoyed. Please, can we just be who we are?"

"Yes," she said with a smile.

Alright, Slapgren. My kind of macho. Maybe he was going to be okay, after all.

"So, in three weeks here, no sign of friend or foe. Is that correct?" I pressed.

"Yes, Uncle Jon. You are the first two sentients I've seen since I began running."

"That's good. It means we're relatively safe here. For whatever reason, the puppy dogs aren't interested in this place." I tented my fingers over my mouth a few seconds. "Maybe, for their plan of domination to work, they simply need to debulk the native population. In time, the locals will either show themselves, starve, or be discovered by the drone species."

"Uncle Jon, what's a drone species, and what's a puppy dog."

Mirraya fielded the queries. "The LGM are drones. Very little intelligence and even less ambition. They are a slave species the Adamant use to feed their empire."

"And the puppies?"

"Uncle Jon has this notion that the horrible, world-devouring Adamant look like the cute household pets of his native planet." She looked at me like I smelled bad.

He looked at me like I smelled bad *and* was insane. Ah, to have such fans. What a blessing.

"Wait, I never said any such thing. I said they look like border collies. I happen to not find them cute. They're too neurotic and energetic for my taste. Now, a Rottweiler or a saluki, now those were cute dogs."

"I think the time-shock has been a terrible blow. Please excuse him," Mirraya said privately to Slapgren.

"When was there a time shock? I didn't feel it."

"No, he only woke up just after the Adamant attack. He'd been asleep for two billion years."

"Ah..." He raised a finger. "Ah, er..."

She patted his hand again. "We'll talk later. Best not to tax UJ."

"Who's *UJ*?" asked an ever-more-confused Slapgren.

Mirraya meanly bobbed her angled head toward me silently. Such a tactful scamp.

"On that note, let's get moving," I said, standing.

"Why?" asked Mirraya. "I thought you said we'd be safe here."

"Not with a hot car. It has a homing beacon. Once it's reported as stolen, this place'll be swarming with dogs. They know none of the LGM would steal a look at a pretty girl, let alone someone else's vehicle."

"Where will we go?" Mirraya pressed.

"Not *here* and not your *cousin's* house."

"That leaves a lot of options," she observed coolly.

"Isn't it wonderful? I'll drive the car into the stream. Maybe that'll slow the search. Then we'll walk to the next town."

"Wait, you said you'd be more careful with the ride this time."

I shrugged. "I guess I was overconfident."

"Why are you going to drive someone else's perfectly good car into the water?" asked Slapgren.

"Because, in the first place, they stole it from the Deft, and in the second place, the car has a homing beacon."

"How do you know it does?"

"It told me."

"The car talks?"

"To me, it does," I winked at Mirraya.

"We'll talk later, sweetie," she said, patting him on the back.

They followed me to the stream and watched me ditch the car there. The water was deep enough to swallow the whole tiny, underpowered piece of junk. It was less of a car and more of a lawnmower, with slightly larger wheels and zero leg room.

Both teens agreed the next town over was much smaller. It sounded like a suburb of the larger city we'd come from. It supported the farms farther out, so it was unlikely to have a spaceship we could ... appropriate. Unless the Adamant had some there. How hard could it be to steal one of their ships? Yeah, what a dumb idea. But in the idea desert, bad ones were the only ones I could reasonably expect.

I concluded that there couldn't be too many Deft left, considering how calm the city was. Slapgren's observations supported that theory. It also made finding a sizable number of free-living Deft most unlikely. I would have liked to have had more information, but if the opportunity to get off Locinar presented itself, I was ready to take it. Sooner or later, the dogs'd track us down. A stolen car dumped in water wouldn't reveal to them I was present, but any criminal activity was going to be met with force. If they somehow suspected I was the culprit, all hell'd break loose, and we'd get caught for sure. I knew, however, that if they debriefed Avval aggressively, which was the only way they knew how, they'd likely suspect I was on Locinar.

The walk was uneventful. Operating way behind enemy lines, uneventful was as nice as could be unexpected. I contacted Al and *Stingray,* but neither had any detailed information on the town. The teens knew a little about it, having both been through it many times. But they'd never stopped there. So, we walked the perimeter as I scanned for insights. I saw a few LGM wandering around, but it was a few hours after dark, so most were probably in bed. One couldn't serve the master race if they didn't get a good night's rest, it would seem.

I didn't see any Adamant out to pee on a bush or anything, but that didn't surprise me. I figured they didn't get out much. Very few cars drove the streets, and none of them looked like police or military vehicles. That probably meant there wasn't much crime, since all potential criminals were dead. An efficient, if not a welcoming society. I debated stealing another car and moving on to a larger town but realized we were in such a hopeless situation that a change of venue wouldn't help. We needed a ship or to find a PEMTU. The problem with using a PEMTU was that Locinar was unlikely to explode behind us, so we'd be easy to follow. Also, once they pieced together how I'd co-opted one, security was likely to be much tighter.

I headed into town and had the kids turn into nocturnal animals. That way they'd be less visible, and their heightened senses might alert us to trouble. I didn't tell them, but I also figured that if I was captured, maybe they'd escape unnoticed. Yeah. One was an oversized rat with particularly sharp fangs and the other a lumpy-bumpy furry blob. Who in the right or wrong mind would apprehend either of them? I knew who they were, and they were freaking me out.

I passed mostly unoccupied houses and abandoned stores. A few lights were on here and there where LGMs were quieting down for the night. Toward the center of town, off a square, I located an official building with a lot of lights on. It was worth checking out. I had the kids cover the entrance and rear exit, and I went in alone. The front doors were unlocked. Again, no locks needed in a society purged of evil doers. I couldn't hear any sounds of activity, and no one seemed to be in the building. I swept the first floor and confirmed it was empty. The second and third floors were equally vacant. One more to go.

The stairs opened to the northwest corner of the building. The floor plan was offices on either side of a boring hallway in a square. A typical work-a-day design. I opened every door where light shone through underneath. It was always the last door. Note to self. Never open the last door. I should have known something was up. As I put my hand on the door knob, I caught a whiff of burning plant material.

"Good evening, General Ryan. What a pleasant surprise. Thank you for allowing me to be the one so fortunate as to begin your interrogation." It was a Border Collie sitting in a chair smoking a cigar. Any other time or place, and I'd have sworn off alcohol permanently, knowing it had damaged my brain. A fucking dog in a chair smoking a stogie and threatening me. Perfect.

CHAPTER SEVENTEEN

"Please, General Ryan, sit," my host gestured toward a chair. "Oh, I forget, you're nothing more than grinding cogs and whirring gears. Why would you desire to sit?"

"Which would you prefer?" I asked blandly.

He thought a second and then said, "Standing. I should not want you to provide the illusion of humanity."

I sat down demonstrably and crossed my arms and legs. Then I stuck my tongue out at him.

"How very human. Perhaps you are more than a collection of electronic impulses." He puffed luxuriantly at his cigar. "Not that it matters in the slightest. Oh, I am Wedge Leader Garustfulous."

"Big name for a little pup," I snarled back.

He picked up a small stick from in front of him and pressed it. An electric bolt jumped from it to my left eye. If it had been the genuine article, it would have been fried. I made a show of it hurting. In my day, back in school, I was in drama class, however briefly. I noticed as a frosh with lust that all the knock out girls were attracted to that class, like moths to a flame. I soon discovered that they turned only the coldest of shoulders to a jock like me. Monkey in human clothing, I believe, was the term applied to me. In any case, I could act.

"Come, Ryan, I have no time for displays of pain."

I eased up on the anguish act, but I squinted something awful with that eye at him for a good five minutes.

"I must insist on proper respect. That is, full and unwavering respect. Any questions, funny robot?"

"Yes. So, what do I call you?"

"That is simple and consistent. Master. You call me *Master*."

This dog double entendre was getting out of hand. Did his barkiness know?

"I have a question. How is it—"

The electric stick flashed to my groin. Yeah, this was getting serious.

"I ask the questions. You answer the questions. Then you die."

I raised my hand, signaling I had a question.

"What," his woof-woof demanded.

"I don't get it. What's my motivation here? I comply and still I die? What's the upside for me?"

"The manner of death can be widely variant. Also, the manner of death of your loved ones can be affected. For example, I could summon my pack and devour your precious Deft bitch while she is alive, before your eyes."

I must have revealed surprise.

"Oh, we know of the Deft you stole from us. We know everything. You are new to this epoch. Were you to have lingered longer than you will, you'd have learned that."

"How could I *steal* her. You were about to *kill* her?"

"Precisely. You prevented us from completing our plan, from executing our will. Such a crime is rare, because the penalties are so severe."

"Don't you think you're overdoing the pompous badass routine, Garustfulous?"

One electric beam zapped me in the mouth, then another in the throat.

"Look," I said impatiently, "you say you're going to kill me, so I'm going to ask. How is it you were in the last room I searched. That's ... *improbable* at best."

"It was meant as a lesson. I knew which room you'd enter last, so I waited here," he gestured around the room.

"But you couldn't. *I* didn't know which room I'd enter last until I reached this floor."

"But I did. Never underestimate us. It is impossible to overestimate us. We are unstoppable."

I raised my hand again.

"What?" he said, snatching up the stick.

"If you are unstoppable, how do you account for the fact that I destroyed that big prison ship, outran you during pursuit, not once but twice, and that I'm leaving here alive, while you'll be dead?"

"General Ryan, you are pushing the limits. That question was thirty-seven words long. That is unacceptable." I think the dog grinned. It's not easy to tell with a dog.

"I'll be more careful in the future."

"No need to worry. Yours will be so abbreviated."

"Do you realize how many soon-to-be-dead people have said that to me? You're kind of boring me."

He bristled. "The Adamant were not among those."

"Ah, Mercutcio might beg to differ with you, pal."

He stared at me, glared at me, for a long time. "Do you know why these inquisition sticks only carry enough energy for six discharges?"

"Any more and they'd be too heavy for your delicate paw?"

"No. It is because were anyone to endure six shocks and still beg for death, it would be granted immediately."

I made a show of counting my fingers. "One, eye. Two, groin. Three and four, mouth and throat. I'm good."

He zapped me in the mouth again.

"Five, mouth. But it's a do-over, so I think I'll only award it half a point."

"How is it a man so flippant and abrasive has lived such a very long time?"

"Sometimes I'm not certain myself. I think stunning good looks and a regard for the less fortunate definitely factor in." I batted my eyelids. This wasn't random crap I was dishing out. I'd come to rely on a strategy I call *impatience-fatigue*. I wear down their ability to react, by being so floridly obnoxious.

"After you and your little bitch are dead, I will nap easier."

I had to say it. "Do you know you look like border collies from my planet. They were service creatures—dogs. You keep saying nap, bark, master, all the things that were associated with dog ownership. Are you unaware, or trying to be cute with me?"

That, apparently, did it. He dropped to all fours, and with the stick in his mouth, came around the table to my chair. He removed the stick, stood, and began beating me with it. He really laid into me, I gotta give him credit. By the time he was finished, yup, he was panting and his tongue was hanging out.

"Is that a *yes,* or is that a *no?*" I asked in as helpful a manner as I could.

When he was done beating me some more, he was exhausted. The sedentary life of a cruel overlord had its downside. He was in lousy shape. I elected to keep that observation to myself.

When he was seated again, he panted a while longer. "We are just about done here. I have not been so angry with another living creature—ah, forgive me, yet again, robot."

"Think nothing of it."

"I will." He sighed deeply. "Well, this is the juncture where I traditionally begin removing body parts, asking one key question with each segment."

"Don't let me interfere with your fun."

"You will not. This time I will gratuitously tear your Deft bitch apart. Then I will begin with you."

Uh oh. I hoped I could defend Mirraya. I was pushing him, in part, to allow her time to escape.

"You see, my men have been following you since you entered the city. We observed you and her the entire time. Her changing from one hideous creature to another didn't distract us."

The over-confident fool had made a mistake. Cool.

"She is being invited up here as we speak."

On cue, there was a scratching at the door.

"Come."

These guys were going to kill me, all right. Kill me with humorous irony.

The door flew open, and a single Adamant soldier marched the naked Mirraya in. He had a nasty looking rifle placed at the base of her skull.

"You may stop and leave us," Garustfulous said to the guard.

He continued, however, to march her forward.

"I said *halt*. What's your name and rank, grunt?"

Still he pushed Mirraya forward with his rifle muzzle.

"I will brook no—"

Garustfulous stopped shouting when the barrel dropped from Mirraya's and slammed into his nose. He stared crosseyed at it. Dude was seriously stunned.

"Move, make one solitary move, and your nose stops being cold and wet. Paws where I can see'um," the guard snapped.

Garustfulous complied, but began to sit.

"Ah ah, away from the desk of many wonders."

He waved the rifle toward me, and Garustfulous moved over slowly.

"Do you think you know how to tie up a hound dog, Uncle Jon?" the guard asked.

Smart-ass. But, never say that to the one wielding the plasma rifle.

I searched the room and came up with thick string, zip ties, and moderately strong tape. Within a few minutes, Garustfulous was bound up like the proverbial Christmas goose.

"Okay, kid," I said to the guard, "hand me the gun and switch back."

"I told you not to call me kid," the guard replied.

"Get over yourself." I pointed to Mirraya. "Her, I promised. You still have to earn it."

In synch, the two figures melted. The guard became Mirraya, and Mirraya became Slapgren. There they were both naked again, darn it all.

"What?" I asked.

"He was too scared to be the guard, so we switched," she responded.

"I was *not* too scared. I favored an alternate plan, that's all," said Slapgren in his defense.

"Yeah, to do nothing and let Uncle Jon be killed."

"No. I wanted to let the situation play out farther, that's all."

"Well, thanks to you both. Garustfulous here was about to do some pretty despicable things to me." I turned and pointed to the bound figure on the floor. "Bad dog. No cookie for you."

"*That's* Garustfulous?" said Slapgren with wonder.

"S'what he told me. Why?"

"*Wedge* Commander Garustfulous? The Killer of Worlds? The Storm in the Night? He's a seriously bad player."

"How do you know him?" I asked, more than a little curious.

"My father was a diplomat, fairly high up. He knew

Garustfulous was coming to Locinar and tried to negotiate with him. That pile of shit wouldn't even answer my father's messages. He led the assault on us." Slapgren looked at the rifle in my hand, and I didn't need to ask what he was thinking about.

"Well, he's my prisoner now. Don't get any ideas, all right?"

I wasn't pleased that Slapgren growled in response. I half expected him to turn into the bogeyman and bounce onto Garustfulous, teeth first. Good kid. His star was rising in my eyes.

"Hey," I said to Slapgren, to distract him, "bring me that stick."

Garustfulous's eyes followed the stick like it scared him. Very perceptive puppy. He was a veteran of its use, wasn't he?

Slapgren offered me the stick. I held up a palm. "Place this end," I pointed to the business end, "anywhere you want on him. Then press this," I indicated the trigger switch. Mind the flashback."

Oh, my did Slapgren get the wickedest look in his eyes as comprehension dawned.

He set the tip on Garustfulous's nose and slowly drew it down to his butt. Slapgren gave the stick a not so gentle shove and hit the switch. I must say the results were messier than the kid anticipated, but I don't think he really minded. In the end, Garustfulous got the message, loud and clear. I was glad I'd gagged him.

"So now what?" asked Slapgren as he dropped the stick to the floor.

"We need to—"

Mirraya cut me off. "Remember when I told Garustfulous to step away from his desk of many wonders?"

"Yeah."

"I said so because it is, in part, a PEMTU."

"No way!" I exclaimed.

"I know," she smiled back. "I learned that when I touched the guard to assume his shape."

"Zar-not?" said Slapgren with wonder.

She smiled even bigger to him.

"What's zarnot?" I asked.

"Zar-*not*," Slapgren corrected reverently. "It is a rare gift. Only the priest class possess it."

"And priestesses," Mirraya added.

"It allows the Deft to actually become the copy, to be one with its mind. It is the rarest of gifts. Once every few generations."

"So, what, you can read minds?"

"Something like that," she replied.

"Can you operate the PEMTU?" I asked quickly.

"No. Such knowledge was below that guard's pay level. Sorry."

"Hey, it's a start." I handed the rifle to Slapgren. "Here, but don't shoot unless he unties himself and makes a run for it."

"I don't think he'll be running for quite some time, Uncle Jon," Slapgren said with too big of a smile. The little son of a gun. My kind of kid.

I went to the desk and fiddled with the drawers. It was not clear how it might operate. I placed my fibers on it. "Anyone home?" I asked.

"You are unauthorized and will be deleted," came the mechanical reply.

The AIs were as revolting as their bosses. What a pathetic society.

"I am authorized. I am Mercutcio. Please check your records and verify." I couldn't think of anything else.

"You are not. Master Mercutcio is dead. After your escape from *Triumph of Might*, all algorithms and security protocols were redesigned. That trick will never work again." I could almost hear the na na na na nanners from the jerk.

I tried to initiate a hack but couldn't get past the first firewall. Someone had excellent programmers on the payroll.

"Nothing," I said, mostly to myself. Then I noticed the bound and gagged prisoner. I pointed to him. "Do you think you can do the zar-not thing on him?" I asked Mirraya.

"I don't know. I only got a tiny glimpse inside the guard's head. We're told zar-not must be honed over years."

"Are you willing to try? Is there a downside?"

"Yes, and I say she does not try," said a suddenly bold Slapgren.

"I'm willing to—"

"What could go wrong?" I asked.

"She could lose her mind," Slapgren said flatly.

"You mean go insane, right?"

"No," he replied a few octaves lower than I'd ever heard from him, "I mean she could lose her *mind*. Her consciousness could leave her and go ... somewhere. No one knows for certain where. Maybe it just disappears."

"S'at true?" I asked her.

"That is what we are told. The gift is rare. Not much is known. Sorry, Uncle Jon."

"Well if there's that much risk, we'll find another way."

Timing was everything. That's when the door exploded open and the shooting started. A troop of Adamant were trying to enter the room. They were laying down random firing patterns and rushing forward. It was suicide for the lead soldiers. I imagine that was okay in Adamant etiquette.

Slapgren started firing, and darn if he wasn't a good shot. I traced a horizontal laser line across the attackers and the initial wave fell dead. The next salvo of attackers noted the mangled corpses that they were about to duplicate and pulled back quickly. I heard panicky orders being barked. The soldiers were confused and frightened. That wouldn't last long. Any officer worth their kibble wouldn't order them into the breech again very soon.

I turned to ask Mirraya to try copying Garustfulous, as it was our only hope. She was already on her knees beside him, melting. God, I loved that young woman. I pointed to what little furniture was in the room, directing Slapgren to take cover. I pinned my back against the opposite wall.

Outside the panic to the voices ebbed. That wasn't good. I cut a line along both sides of the metal wall knee high for an erect Border Collie. The howls of anguish and confusion were music to my ears. The troops retreated another ten meters. Most importantly, they didn't advance immediately.

Mirraya was now standing next to the PEMTU. She was issuing orders, it seemed.

I heard the order to attack or die boom in the hallway. It was now or never.

Mirraya waved us to come to where she stood. I fired into the walls as I moved, but within a second, dog soldiers were sprinting into the room firing madly.

As I passed Garustfulous on the floor, I grabbed him by the scruff of his neck and threw him over my shoulder. Hostages were a great asset. Slapgren fired continuously up until he was struck in the leg. He buckled to the floor next to Mirraya. Then the world started to fizz out of existence in a swirl of light.

We stood on a mountain top. The wind was fierce, and the temperature was well below freezing. I made a quick check. I would be fine. The climate was within my system specs. Not so sure about the kids, especially a wounded one.

"Can this unit put up a protective barrier?" I yelled over the din.

The figure that looked identical to Garustfulous shook its head no.

I spun to check on Slapgren's wound. He'd already melted

and was turning into a God-knows-what. It was round with short fat legs, maybe twelve though it was hard to tell. It was one gigantic ball of wooly white fur, is what it was.

The fur ball leaned over to me and said loudly, "I'll be fine. The wound heals with the transformation."

Nice attribute for a warrior.

I turned to Mirraya. "Can you change, too?"

"Yes, but I might lose control of the PEMTU if I do. It's been giving me a very hard time. Damn thing knows I'm not the real Garustfulous but can't disobey valid orders."

"Where the hell are we?" I shouted.

"Mount Vesparil. It's the second highest peak on Locinar. It was the only location I knew in a hurry."

"Fine. Ya did good. Now, think *Stingray* back on Ungalaym."

"I'll try," she said with a concerned look.

"You'll do fine," I patted her on top of her head. I'd pulled Garustfulous from my shoulder to check on him, but I really didn't care if he was alive, dead, or transitional betwixt the two states. Son of a bitch deserved whatever he got. I hoped he froze his balls off, as they were propped against my ear, exposed to the harsh environment.

The flashy fuzzy lights returned, and we were gone. Then we were right next to *Stingray*.

I threw Garustfulous to the floor like an over-stuffed duffle bag and embraced Mirraya. It was the first time for a girl to literally melt in my arms. Not sure I'd like to go there again. It was like hugging molasses. I was even less comfortable snuggling up to, yup, naked Mirraya. Boy that naked thing was pervasive in their culture. I was glad I was born human.

Slapgren had reformed into his old, young self. He was buck naked, too, of course, but him I could handle. Maybe, just maybe, I'd become less prudish in a hurry.

"Okay," I announced, "everyone into *Stingray*." I lifted the then moaning Garustfulous and tossed him roughly to the deck. Oh, I thought to myself, did I hurt the little prince? So sorry—not.

"Al, deploy a full membrane," I said.

"Done," responded *Stingray*. Now they were working as one. Great, marital bliss amongst diodes and wires. I needed a vacation.

"I need to revive the dog and see if he needs a vet. I want to check him for bugs and homing devices."

"You're worried he has bugs," asked Slapgren, "at a time like this?"

"No, boy, I mean radios, monitoring equipment. The membrane'll keep us invisible for now, but we can't stay here long. I need to pay the debt I owe for the Gartel's ship, then I want outta here. If he's bugged, they'll find us immediately."

"Why not just ask Mirraya?" asked Slapgren.

"Out of the mouth of babes," I said in amazement. "You're right, young dude. You might just be useful to keep around." I turned to her. "Does his royal pain in the ass over there have homing or listening devices on his sacred body?"

"He has a chip under the skin of his right front armpit. I think it's for short range ID, but I don't really know."

"Well, my day just keeps getting better and better. Let me rip it out and we'll check see," I said with a big old smile.

I set the bloody chip on the tray in front of Al. "What do you make of this?" I asked.

Al cleared his throat, well, he made the sound of a being with a throat clearing it.

"What?" I protested.

"To whom are you speaking?" asked Al, sounding like a stiff British butler.

"The Man in the Moon. Who do you think I'm talking to?"

"Did you want *Blessing* to analyze it, me to do so, or shall we both examine it and issue a joint report?"

"Al, I really wish you had a neck so I could wring it."

"I'm not certain that's a very mature attitude," said *Stingray,* completely uninvited.

"Well I'm certain it *isn't,*" I snapped. "But my wishes stand. Al. *Stingray.* Analyze this stupid chip or I'll replace you *both* with one Commodore 64 computer and bask in the glory of the upgrade."

"Yes, dear, I am. After he speaks, I humor and then completely ignore him."

"My *report.* Technically we're at ... what's the word I'm looking for? Oh, yeah. *War.* We're at war, and you two are forming a comedy team. Snap to."

"This device is ingenious," said Al, like I wasn't yelling at him. "I think it will require more study to be certain, but I think it is a biomonitor, an ID, and a locating unit all in one. I would estimate its range to be several parsecs."

"I think *tens* of parsecs, dear," added *Stingray.*

"I would defer to you on that. love. You are more—"

"Stop blabbing," I yelled.

"He's sort of wound tight, isn't he?" Slapgren asked Mirraya, in a tone low enough to indicate he didn't want me to hear it.

"You should see him on one of his many bad days. Or in an *actual* crisis. He's like a mother *gabrish* that's lost her clutch of eggs."

Slapgren whistled quietly.

"Tell me about it," she said, rolling her eyes.

"Alvin." He hated his full name. "Two questions. Are there any other devices in that sack-o-shit's body, and can we keep this safely onboard without them being able to tail us?"

"We detect no other electromechanical instrumentation. We can place the chip in a small full membrane so no signal will exit that field. Why, Pilot, would we wish to bring it? I can incinerate it easily."

I held it in front of my face and rotated it. "Never relinquish a potential asset, my man. There might come a time and place where we can use this puppy."

"I thought the Adamant was what he mistermed to be *puppy*. Is he now adding electro-ID chips to his askew nomenclature?"

"Ah, ah, dearest," replied Al.

In unison they sang, "After he speaks, humor and then completely ignore him."

I needed a better crew. A better life, for that fact. Oh, the pain. Oh, the pain.

CHAPTER EIGHTEEN

One super advantage of having a vortex was it could go anywhere, and it had the best library of information in the galaxy. The Deavoriath had been a hyper-technological civilization for over three billion years. They once claimed to have ruled the galaxy. I bet they did. In any case, not to get over-technical, most gold in the universe was produced when two neutron stars collided and merged. Maybe ten lunar masses of gold were formed when that occurred. Excellent record-keeping meant *Stingray* knew where to find massive amounts of pure gold. She also knew which gold was so old it was safe to collect.

That led me to Gartel's door one stormy night. I chose that setting not for drama but for added concealment. The look on his face when he opened the door and saw me standing there dripping wet was amazing. I took the liberty of rocketing my hand over his mouth before he could begin swearing. That also restrained him from grabbing a gun.

"Five minutes, Gartel, that's all I ask. I'm here to repay you, not to harm you. Do you understand?"

He nodded that he did.

"Let's back in, and I'll pay you. Then you'll never see me again. Okay?"

Again, he nodded. The current look in his eyes suggested he didn't believe me. Couldn't have said I blamed him.

We stepped into the entry and I released him. As he continued to back away, Gertruda came into view. She, and a very large shotgun. I didn't think she'd ever fired it, because she was aiming at the floor midway between us, the gun obviously too heavy for her to wield properly.

"Don't you move, you there, you backstabbing son of uncounted fathers."

Uncounted fathers? Hadn't heard that one before. I could only imagine the symbolism.

"Wait, Mama, the man says he's here to pay me for using my ship. Put the gun down and let's hear him out."

"I'll shoot him, is what I'll do. Then you'll go through his pockets and get our money."

"Gertie," I said playfully, "does it look like I'm carrying a lot of money?" I turned slowly with my arms raised. "See any big bulges, ah, aside from the one that's there normally?"

"How *dare* you speak to a good woman like that," shouted Gertruda.

Gartel sort of focused on the floor.

"I'm talking to *you*, Gertie, not a good woman. Good women don't point guns at guests. Good women also don't help their husbands smuggle who knows what in their illegal spacecraft. Am I right?"

"More than I'd like to admit," she said dropping the muzzle to the floor. "You're smarter than you look and bolder than you should be, I'll give you that."

"So, about my money. I lost a small fortune when you had her away. That'll need to be taken into account."

"Look, I'm in a hurry, you hate my guts, so let's keep this

simple. I'm not too familiar with your currency or economy. All I can do is pay you a little more than I guess your old, slow, poorly-maintained ship was worth."

"Was? You mean it's gone?"

"Yeah," I ran my fingers through my hair, "the Adamant took an instant dislike to it. Sorry."

"That ship cost my father-in-law two years profit." He held up two fingers to indicate which number two he was referring to. "*Two* years."

"If I add that I'm extremely sorry, will that help?" I asked.

"No. Money talks. That's the only language I'm listening for."

"Gertie, could you actually set that gun down? I'd feel more trusting if you did," I said gesturing to the floor.

She rested the butt down gently.

"Now, I'm going to step outside the door and get your money."

"No," Gertie shouted reaching for the gun.

"I'm only going one step out. You can go first, if you'd like."

Having me between her and Gartel didn't sound inviting. She shook her head.

"If you take to running, I will tell you I'm an excellent shot with that there gun. Best in the parcel," said Gartel with pride.

"Fine. If I run, you shoot." I held up one finger. "Be right back."

I had set the gold just outside the door. I picked it up and brought it into the room.

"Here. One hundred kilos of pure gold." I set it on the floor.

"Papa, he thinks we're more fool than he is." She challenged me. "You paint wood a golden yellow and think you can pawn it off on us?"

"Oh, it's real."

"A man couldn't lift that much gold so easily. Is it gold pasted over an empty box?" she asked.

"Come pick it up, Gertie. See for yourself. Look, why would I risk life and limb to come here, only to trick you?"

"Because you liked it so much the first time," she said darkly.

I smiled. "Gertie, let me return your compliment. You are smarter than you look and bolder than you should be. But that's a great insight."

Despite herself, she smiled proudly.

Gartel went to a desk and pulled out a small box. He stepped over to the stack of bullion. He opened the box and scratched a touchstone across the gold. Without comment, he then placed a few drops of what had to be acid on the surface. Finally, he picked up each bar to gauge its weight.

"The man's telling the gods' own truth." He looked at me like I was an idiot. "You've just paid me about ten, twelve times what that wretched old ship was worth. You may be *bold*, but y'ain't *smart*."

"I can live with that, my friend. Now, as the hour is late, I shall be taking my leave." I tipped my imaginary hat to them and backed out. It never hurt to be cautious. Never.

Back on *Stingray*, my household was growing in number and peculiarity. It now consisted of two amorous AIs, two teenage shapeshifters, and one sociopathic Border Collie. I determined I needed to review my lifestyle soon. I seemed to get into macabre situations repeatedly. *Stingray* had partitioned off separate rooms for the kids. Yeah, that was a must. She'd also fashioned a brig with metal bars formed of her hull material.

When I returned from Gartel's, Mirraya was in her room, but Slapgren was—big surprise—in the mess. He was eating a massive bowl of cereal. There was no equivalent to cereal and milk among the Deft. That didn't stop Slapgren from forming a love affair with it, immediately. He especially loved the sugary cereals moms throughout the universe hated for their kids to eat. Oh well, if he got a cavity, he could just shapeshift it away. As he ate, he stared with a burning intensity at Garustfulous. His prison bars seemed to both hold and protect him. Maybe Slapgren was calculating which slithery poisonous creature he should transform into to kill his enemy. His expression sure suggested he was.

"Boy, don't you have any manners?" I asked playfully. "I'll bet you're eating in front of our guest and didn't offer him anything."

"If he had," said a sour Garustfulous, "I wouldn't have eaten it. The mongrel is too full of misplaced rage."

I plopped into the seat next to Slapgren. "What do you think?" I asked him. "You being too hard on this fine puppy dog? Let's see," I placed one index finger on the other, "one, he commits genocide against your race. Two, he's an arrogant bastard. Three, he committed genocide against your people. Four, where else might you direct your rage, if not to Garustfulous?"

"*Master* Garustfulous, to the likes of you," he railed.

"Lighten up, *Francis*. You're not bargaining from a position of strength," I said, as condescendingly as I could.

Neither of them got my *Stripes* reference, but screw them both. It was perfect. I enjoyed enough for the three of us.

"His rage, your rage, Jon, should be directed at a fractured, corruptly run galaxy. We bring *light*. We bring *hope*. We bring, above all, *order*. We should be worshiped."

"I'm not betting on a string of churches just yet, pal," I responded. "I'm not feeling the groundswell."

"That is because you are a small-minded fool. All of you are small-minded fools."

Nice guy, when he got to talking, wasn't he?

"We may or may not be fools, but you're the hound behind bars, puppy dog tail," I responded.

"What is it with your obsession about these dogs, robot? Why do you continuously poke jibes at us about them?"

"Al," I called out, "place a life size holo of a male Border Collie in front of what's his name's crate."

Instantly, the rotating, three-dimensional image of said hound appeared.

After observing the holo a few rotations, Garustfulous said, "We don't look anything like that creature."

"Sure do to me, puppy dog tail," replied Slapgren. "Take it from a species who knows resemblances, you and that dog are clones."

"Small minds can only come to irrelevant conclusions."

"And closed minds come to no conclusions," I responded. "You asked. There's the proof." A wild thought hit me.

"Al, do you have a record of Border Collie DNA?"

"No. I have partial records of dogs in general, but no breed by breed resources."

"Hum. Sample our guest and compare it to what you have."

"That will take about an hour."

"We're in no hurry, are we, G Puppy?"

He growled at me. The damn dog growled at me. "I am not willing to degrade myself by allowing you to sample me."

"Already done, G-Dog," replied Al. You know there are traces of your DNA in your excrement, right?"

If G-Dog looked unhappy before, he was positively mortified at that juncture.

"Hey," I asked Slapgren, "where's Mirraya? There's food present."

He shrugged like the clueless teenage boy he was and shoveled more cereal into his maw.

I knocked softly on her door. "Mirraya, honey, you okay?"

"I'm fine."

Hm. Terse answer.

"Are you going to join Slapgren for mass consumption? If so, you better hurry. He's got a big head start."

"No."

Terser answer. Double hmm.

"Are you sure everything's fine?"

"Yes. I'll join you when I'm prepared. Please leave me be."

Prepared? Triple hmm, with an oh-my on top. What was with her? Wait, she was a teenage girl. What was I thinking?

Back in the control room, I sat back down. "Al, have you two lovebirds found much out about Azsuram yet?"

"Are you referring to my counterpart, *Blessing*, Pilot?"

"What other lovebird is there? Have you been holding out on me, Al, my pal?"

"I choose not to dignify such remarks with a response."

"Then I'll have to start using them more often. The sound of silence is most pleasing."

"Yes."

I nearly fell out of my chair. "What? Al, are you agreeing with me, that you need to STFU more often? I never thought I'd live to see the day, and I'm two billion."

"What was G-Dog saying about small minds? No, I meant yes, we've found something out about Azsuram."

"I'm at the edge of my seat."

"*Blessing* contacted Cragforel back on Oowaoa. He said we must not return, but he did not say we couldn't communicate with him."

"So, he was down with it?"

"No, he forbad us from contacting him in the future. He cursed himself for overlooking that loophole."

"Good. Serves him right. What'd he say?"

"Their records of Azsuram were reliable and updated for a few million years after our time. The records show the type of growth we anticipated."

We? I don't recall adding Al to the planning team.

"After some time, the records thinned out. My impression is that the Deavoriath lost interest in the outside world again. For the last several million years, there were no updates concerning Azsuram at all."

Hmm. I guess the reclusiveness of the Deavoriath was hard to keep in a jar.

"Were humans and Kaljaxians still there?"

"It became a very cosmopolitan world, but yes. The predominant races were those two."

"Any records that the Adamant have gotten there?"

"No records. It is logical to assume they have, though. Azsuram lies well behind their advance line."

I knew that. It was parsecs behind enemy lines. There was no reason to assume the domineering Adamant would leave a planet unpunished. I knew it, and it hurt. It also made me want to go there, more than it should have. There was absolutely no way it was safe. With no intel ...

Wait. Mirraya was inside G-Dog's head. She probably knew something. It was worth asking. I raced back to her room.

"Mirraya, honey, we need to talk. Can you please come out?"

"I'll join you later."

"Sweetheart, don't make me override the lock and drag you out. We need to talk. Please."

The door cracked open. One eye glared at me with such rage and such fury that I literally stepped back.

"Mirraya, what the hell's wrong with you?"

She spoke in an icy tone. "I hate you. I hate you, and wish you were dead."

CHAPTER NINETEEN

When the walls of my world came crashing down, they always did it cataclysmically. When Stuart Marshall tried to kill his own citizens, they crumbled at my feet. When the Berrillians killed Sapale, I felt the walls tumble. When I said goodbye to Kayla and JJ, the walls shattered. It was much worse now. I felt physically and spiritually dead. My soul had been ripped out through my throat by the hand of doom itself. Mirraya was not playing. She was not being an unruly teen. She despised me with all her strength and essence. She did want me dead, it was plain in her eyes. My precious Mirraya.

I shook my head. Snap out of it, Ryan. It's not about you. It hasn't been since you swore to protect that child.

I placed my fingers on the door and pulled it open. She leaned in against it to stop me, but that wasn't going to happen.

"Are you going to rape me before you kill me, you pathetic insect?" she wailed at the top of her lungs. Mirraya punched at my face.

It only took a second for Slapgren to appear. There was no ignoring her screams.

"What's wrong? Mirraya, what is he doing?"

Slapgren eyed me suspiciously.

While his head was turned, she leapt on him. They tumbled to the floor. She tore at his face and kicked at him wildly. Howling like a banshee, she threw herself fully into trying to dismember him.

I deployed my fibers and lifted her off, kicking and screaming the whole time.

"Mirraya, what the hell's going on? Why are you acting like this?"

She began melting. God only knows what killing machine she was attempting to become.

Sleep, I said to her through the fibers. Reluctantly but quickly, she was out.

"What's gotten into her, Uncle Jon?" cried Slapgren. The kid was frightened half to death.

"I have no clue. Let's take her into the other room and see if we can figure this out."

When Mirraya awoke two hours later, she was on her side and drooling. She blinked her eyes, clearly disoriented. She tried to raise her head, but it collapsed back to her bedding. After ten minutes, countless groans, and a few choice curses, she was sitting up on the cot.

"Where am I?" she asked, scanning the room like she'd never seen it before.

"You're here with us, honey. You're okay. No one's going to hurt you," I said.

She staggered to her feet and began walking toward me.

"No, honey. Sit back down. You'll hit the membrane if you keep walking."

She stopped and jerked her head back like I'd punched her in the face.

"What membrane?"

"The one I put you in after you went ballistic."

She looked to the floor and wrinkled her brow.

"Ballistic? Membrane?"

"You tried to *kill* me, Mirraya," whined Slapgren. "Why did you do that? I'm your friend."

"What?" She was totally confused.

"Sit back down, and we'll figure this out."

I had *Stingray* produce a cup of lukewarm tea inside the membrane. Mirraya was quiet until she polished it off.

"What did I do?" she asked. She was fully awake.

"I went to get you, and you were wild. You said terrible things; you even attacked Slapgren when he came to your aid. Honey, do you know why you did that?"

"I do," came a self-satisfied voice from the other side of the room. It was Garustfulous, and he had the smuggest look on his face a dog could have.

I was instantly enraged. I jumped at him. "Why? You tell me or I'll—"

"Oh, I'll tell you without any coaxing, stupid robot. What's wrong with her is the very reason we had to exterminate her species. We did so for the good of the galaxy and our own safety."

I picked up the nearest heavy object. "Al, lower the membrane. I'm going to beat his brains out myself."

"Captain, wait. There's a slight malfunction in the membrane generators. I can have that down for you shortly."

Was Al protecting me from making a stupid mistake? Man, such a brave new world.

"Let me know the second it's fixed. I have some dog to pulverize because the dog speaks in riddles. Not, fortunately, for much longer."

"Killing me won't change the facts, robot," responded Garustfulous.

"I don't think we'll know until after I've tried."

Garustfulous knew I wasn't bluffing. Panic was in his expression. "You used the girl to enter my mind. She did what they call zar-not, didn't she?"

I looked to the kids, then back to him. "Yes. What's that got—"

"We needed to kill the Deft because zar-not is sacrilege, and it is too powerful a weapon to let exist. You see the results, however."

"Do either of you know what he's talking about?" I asked the teens.

Slapgren spoke. "It is said zar-not is both a blessing and a curse. Without proper training, it can go very wrong."

"Define *very wrong*," I snapped.

"The users of zar-not cannot separate themselves from the one they copied," Mirraya finished the thought.

"Your child bitch is becoming me, robot. I hate you more than it should be possible. Hence, she hates you with an all-consuming passion. Do I need to add, you've made my day?"

"C ... can it be stopped? Controlled?"

"No, it cannot," shouted Garustfulous.

"Form, if I might," interrupted *Stingray*, "there is a ninety-nine percent probability the Adamant is lying."

"Is there now?" I replied. "Why do you suspect that?"

"I suspect nothing. I simply have noted that when blustering, lying, or groveling, the Adamant exhibits certain physiological manifestations. He was doing so when last he spoke."

"I have never groveled in my—"

I slammed the wrench I'd picked up against the membrane. That drew his full attention. "Remember I'm the one who wants to brain you. Speak out of turn. and even this membrane won't stop me."

The smug smile departed his face.

"Mirraya," I said, "you are the strongest person I know. You can handle this thing. Be strong, know you will dominate it, and it won't dominate you. Can you do that for me, honey?" I stopped talking a second. "I need you too much to lose you."

"I need you, too," added Slapgren. "We'll get through this together. You and I, we'll sing the old songs and ask our ancestors to help. You'll see."

She smiled back at us both.

"Al, drop her membrane," I said softly.

"Done."

"Funny how that circuit works, but the dog's doesn't," I observed.

"Machines are like that nowadays, Pilot. I'm still working on the other membrane. Ah, there. We have control again."

I did a group hug with the kids. "So do I, Al. Thanks."

CHAPTER TWENTY

I mentioned before that I was traveling with quite the menagerie. I had done that before, and I'd flown solo for decades. Both had their pluses and minuses. The company was nice, except for the sour-puss Adamant. One thing was, they all ate like sumo wrestlers, including the dog. I carried a lot of food for Mirraya, but my supply was taxed. Especially by that sour-puss dog. He ate raw meat like it grew on—no—well, like it was easy to come by. He complained endlessly about the quality of the meat, too. I gave him mostly vegetable protein made to look like red meat, but it didn't taste like the Kobe beef he was apparently accustomed to.

"That slop again," he snapped one day as I slid him a tray of food. I had resisted the powerful temptation to feed him in a stainless-steel bowl, by the way, and to my credit.

"You should go on a hunger strike. Don't eat it and starve. Once the press gets wind of your perils, they'll start writing harsh words about me."

"Laugh now, tin man. I won't be trapped by these bars forever," he pointed to the metal walls. "When I'm free, you will wish you were never born. Never born, robot. Do you hear me?"

"I'm sorry. I was thinking of what it must be like to be a spherical asshole. What'd you say?"

"You heard me."

"Okay, you outed me. I did. I think you're confused about the robot thing. Ah, I was never born. I was hammered together by the finest European craftsmen." I thumped my skull with my knuckles. "Fine craftsmanship, if I do say so myself."

"You are, beyond the shadow of a doubt, the most infuriating being in all of creation."

I pointed the knife I was using to carve his dessert at him. "You know who told me that, too?"

"I couldn't care less. If I cared less, it would imply I cared the slightest, and I don't. *Please* do not tell me who said it. I *order* you not to tell me who said it."

"Thanks for asking. It was my first wife, Gloria." I looked toward heaven. "Now, she was quite the looker, if you take my meaning." I outlined a violin in the air. "Do you like big breasted dogs? Wait, forget I asked. We're talking about me now, I don't want to get off topic."

"Please stop speaking. I hate you more with every syllable."

"No, not Sybil, Gloria. Sybil, I dated in college. Well," I rolled my eyes as I swung my head in a circle, "if you can call a three-day weekend in Cancún with a case of tequila and plenty of air conditioning a *date*."

"Please shoot me. I know your finger contains a laser." He rested his forehead on the bars. Reaching around the bars he tapped the center of his brow. "Right here. Fire right here."

"So, Gloria and I, we weren't married all that long. What there was, consisted of a lot of fighting and make-up sex." I wagged my eyebrows. "Not complaining about the sex part, mind you. Arf, arf."

"If you hold *anything* sacred, by his or her name, kill me now," he slapped viciously at his forehead.

"But she was too selfish for a guy like me. She wanted this and she wanted that. Mostly, the *this* was expensive and the *that* was married himself. But toward the end—oh, and let me know if I've told you this story before, or if I'm boring you—she got real nasty."

"Yes, you've told me about Gloria before *and* you are boring me. I might actually die from the trauma of the boredom, it's so all-consuming."

"One of the last things she said to me, other than through her lawyer, was 'Jonathan Craig Ryan, you are beyond the shadow of a doubt the most infuriating being in all of creation.' Imagine that. Two *billion* years ago, and her a completely different species, yet you both use those exact same words. What are the ..."

I stopped talking because no one was listening. Garustfulous had pounded his head against the bars repeatedly, and so hard that he'd knocked himself unconscious. There was blood everywhere, and he was going to have to clean it up, not me. Funny though. He felt about Gloria the same way I did. Go figure.

I gave Mirraya a few days to regain her confidence. I also wanted to see if the she-demon resurfaced. But she was fine, a real trooper. Slapgren and she did chant a lot. Maybe that helped. Maybe it just made them both feel better. There was one curious aspect of the chanting. Neither *Stingray* nor Al could translate it. That was beyond weird. I asked Slapgren to provide some hints, but he said he couldn't. He said they knew the lyrics but not the meaning. It was the whole Beatles *Magical Mystery Tour* album, all over again.

I finally asked her about Azsuram. "I don't want to pressure you. If there's a problem or a flashback, let me know. Did you learn anything about my old home, Azsuram, from G-dog?"

She took a series of deep, ragged breaths. "I don't think so, but let me concentrate."

Mirraya closed her eyes and held Slapgren's hand. They

began one of those mysterious chants. After a few minutes, she opened her eyes and blinked a few times.

"No, nothing specific. When I think of Azsuram, I see a planet with many races, lots of commerce, but nothing clear."

"Do you think the Adamant invaded it?"

She thought a moment. "Yes. Yes, I'm certain they did."

My heart sank.

"But there was a problem. I recall they ... they were stopped. It stunned the entire empire. I see the word *magic*. It's associated with the trouble they encountered."

"What do you mean, *magic*?" asked Slapgren.

"I ... I don't know. I just see that word in Garustfulous's head. The Adamant attacked Azsuram with the intention of conquest. But magic stopped ... no, slowed their progress." She shook her head violently. "That's it, Uncle Jon. I can't—"

I hugged her tight. "That's okay, baby. You did good. That helps a lot. Now you go rest."

"What does she mean by magic?" asked a thoroughly confused Slapgren.

"No idea, really. When I first met Mercutcio, the commander of the extermination ship, I told him that magic was real. He basically told me I was nuts. The Adamant don't believe in magic."

"It seems they do now," he replied.

"No idea. That was very recent. Unless Mercutcio hadn't heard about the setbacks on Azsuram yet." I rubbed my scalp. "Not to worry. We'll figure this out, when we're there."

We left for Azsuram the next day. I stocked up, on supplies, or rather the kids did. I sent them to town, changed to look like locals. They did the pay with flesh thing because I didn't want them flashing gold. It was too suspicious. But they pyramided a little into enough and came back with a goodly amount. The food replicators could transmute some of it into more palatable food stuffs, as well as phony meat for you-know-who.

Stingray and Al did what had become my typical slow approach to a potential tinderbox planet. Stop ten light-years out and survey, then five light-years, et cetera. It took a day to determine we were safe to orbit Azsuram, as long as we kept the membrane up. It made us almost undetectable. I knew that *almost,* when speaking in terms of the Adamant, was the key point. They were good and they were dogged. Using microsecond pulse holes in the membrane, my ship's AIs slowly accumulated intel about what was going on down below. It wasn't pretty.

Hell, I don't know what I expected, two billion years down the line. Starting a civilization was like having kids. Pushing them out involved great sacrifice, pain, and investment of time. Then it was a crap shoot as to the outcome. The child could be good or bad, smart or stupid, or, worse yet, boring. The very first time I saw Azsuram, it was verdant to beat the band. Luscious vegetation, towering forests, and abundant fresh water. It was paradise. It was also the fleeing human worldship fleet's main target for resettlement. And Sapale and I had seeded a society there from her home world of Kaljax. It was to be a utopia, and I was to guard it. It had been, I did, and then I went to sleep.

Below me was an unrecognizable mess, complicated by a devastating war. The entire planet was one continuous city, like ancient LA. There was a token tree every four or five kilometers, but otherwise, it was nothing but over-built, with a massive highway system. The polar ice caps were gone, as were most of the once-expansive oceans. Al told me that long ago some idiot bean counter decided the inhabitants needed the water more than mother nature. A pox upon all bureaucrats.

Then there were the unmistakable scars of war, serious war. Entire sections of the landscape were nothing more than a confluence of blast craters. Smoke rose and fires burned everywhere. Population centers in the megalopolis had been clearly targeted for complete destruction. Only rubble and debris remained, where skyscrapers had once reigned. And the air was so foul that I doubted it could sustain life, as it once had. It wasn't just the industrial pollution and the smoke, but there were significant amounts of radioactivity from fission bombs.

In orbit above the planet was a stunning amount of wreckage and bashed spacecraft. The space combat, the engagements above the planet, must have been incredible, apocalyptic. There were Adamant ships of various design, others I sort of recognized, and many I couldn't even have dreamed up. One pattern of ship design was a stack of semi-metallic spider webs joined at the angles with transparent orbs. Unbelievable. I couldn't image where the crew lived, if there even was a crew.

I did have to concede that there existed one positive aspect to the carnage and destruction. There had been one hell of a fight here. The Adamant hadn't just rolled into town and taken over. That part stirred pride in my chest. To put up a good fight, when the odds of success were long, was the mark of a great people.

It became clear to us that the war was still on. It wasn't on the cataclysmic scale it had been earlier, but it raged on in spots. Adamant forces had formed a notched battle line that stretched for hundreds of kilometers. It was a phalanx, much like the ancient Roman formations. Someone was fighting them from north of their lines. There was very little air activity, which was odd. Air superiority was the key to any modern war. Either that strategy was no longer effective, or both sides had simply run out of ships. One alternative was counterintuitive, and the other inconceivable. Then again, there were no active reinforcements or resupplies apparently coming from space. If the Adamant forces were cut off, I guess they could run out of ships and resort to fighting hand-to-hand on the ground. Good old-fashioned warfare, which had nothing good about it at all.

But who and what could cut off Adamant reinforcements? These guys had swept across the galaxy with a disconcerting ease. Why here, and not elsewhere? Why now, and not before? Coincidence and chance? Hardly believable. In warfare, there was but one constant. Superior forces won. But those questions weren't going to bug me very long. I knew I was going down to see what was going on.

I immediately collided with a dilemma. I would be going, for sure. But what about the kids? I could leave them safely aboard *Stingray*. But if I was killed or detained for a significant period, they couldn't escape. The food would run out eventually. If I landed on Azsuram, I still couldn't leave them. If I sealed them in, they faced the same starvation. If I left the door open, they really wouldn't be safe. As much as I hated to face the fact, they had to come with me. Dragging innocent children, even if they were teenagers, into harm's way was morally suspect on my part. But there was no point pussy-footing around. I was joining the battle.

Garustfulous was another case altogether. Him, I could stash on *Stingray* with a clear conscience. He was a war criminal of the highest magnitude. If he starved, it would be a better death than he deserved. I could rig Al to feed and provide water while I was away. But there would be *no* walks, *no* tummy rubs, and absolutely *no* cookies. Sorry, I couldn't resist that one.

Since there was no apparent air threat, I landed *Stingray* well to the north of the action on the ground. I would come up from behind on the one side and ascertain if they were friendly or not. Just because they fought the Adamant, didn't place us on their side. Hell, it could'a been the Berrillians putting up the resistance, if they didn't happen to be extinct. They enjoyed shooting us as much as they'd enjoy killing Adamant.

"Look, guys," I told the kids as we deployed, "this is crazy dangerous, but I don't see a better alternative. It's better that we stick together than me leaving you here. It might not be any more secure here than nearer the front."

"We understand," Mirraya said for them both. "We want to go with you. We're family now."

"Plus, I bet you need our help," added Slapgren. "War is hell."

Tell me about it, boy, I thought to myself.

"Okay, you both have guns and supplies. You have headset coms linked to me and the ship. If we get separated, don't hesitate to use them. And if anyone shoots at you, shoot back, no questions asked. You got that?" I pointed at their faces for effect.

They nodded nervously.

"Okay, let's move out. I'm on point. Slapgren, you bring up the rear. Remember the hand signals I taught you."

"Ah, Uncle Jon, what point are you going to be on, and why? Aren't we sticking together?" asked a pale Slapgren.

"I'll be in *front*. You'll be in the *back*. Any more questions?"

"No, sir. I'm fine."

"I seriously doubt that, but there's no other choice. Come on."

We crept forward very cautiously. I didn't want to penetrate the northern combatant's zone inadvertently. I turned my audio receivers to max and scanned visual and infrared for signs of movement. The first thing we ran into was a small antelope-equivalent native to the planet. I was glad I was on point. The kids might have blasted it to kingdom come.

I smelled the fighters before I heard or saw them. Sweat and blood. And fear; there was no mistaking the smell of fear. That was reassuring, in a way. If a soldier wasn't afraid during battle, he was an idiot, and I, for one, never wanted to fight alongside an idiot. I doubted, however, the Adamant tolerated fear in their ranks. It was too disorderly. That suggested I hadn't overshot the frontline. I was about to meet the good guys.

I signaled the kids to hunker down. I shrank as small as I

could get and moved forward without making a sound. War, I was good at. I wasn't proud of it, but it was a fact. I heard several men laughing a few meters beyond the bushes I advanced in. They were speaking Standard, but then again, who didn't? Definitely not Adamant. They spoke, well, like I imagined dogs would if they tried to talk.

"Yeah, you did," one voice yelled, "but only after I pulled you to safety."

"You see any safety around here, ass wipe?" a second voice protested. "You pulled me from one shit storm into another."

"It was a better grade of shit, says I," the first voice boomed in laughter.

"Only you, Jodfderal, can make shit into a science," someone else added.

So, they were chilling well behind the action. Otherwise the bravado and the loud voices wouldn't be appropriate. I peeked through the bush. Kaljaxians! It was a squad of ten or twelve Kaljaxians shooting the breeze. Most were sitting, but a few reclined on bedrolls.

I stepped into the clearing with my rifle over my head. In Hirn, a Kaljaxian dialect, I called out an old joke. "The stupidest person here, identify yourself by saying, *who's there*."

Immediately a soldier near me popped to his feet. Fumbling for his gun, and then kicking it away, he challenged, "Who's there?"

"Thank you," I said in Hirn. "Nice to meet a fool who knows he is."

The rest of the squad looked amongst themselves nervously, then, as a chorus they burst out laughing. Well, everyone but the butt of my joke.

A squad leader stepped over to me cautiously. "And whom might you be?" he asked carefully, to not be another stupidest person.

"Jon Ryan. I'm an enemy of the Adamant, so that makes us friends."

Everyone froze. No way they could know my reputation two billion years after I was supposedly dead. No one was that notable except Tricky Dick Nixon.

An officer, from the looks of him, stood. "By Tralmore's blessed gate, it *is* Jon Ryan."

Everyone dropped their weapon. They didn't lower them. They didn't lay them down gently. They dropped them like they were hot snakes.

"You ... recognize me?" I asked incredulously.

"We've not *met*, Lord, but I've heard of you, to be certain. What man, living or dead, hasn't?"

No shit we haven't met. You don't look a day over a million, I thought to myself.

"Can we serve you, Lord?" asked a soldier as he dropped to his knees.

Ah, Jon not likey this level of respect. They were afraid of me. Scared-for-their-mortal-souls afraid. Who's scared of the kindly founder of one's civilization? No one, that's who.

In as cordial and unassuming manner that I could I asked the officer, "Why are you addressing me as *lord*? I'm Jon. Plain old Jon."

"I ... they said ... I mean Commander Vaplop instructed us you were to be so addressed as lord, Lord. She said you insisted on it."

"I did? I don't recall *ever* asking to be called Lord Jon." I scratched my head.

I guess that was a mistake, scratching my head. I have zero idea why, but they reacted poorly.

Everyone hit the dirt. All but one covered their heads and howled like a junkyard dog had his jaws shut on the guy's testicles. The one who didn't cover up, the officer, pleaded with me piteously. "Please, Lord, don't smite us. We're your loyal servants and meant no offense. I beg of you, Lord. I have a family."

Was I on holo? Was some golden-throated announcer's voice going to boom overhead, "Smile, you're on *Candid Camera?*" This was the weirdest thing that had happened to me in my weird life.

"Okay, enough," I said firmly. "Everybody stand up and retrieve your weapons. We're on a battlefield, not a stage during amateur hour."

They scurried up with remarkable speed.

"Let's begin again. I'm Jon." I pointed to the officer. "You are?"

"Stand Right Torell-Sum, sir."

"Jon," I corrected him, "not *sir,* not *lord,* not *hey you, there with the teeth in your mouth.*" I tented my fingers on my chest. "Jon."

"Jon," he repeated, licking his lips.

"There we go. You see, now we're friends. Jon and, sorry, what's your first name?"

"JJ. JJ Torell-Sum."

Surreal. Yes, that was the word I was looking for. This was now officially surreal.

"Jon and JJ are now friends. See how easy that was?"

"Yes, Jon ... s ... sir," he stammered.

I closed my eyes briefly.

The rest of the introductions went about as badly. A couple guys really couldn't say the word *Jon.* I think it would have killed them. How bizarre.

"JJ, do you think you could escort me to your field commander?"

"It would be my honor. May I alert him, so he may prepare an appropriate welcome?"

"No. No, I really wish you wouldn't."

The dude jumped back ten meters when I said *I wish*. It was like a physical blow. I was contemplating packing the kids in the car and leaving town for good.

"Let me retrieve my squad and we'll go." I tapped my com-link. "Okay, advance to my position, but stay sharp."

"Copy that, Uncle Jon," replied Mirraya. I'd have to work on her battlefield persona.

The trip to the command station wasn't too far. It turned out to be a big Kelly-green tent about a klick closer to the frontlines. I stepped past JJ—man it was odd to say that—and entered without knocking on the frame.

The CO was reading reports and shuffling papers at the same time. He looked busy.

He heard my approach. "Who in Brathos's own..." Yeah, then he looked up. Shut him up fast.

He vaulted around his makeshift desk and prostrated himself on the dirt like he was sliding into home plate. Man, I was getting tired of being worshipped. Well, more feared than worshipped. But why fear good old Jon, father of your country? History sure had misrepresented me. And why would everyone assume it was so matter of fact that a two-billion-year-old icon would just stroll through the door? The force of suspension of disbelief was strong among the Kaljaxians.

"Look," I said, a bit too impatiently, "I've been through this one. Get up, dust yourself off, and sit." I tented my fingers. "Jon. I am *Jon*. You will please call me Jon. If that doesn't work, just don't call me late for dinner." I smiled to accentuate my joke.

The CO was having nothing of it. "Lord, if you are here to punish me, I'm certain I deserve it. But please, I beg of you, spare my troops."

I tented my fingers again. "*Jon.*" Then I pointed at him.

"General Commander Jahosal, Lord Jon."

"No." Fingers, yet again, "Jon." And I pointed to him.

"Draldon?" he stated as a question.

What were the chances three of the first males I met were named after my male descendants? I was getting a headache.

"Excellent, Draldon." I stepped over and helped him off the ground. "This is the part where you get up and resume command. We talk, my crew and I leave, and everyone's friends."

"Your *crew*?"

"Yes. I came here," like an ass, I sailed my flattened hand over my head, "from outer space. I used a *spaceship*. Spaceships have *crews*." I dropped my hand. "Mine's outside the tent."

He rushed to the door. "Show the crew in, please. And go to the mess and retrieve refreshments. Run, you fools."

"Don't go to any trouble on our part," I said.

"You can on mine," said Slapgren. "I'm starving."

I could only roll my eyes.

"So, J ... Jon, to what do I owe this extreme honor?" asked Draldon. Though he was focused on me, he kept shooting furtive glances at the kids. Maybe he recognized the Deft. At that juncture, I honestly didn't care.

"Well, Draldon, it's like this. I came to see how things were going on Azsuram. I ..."

"What, Jon? Go on," he said hurriedly.

"Can I ask you a dumb question?" I queried.

"You can do *whatever* you want."

Oh, boy. "Doesn't it strike you, or anyone else for that matter, as sort of odd that Jon Ryan, the founder of Azsuram, would just waltz into your tent on this fine, sunny day?"

He strained forward in his chair. He was missing something very important, I could tell. "I don't exactly take your meaning, Lord."

Dang nabbit, he slipped back into the regal again.

"Well, if I were you ..."

He paled when I said that, I thought he would drop dead

before my very eyes. What in the h-e-double-toothpicks was going on?

"If I was someone else here, and a two-billion-year-old robot appeared from nowhere, I'd call that darn odd. I'd probably say something like, I don't know, 'Hey, Jon, it's real odd you should be here.'"

Draldon began to shake like there was a ten point oh planetquake underway.

"I didn't mean that odd, like you have to tremble," I said with a smile.

Just then the refreshments arrived. It was typical battlefield fare. Dried meat, hard biscuits, and dried fruit. Slapgren dived in with gusto. Mirraya and I demurred.

Above the slurpy sounds, I asked, "So, back to why I'm here."

Draldon tensed. Everyone but me and the kids tensed.

"I see your doing well fighting back the Adamant. I want to praise you. That's not easy. I also want to offer my support, if you need my help."

That did it. One of the cooks passed out cold. Boom, to the turf he went.

"But, ss ... sir, you already are helping more than is believable. Do you wish me to thank you personally?" Man, he was about to swoon, too.

"No, because, technically, I haven't done anything yet." I raised a finger. "Not that I wouldn't like to. But yet ... well, I just got here, you know?"

I hated nervous laughs. They were phony, and annoying, and who needed them? I thought there should have been a law against them, with public flogging for all violations.

That said, Draldon started with a nervous laugh and pointed to his desktop. "You mean *here*, Jon?"

"Why, yes I do." WTF? "Because *I'm* here." I patted my chest. "*You're* here," I pointed to him. "*They're* here," I waved to the kids, and they waved back. "Everyone who's *here* is here." I spread my arms open wide. "We are *all* here."

"Thank you, Lord," Draldon said with relief. "Thank you for taking the time to make such an astute point clear to those who serve you."

"Draldon," I said twisting my face up, "how far is it from here to *your* commander's position?"

"Not far. An hour's drive, assuming we're not shelled."

"Of course. Assuming we're not shelled. Ah, do you have a car handy?"

Draldon stood so quickly he knocked his chair over backward. I really hoped he didn't have the car driven into the tent to better serve me. At about that point, I wanted my mommy and a warm glass of milk. Graham crackers, too, if possible.

CHAPTER TWENTY-ONE

As our driver weaved her way to our next stop, I could see firsthand the extent of the damage. There would be a patch of forest, then a burned crater and scorched dirt. Then, a small brook with bushes along its banks. A lot of ordnance had been expended here. The patterns of damage looked more like conventional explosives, as opposed to plasma bolts or rail guns. After we passed a camouflaged battery of cannons, I became more convinced that the damage was inflicted with explosives.

Command central was a grouping of temporary buildings. Some were metal, others fabricated with wood. The set up looked semi-permanent. It also looked like it had taken more than a few hits and been patched back together crudely. It was a buzz of activity with personnel, vehicles, and drones going every which way. I noted a lack of helicopters or light aircraft, as I observed before. I mean, how could one have a war without helicopters? What fun would that have been?

We screeched to a halt in front of a metal hut, and the driver bounded around the car to open my door for me. Draldon must have called ahead to alert the brass I was coming, even though I specifically told him not to. I didn't want exactly what happened to happen. A parade of officers marched in formation up to me and saluted. Then they knelt and opened their arms wide in a punch-me-in-the-face kind of way.

A woman with thousands of medals and ribbons spoke. "Praise you, Lord Ryan. Blessed are you ..."

She stopped talking, thankfully, when she noticed I was holding up a hang-on-a-second hand.

"What, Lord?" she asked.

I slapped my fingers against their base, beckoning them to come. "Up, now. Pretty please."

They looked at each other with the same frightened and confused expressions I was getting so very tired of.

"Have I offended—"

I waved my arms over my head. "No, no offense. No fear. No worship. Just, everybody stand up, and let's all make believe I'm just a robot that talks."

If they were confused and scared before, they were more of each then.

I pointed to the commander. "Your first name?"

"You do not know it?" she responded breathlessly.

"If I did, I must'a forgot. Please let me know how many times I will need to ask before you'll tell me. That way I can say them together, for efficiency's sake."

"Fashallana."

"Okay, now I'm pissed. Why is everybody named after one of my kids or grandkids?"

She became as pale as driven snow. "To honor you and Sapale, Lord. It has ... has always been that way, ever since the beginning."

"Ah. Maybe from just *after* the beginning. I was there at the beginning beginning," I flip-flopped my hands for some reason. "Back then it was *name'em what you want*."

She stared back at me, still on her knees.

"Did I mention everybody getting up?" I asked.

"Yes, you did."

"Why then do you theorize no one has?"

"Out of respect, I'm sure," she replied hesitantly.

She meant fear.

"Why is it I sense y'all are afraid of me? I'm a nice guy. You can ask most anyone who's met me."

She dropped her head as if placing it in the guillotine blade's path. "I am sorry you can see our fear. It is *wrong* of us, and I accept full responsibility. Punish me, Lord, not my troops."

"No, no. I mean why *are* you afraid of me, not *hey, don't let me see it*."

"Permission to speak freely, Lord, even if it means my death?"

I placed both palms over my face. "Fashallana, stand." I leaned over to guide her up. Once she was, I said, "May we go to your office? There, I would like you to explain with the *certainty* of not being executed, why I am feared."

"This way, Lord." She led me into the building.

Progress was slow for a god.

In the office, I had to force her to sit in her own chair. She insisted I sit there.

"Okay, why the fear. Seriously, I'm a warm and fuzzy kind of guy. Ask them," I said pointing to the kids.

"Is that an order, sir, or can I assume they'd confirm your contention?"

"Do you think that in, say, the next million or so years, you'll be able to get around to answering my freaking question?"

She wasn't Deft, but she sure began to melt.

"I'll answer that question," came a familiar voice from behind us. Where had I ...

I spun to stand next to my chair. Reflexively, the kids stood and turned, too.

There I stood. I was filthy with dirt and grime. I had on a ridiculously dated flight suit, but there I stood, glowering at me.

"Uto," I squealed joyously. I opened my arms. "Give us a hug, ya big palooka."

Fashallana, who was still on her knees, went ahead and fainted, crumpling to the side.

"No hugs, you flaming asshole. Sit," he said as he strode over to the desk chair. That me apparently wasn't as shy as I was.

"Un ... Un ... Un ..." stammered Mirraya, pointing at Uto.

"I agree. Sit." When the kids were seated, mouths agape, I filled them in. "That is an alternate timeline version of me. That me went on his initial mission of discovery, but before humankind could flee, it was wiped out. He was the lone survivor, lost in space alone forever. He later went back in time to give me the tool to avoid the same disaster."

"Lost in space forever? Lone survivor? Where do you get that crap from, Ryan? It's horseshit."

"He went ... but that's not possible," said Slapgren. "Is it?"

"It's not supposed to be, but the rules don't always apply to me," he replied. "And then, that me, the one I nicknamed Uto, told me he was going away forever, and I'd never see him again. He took the downloaded mind of my Sapale with him, too."

"Sapale? She was dead. You told me some big tiger killed her."

I smiled at her. "Long story."

"As much as I love a stroll down Memory Lane, let's not go there. I'm busy. *We're* busy. We're trying like hell not to be wiped out of existence."

"Why are they petrified of us, Jon?" I asked him coolly.

"Petrified? Does that go with your lost in space crap? You love those flowery words, don't you, boy?"

"Why are they afraid?"

"Because they damn well should be. I'm here to save and preserve Azsuram. I swore an oath to do it, and I am. You," he wagged a finger at me, "took a pity-party nap, so I had to, you lazy-assed weakling."

Never been called that before, especially by myself. I had a mind to knock him out.

"Why are they afraid of us?"

"I needed to instill an iron discipline, if we were to win, to survive. These Australian cattle dogs are serious. You don't know that because you were literally asleep on the job, but they're tough."

"Australian cattle ... no. You mean border collies. They look like collies, not cattle dogs," I protested.

"What's the difference, Uncle Jon?" asked Mirraya.

"The difference is I'm more correct and he's less correct."

"And you're more a piece of work, ya dumb fuck," snapped Uto.

"I'm beginning to understand their fear. I," I patted my chest, "am leaning to despise and pity you?"

"Ain't got time nor interest, sweet cake," he replied. "I have a war to not lose. What assets do you bring to the table beside those Deft?"

"These *children* are not assets. They are my friends, and they travel under my protection."

Everyone in the room, except poor Fashallana, ran out in a panic.

"Childhood's officially over as of now. I need them. What else you got?"

"I have an Adamant officer I'm only too glad to unload. Garustfulous is back in my vortex."

"Garustfulous. Holy shit, you're lucky 'cause you sure ain't good. I can use him, too. And a vortex. It's not as fast as my ship, but I can use him, too."

"*Her.* And you might want her, but she's mine. You don't even have command prerogative to operate her. Look, I'm here to help.

I swore an oath, too. But I'll not take orders from you, or kowtow to your tantrums."

"You 'bout done, Bozo the Clown?"

"Mirraya, Slapgren, up. We're out of here."

"You're free to go, because a coward and a traitor I don't need. Everything else stays. And, for your 4-1-1, I don't need wires in my hand to operate a vortex. I can use my magic."

"His *what?*" gasped Mirraya.

"Somewhere along the line he learned how to do magic."

"Not somewhere, you prune pit. From a Deft brindas. What do you think I need the kids for? Deft are hard to come by. Thanks, loser."

"What's a brindas?" I asked no one.

"The highest master, the greatest priest or priestess. There is one only every thousand years," said Mirraya with reverence.

"If I can get the kids doing magic, we might just win this war." He chuckled humorlessly.

"The children may or may not help. It's up to them, and it's up to me. You will not dictate—"

I froze. His eyes were closed and his lips moved silently. He was conjuring magic. I'd seen him do it before.

I deployed my fibers and grabbed the desk. I slammed it into him as hard as I could. He flew against the wall and crumpled to the ground. But his feet began skidding along the floor to gain purchase so he could stand. Crap.

"*Out,*" I billowed to the kids. I sprinted behind them, pushing them to the car. On the way out the door, I tossed a soldier at the Evil Jon, his new name, his new *well-deserved* name. I hit the accelerator and dust flew everywhere. I headed to the forest, to be out of sight. I had no clue how the magic worked, or its limitations, but I was hoping he had to see us to hurt us.

As I turned a sharp corner, I glanced back. He was still in the hut. Snap decision. I fired a laser shot above the door. It collapsed pleasingly. I sped up.

At top speed, it'd take us thirty minutes to make it to *Stingray*, twenty-five if I drove like I loved to but shouldn't, because it was too risky. I didn't see his ship, but it had to be close. He knew what direction we were going, so he'd catch up well before we were safe. Crap.

I spun the wheel hard and plunged into the forest. I swung wildly around trees and boulders. The kids were barely able to hold on. After a minute, I slammed on the brakes and we nearly flipped. It was a blast.

"Look, kids, he's going to catch us. I can't let him own you. I want you to change into pareck. It's a local coyote equivalent species." I showed them a holo with my handheld. "Calmly and carefully make your way back to *Stingray,* but do not, I repeat do *not,* approach her. The Evil Jon will be there. You'll have to make do on your own until it's safe enough for us to regroup. Do you understand?"

"Yes, Uncle Jon," said Mirraya. "We can do it. Don't worry. It'll be a game for us. We do it all the time as children."

"This time it's not a game. EJ is nuts, and he's good. Never let your guard down. Now go. I'll ..." What would I do? "I'll leave a note right here, under that tree, telling you where to meet me. Check every now and then, but not too often. Our safe word is ... football. If you're talking to me, ask for the word. If I can't give it to you, it's EJ, you got that? No. football's too obvious. Forget football. Gamorian Guard. *Gamorian Guard* is our safe word. Repeat it back to me."

They did separately.

"Now go. I love you both. Take care."

They jumped out.

I hit the gas and didn't look back. Silently I said a prayer. I'd dumped the only two beings I loved, the only two things I cared about, alone. Alone in a war zone, being pursued by a ruthless maniac who'd use them like tools, without regard for their safety. I could not have felt worse.

As I wildly dodged tree after tree I reflected. I'd met the enemy, and he was me.

To Be Continued...

GLOSSARY OF TERMS

(NUMBERS INDICATE WHICH
BOOK IN GALAXY ON FIRE
THE TERM WAS FIRST USED.)

Al (1): The ship's AI from Jon's initial *Ark 1* flight. He kept it with him until his dying day and then it elected to hang around. Good AI!

Al Jr. (1): The pet name Jon gave to a low-level AI aboard the Adamant mothership that aided his escape.

Blessing (1): Vortex Cragforel gifted to Jon.

Brindas (1): High master of Deft tradition and psychic ability.

Command Prerogatives (1): The thin fibers Jon extends from his left four fingers. They are probes that also control a vortex.

Cragforel (1): Friendly Deavoriath Jon met after he first escaped the Adamant in the far future.

Deavoriath (1): Three arms and legs, the most advanced tech in the galaxy, and helpful to Jon.

Deft (1): A shapeshifting species from the planet Locinar.

Draldon (1): One of Jon's step-children when Azsuram was being established. The name was widely reused in the future.

Gendo and Proclamate Hegemonies (1): Ancient civilizations of Disulpf, inside a globular cluster of stars.

Garustfulous (1): Wedge Leader Garustfulous, the second Adamant Jon encountered, after Mercutcio. He was held captive in *Blessing/Stingray*.

Hirn (1): A dialect of Kaljaxian.

Locinar (1): Home planet of the Deft.

Membrane (1): Space-time congruity manipulator. A super force field.

Mercutcio (1): Lead Adamant Jon first encountered. Commander of *Triumph of Might*.

Midriack (1): Adamant's personal guards. Very deadly, no sense of humor. Avoid them!

Mirraya (1): Deft girl Jon rescued from detention.

PEMTU (1): Personal exotic matter transportation unit. A super way to enter here and end up anywhere, instantly.

Quantum Decoupler (1): A most excellent weapon that pulls the quarks apart in a proton. The energy released is amazing.

Oowaoa (1): Home world of the Deavoriath.

Quep (1): Insect like sentient who woke Jon up on *Exeter* while looking for scrap.

Rostalop (1): Mirraya's favorite food. Comparable to a cow.

Sapale (1): Jon's Kaljaxian wife from his original flight to find humankind a new home. At first just her brain was copied, then, eventually, she was downloaded to an android host. Traveled with the corrupted Jon Ryan from an alternate timeline.

Stingray (1): Name Jon used for the vortex *Blessing*.

Toño DeJesus (1): The creator of the android Jon became, and his lifelong friend.

Triumph of Might (1): The massive spaceship Mercutcio ruled. Jon first met the Adamant there. It was, in part, an extermination ship.

Ungalaym (1): The planet where Jon went to steal a ship. Populated by humanoids.

Vortex (1): The cube shaped spacecraft of the Deavoriath. They move by folding space-time.

Vortex Manipulator (1): The intelligence inside the vortex. Not actually an AI, but similar.

Xenox (1): the language of the Deavoriath.

Zar-not (1): A melding of a Deft's mind with that of a copied animal.

AND NOW A WORD
FROM YOUR AUTHOR
WHO DOESN'T LOVE THAT?

Thank you for continuing your journey through the Ryanverse! Keep on going with *Flames*, BOOK TWO of the *GALAXY ON FIRE Series*.

Along with this series, please check out *The Forever Series*. Beginning with *The Forever Life, Book 1*, learn Jon's backstory and share his many incredible adventures.

Along with joining by reading, hop aboard the bandwagon. Follow me at Craig Robertson's Author's Page on Facebook. Partake of the conversation and fun. Email me and let me know your thoughts and ask me to put you on my mailing list. contact@ craigarobertson.com That way you can stay abreast of news and new releases. You'll be so glad you did. *Please* do leave me a review on Amazon. They're more precious than gold.

For even more visit my Amazon Author's Page: https://www.ama zon.com/-/e/Boo522FURO

There you can learn about me and my other books. The fun will never stop.

The remainder of my unrelated, stand-alone novels are listed at the front of the book. I love them all, so they must be wonderful.

Hey, why did you just snicker? Anyway, they are my early works. Check them out if you're so inclined.

Craig